HISTORY MAY BE WI
VICTORS, BUT IT IS
WRITTEN IN

Often the difference between a win or a loss comes down to the smallest moment, the smallest shift. A bit of luck. This anthology of twenty alternate history short stories revisits several of those pivotal moments and imagines what might have happened if things had gone just a little bit differently. The authors have drawn upon the whole timeline of history to tell stories of Scottish kings and Russian czars who lived instead of died, of wars whose outcome hinged on one person's single choice, and of inventions that might have changed the world.

The collection is filled with familiar figures—including Billy the Kid, Vlad Dracula, and Jack the Ripper—as well as stories exploring two very different fates of the Roman Empire. The anthology also includes an alternate history from the fictional world of *The Great Gatsby*. Some stories look at events that have not yet happened, and a few blur the meaning of time itself. History can be surprisingly malleable if we simply look at it in a new light. And, with a bit of luck, the stories that connect the past to the present can lead us into a world we never imagined.

A Bit of Luck is the ninth anthology edited by Lisa Mangum and published by WordFirePress. Profits support the Don Hodge Memorial Scholarship fund for the Superstars Writing Seminars.

A BIT OF LUCK

A BIT OF LUCK

ALTERNATE HISTORIES IN HONOR OF ERIC FLINT

Edited by
LISA MANGUM

WFP
WordFire Press

All rights reserved. No part of this book may be reproduced or transmitted in any form or by any electronic or mechanical means, including photocopying, recording or by any information storage and retrieval system, without the express written permission of the copyright holder, except where permitted by law. This novel is a work of fiction. Names, characters, places and incidents are either the product of the author's imagination, or, if real, used fictitiously.

The ebook edition of this book is licensed for your personal enjoyment only. The ebook may not be re-sold or given away to other people. If you would like to share the ebook edition with another person, please purchase an additional copy for each recipient. Thank you for respecting the hard work of this author.

EBook ISBN: 978-1-68057-611-5
Trade Paperback ISBN: 978-1-68057-612-2
Jacketed Hardcover ISBN: 978-1-68057-613-9
Library of Congress Control Number: 2023947220
Cover design by Miblart
Kevin J. Anderson, Art Director
Vellum layout by CJ Anaya
Published by
WordFire Press, LLC
PO Box 1840
Monument CO 80132
Kevin J. Anderson & Rebecca Moesta, Publishers
WordFire Press eBook Edition 2023
WordFire Press Trade Paperback Edition 2023

Printed in the USA
Join our WordFire Press Readers Group for
sneak previews, updates, new projects, and giveaways.
Sign up at wordfirepress.com

For Eric Flint

CONTENTS

1. For Want of a Hat   1
   Kate Dane
2. Not on Our Watch   8
   Kevin Ikenberry
3. Syracuse, the Eternal City   18
   Stephen K. Stein and Carolyn Ivy Stein
4. The Doom of Egypt   39
   Julia V. Ashley
5. Divine Calm   54
   Charles E. Gannon
6. A Ruinous Rent   67
   L. A. Selby
7. A Brother's Oath   80
   L. Briar
8. Xiào Shùn   100
   Lehua Parker
9. Kutuzov at Gettysburg   116
   B. Daniel Blatt
10. The Notorious Lawman Billy the Kid   134
    Edward J. Knight
11. Out of Habit   152
    Julie Jones
12. Aces High   166
    Jennifer M. Roberts
13. Rufus and the Wizard of Wireless   176
    Stace Johnson
14. G-Gals   194
    Kendrai Meeks
15. Collateral Loss   212
    Fulvio Gatti
16. Boulder Choke   216
    Carrie Callahan
17. This Was Your Life (Play It Again, Sam)   230
    Mary Pletsch
18. The Unnamed   252
    Gama Ray Martinez

19. Three Times the Power, Four Times the Pain *Akis Linardos*		268
20. Entropy Ranch *Kevin J. Anderson*		278
About the Editor		307
If You Liked …		309
Other WordFire Press Titles Edited by Lisa Mangum		311

1

FOR WANT OF A HAT
KATE DANE

Shopping malls were the last place in the world Eric wanted to find himself. Well, not the very last place—that would be a graveyard. People rushed every which way, jabbering and lugging packages, being transfixed by whatever caught their eye, and stopping short to become traffic hazards. Stores tempted passersby with window displays and bludgeoned them with sales signs and perfume and music. Queen's "The Invisible Man" was playing.

That was him. Invisible. He had to change that.

Shops offered bright colors and clothes to outfit everyone from showgirl to clergy. Tech gadgets you'd need to be a wizard to unravel. Some focused on single items like purses, stationery, pens, games, pets, rocks, pet rocks.

Everyone but him seemed laser focused on buy, buy, buy.

Actually, a lot of places besides graveyards would rank below shopping malls. Sewers. Battlefields. Maybe not battlefields. In a war, the enemy on the ground, the mission, and the stakes were clear. And actually, graveyards might not be so bad, unless you were the corpse. Though if you were dead, you wouldn't care about your surroundings.

He had come to the mall, searching the temple of consumerism, to buy a brand. Not a brand label, but an author persona for conferences.

Dress professionally, but memorably, experienced writers had advised. Find clothes that were identifiable and, preferably, associated with what you wrote. Wardrobe posed a problem for the author of *Mother of Demons*. He wasn't walking around with a pitchfork or horns.

What he needed was something comfortable yet distinct. Something that said *I am writer. Read my books.*

A hat store caught his eye. No, not a hat store. A *haberdashery*. Serious hats, an upgrade from horns. Some not so serious. Walking around with an aviator hat trimmed in fur would make him look like a Wookie ate his head. Another hat looked like an upside-down plant pot with a floral border. Nope.

Others looked wearable. A slouchy fedora, though he'd skip the feather. A straw hat. A black one, like Oddjob's hat, the one he threw to cut off a statue's head in the James Bond film. Black and a bit different.

Hats added distinction. The right hat would shape his future.

Not a ball cap or a beanie. A hat proclaiming readers would enjoy his novels.

Eric stepped into the store.

A boy, maybe six, with floppy hair and a Han Solo T-shirt looked up at him. He twirled a laser blaster and looked as if he hoped aliens would appear so he could blast them. Beside him, a woman with a hat bearing a lethal-looking flower talked to a blue-suited and black-tied clerk.

"May I help you, sir?" This clerk wore a brown tweed suit and a tie in designs of green and brown, a woodland forest look if you manicured the trees.

"I'm looking for a hat."

"You've come to the right place." The clerk's smile invited him to the inside club of hat-wearers. "What are you interested in?"

"The black one, there." He pointed to Oddjob's hat.

"An excellent choice." The clerk picked the hat from the stand. "The bowler hat was created in England in 1849 as a protective hat for gamekeepers. When the nobleman who commissioned it came to pick up the hat, he placed it on the floor and stomped on it to test it. The hat survived, and he paid twelve shillings."

"I imagine prices have gone up. Can I stomp on this one?"

"Yes, more than twelve shillings. No, we don't encourage customers to step on our hats."

"Too bad," the boy muttered. "I'd like to stomp them all."

"This hat has a distinguished history in America, too," the clerk continued. "The Earl of Derby originated a small horse race that took his name and has run for decades: the Kentucky Derby." He held the hat out. "Bowlers were worn by stylish racegoers to the Derby, and the hats became known as derbies. Enjoy the comfort."

Eric put on the hat. It settled comfortably as if shaped for his head. Black and distinctive. Not a tall top hat. A working hat for gamekeepers and associated with the Kentucky Derby. It could become his signature garb.

"This hat has graced men such as Billy the Kid and Winston Churchill. Liza Minnelli wore a bowler in *Cabaret*."

"Along with fishnet stockings." An idea formed. War and betrayals not set in the modern world or even World War II like *Cabaret*. He could write stories of Americans dropped way back in history. They'd have modern knowledge but the limitation of being a small group facing a world where everyone else saw things differently. Time and space would fracture into shards, and the shards would be displaced. His heroes should be tough. Not military or smart college boys, but hardworking Americans. Coal miners used to dirt and danger.

The clerk wouldn't stop yakking. "Think about on-screen heroes: Patrick in the *Avengers*, Charlie Chaplin, Stan Laurel and Oliver Hardy."

"Charlie, Stan, and Oliver were never heroes. If you're talking films with bowler hats, what about Oddjob?"

"Memorable, but not the type of person we wish to associate with the bowler hat." The clerk had gone stiff.

Eric turned to the boy. "What do you think?"

"It's a sissy hat. The edge curls." The boy's lip curled to match. "You need a cool hat. A cowboy hat with a big brim, one holding ten gallons."

The woman turned. "We don't say words like sissy, do we?"

The boy shook his head. "No, Mama."

Her gaze assessed Eric from top of hat to toe of shoes. "The hat makes you look like a gentleman."

The boy's mouth scrunched.

"The bowler isn't the hat for me." Eric removed it and handed it to the clerk. "I'd like a cowboy hat, a dark-colored one, but not black. No feathers."

The grin on the boy's face would have lit up an eclipse.

The clerk returned the bowler hat to its stand, went into the back room, and came back with a hat saying Texas with style. "This is a granite-colored Stetson with a hand-painted belt buckle accessory on the brim. The hat is fur felt with a leather sweatband and satin liner for working comfort."

The Stetson had a rakish sense of humor, one side angling up more than the other in a wry smile. Three dents adorned the top, a deeper one in the center and matching ones on either side. Not a snooty hat, a working hat.

"Creases used to be made in the hat by hand. Reportedly different ranches had different creases. Now the hats come—"

"Pre-dented at no extra cost." Eric took the hat, put it on his head, tilted the brim back. He could feel the open range blowing through him. This hat demanded humor, not seriousness. An Old West version of Indiana Jones. He looked down at the boy.

The boy looked awestruck. "You're almost as good as Han Solo."

"I'll take it," Eric said. A world was forming in his head, one where cowboys, American Indians, and sheepherders formed alliances instead of battling. Together they'd guard the West, using ray guns and magic spells to trap Easterners and their uncrushable bowler hats made in factories east of the Mississippi.

He could tip this hat to Han Solo, too, who wouldn't be caught dead wearing a bowler. A black vest over a white shirt like Han and the Stetson on top. Eric had his conference look. Problem solved, professional writer on the road.

In Eric's world, buffalo would roam free, train tracks would never scar his Western landscape, and the profiteers could cannibalize each other. He'd take the flexible Stetson, dented but still functional, and add humor to a truly Wild West.

Forget about demons. He had history to rewrite.

ABOUT THE AUTHOR

Kate Dane writes quirky stories, often with romance and magic, always with hope. Eric Flint published her first novel, a werewolf romance entitled *Sit. Stay. Kill.* This is her first alternate history story.

2

NOT ON OUR WATCH

KEVIN IKENBERRY

The operations officer's startled voice woke the captain from what passed for sleep on a combat cruise in disputed territory. "Captain? Sorry to rouse you. There's an unknown vessel off the port side. Could be our target."

The captain grunted and rolled off the small, but functional bunk. "Maintain course and speed. I'll be right there."

Commanding a ship of the line meant there were tasks and minor emergencies almost every day. Those few quiet days of transit where no urgent communications arrived, no significant navigation challenges were present, and even the environment cooperated were a blessing and allowed thoughts of home to intrude during the duty day.

Since passing into disputed territory, though, every waking minute was filled with inspections, drills, and constant vigilance. As such, there would be no sleeping in the Captain's Quarters for the foreseeable future. The cabin's proximity to the bridge eliminated the most critical element on their side: time.

Vigilance was eternal in time of war. Even the hours meant for rest required a few people to remain ready for action. The captain stood and straightened himself, trying to appear fresh and rested, before walking out of his cabin.

"Captain on the bridge," the officer of the deck called.

"Sensors, report."

"Contact bearing one hundred eighty. Speed steady at thirty-four." The sensor technician replied without looking up from the screen. "Appears to maintaining course and running silent, Captain."

"Very well, maintain passive measures." For a moment, he considered calling the ship to battle stations, but the voices of mentors past said to let the situation develop. Gather more information. With no other vessel in observation, there would be plenty of time to maneuver if the situation called for it.

"Monitor all frequencies for communications," the captain replied and moved to the command chair. The officer of the deck resumed a position to the side of the command chair, ready to assist as per their station. "If they broadcast, jam their transmissions."

"Aye, Captain."

Peering through the bridge windows, the captain squinted into the black for a long moment. He almost asked for a better bearing on the target until a tiny light flashed once against the black sky.

There.

There were no distinguishing characteristics on the enemy vessel from their current distance. He turned to the operations officer. "Is that the target or something else with spectacularly bad timing? What does intel think?"

"Heavy attack vessel, Captain. Appears to be moving at flank speed." The operations officer consulted the central console. "We have nothing else on our sensors in all directions. Given what we know of the attack profile, the unknown contact matches the intended enemy vessel with total confidence, Captain."

"Time to intercept?" the captain asked.

"Unknown. Target speed is fluctuating as predicted," Operations replied. "Vessel appears to be braking. Possible aspect change to target."

The captain bit back an epithet. If the vessel turned more toward them, any enemy forward passive sensors might pick up their presence. Possible courses of action flooded through the captain's mind. Experience said to explore the possibilities and take quick action. If chosen correctly, they could avoid detection until a time and place of the captain's choosing. If not, putting the ship in the best possible position to defend itself was paramount.

The captain turned the chair back to the left and squinted into the night. "Helm, come left twenty degrees. All ahead full."

"Left twenty degrees, all ahead full," the helmsman repeated.

As the cruiser turned, the captain gave a moment's consideration to the situation before deciding to wake the crew. The enemy vessel, now identified on a trajectory like its predecessors, had reached their defensive boundary and could not be allowed to reach its intended target.

"Confirm defensive boundary," Operations called.

Action was necessary. "Weapons, I want a shooting solution on that target now. Chief of the Watch, sound general quarters and set hands to action stations."

The Chief of the Watch, the senior enlisted leader aboard, stepped forward. "Aye, Captain."

A moment later, alarms brayed, and the mostly sleeping cruiser sprang to life. As it did, the console buzzed, and the captain picked up the private line. "Captain."

"Intel. Assessment on the suspected target is complete."

"Standby, Intel." The captain squinted into the dark again. "Weapons, prepare to spin up missile launchers three and four. Set autonomous guidance."

"Pre-loading missiles three and four, Captain."

The captain inhaled deeply. "Let me know when you have a solution."

"Aye, Captain. Range to target is one hundred twenty and rapidly decreasing."

For once, they'd anticipated an attack on a potentially prosperous target and managed to move a ship of the line into its way. Any impact on the target site might change the course of history. To stop it, the captain needed information and intelligence. "Intel? What is it?"

"Estimated target impact point is twenty-two degrees above the planet's equator. There are land masses and a significant ocean in the impact zone. Resulting waves would be catastrophic for most of the surrounding region," Intel replied. "Captain? There are over six million life-forms in the impact zone, and more than six hundred billion life-forms on the planet itself."

"Evidence of active civilization?" the captain asked. "Technology levels?"

The captain heard Intel take a long breath. "Negative on active civilization. Technology level appears to be zero. Though there are inhabitants who seem to move, communicate, and even hunt together. This barely meets the engagement criteria, Captain." Intel paused. "Not presuming to try to—"

"Time to engagement zone is one hundred and sixty-seven zetas, Captain," Operations called. "Shooting solution identified."

The Captain nodded. "Intel? What's your predictive assessment?"

"The inbound attack vessel is an attempt to stop planetary development, Captain. It fits the standard profile for enemy interdiction missions," Intel replied. "While the planet is uncivilized, the fauna present, and the planet's atmosphere and natural resources, would suggest that it be a potential colonization target."

"Like their last two hundred and six attacks," the captain mused. "At least we're in time to stop this one."

For a change, he added silently.

"Affirmative, sir," Intel replied. "Further simulations are inconclusive. Carbon-based life-forms are difficult to predict, but there may be some benefit gained in allowing the attack vessel to strike its target."

"Why?"

"There is no guarantee the current life-forms will progress enough to reach civilization, much less one that is technologically evolved. Amphibian-related life-forms are typically unstable and unable to use tools. And these are quite violent," Intel answered. "Our reconnaissance drone is broadcasting now. On screen, Captain."

Everything pointed to the planet being mostly temperate, unlike most water-based worlds they'd seen in the galaxy. The fortunate combination of a relatively low-energy yellow star at the proper distance to ensure a majority of the water stayed fluid suggested promising things for the planet. As the drone descended quickly over the ocean, streaking toward a narrow ribbon of shoreline, the captain saw creatures flying in the blue and white skies. Lush vegetation appeared to cover the landmass near the ocean's shore. Amongst it, bipedal creatures moved.

Sensing movement, the drone slowed and circled over the land. There were other creatures present now. Four-legged beings of all sizes, large and small, moved amongst the even smaller, similar two-legged ones in apparent harmony. Some moved fast, alone, while others traveled in coordinated herds. Bodies of water inland from the sea teemed with life. All of it peaceful and seemed somewhat hopeful to the captain's jaded senses.

An unharmed world with unlimited potential. Water. A clean, nitrogen-rich atmosphere. There could be—

A flurry of movement on the ground below the drone caught the sensor's attention. Smaller creatures darted away from the water's edge. Avian creatures exploded out of the trees, shrieking in trumpeting tones the captain never imagined. A two-legged creature with a long tail darted toward the thicker vegetation and leapt toward the promise of concealment but failed to reach its destination. A larger, bipedal... thing lashed out. The larger head and gaping jaws easily snatched the smaller creature mid-flight and bit down. With its meal safely in its mouth, the bigger creature lashed its head from side-to-side several times, leaving the smaller creature hanging limp. Dead.

The captain breathed for the first time in many zetas. *Such power. Such speed. Ferocity. What if they could be our allies and not some smaller, technologically advanced derivative?*

I will not repeat the mistake I made at Kyton-four.

The captain consulted the command console. "Intel?"

"Here, Captain," Intel said over the still open line. "The long development cycle shows a more adept, more technically focused species could emerge in the aftermath of an attack vessel strike. Either mammalian or insectoid-based species could thrive in that event. Though, the damage to the planet and its current ecosystems will be catastrophic. It will be many zarillium before this planet will be viable after a strike."

"Understood." The captain disconnected the line and turned to Operations. "Get us within range to ensure that the attack vessel is destroyed by our fire."

"Aye, Captain." The operations officer picked up a device and pushed another button.

"All hands, this is the captain. We've positively identified the enemy attack vessel and are moving to engage. Prepare for combat operations in case the vessel has a hidden escort. All defensive and offensive weapons are to be loaded. Do not fire unless they fire upon us."

The captain paused and took a breath. "Far too many times we have been unable to even approach an enemy attack vessel. Two hundred planets and countless life-forms have died as they continue to wipe out potential threats. Those threats to our enemy's advance would be our allies in this long fight. As we've done before, we will again. For the Union."

The captain turned to Operations. "Helm, all ahead flank. Ops, prepare defensive countermeasures. Standby to fire missiles three and four."

"Missiles three and four ready to fire and solutions loaded," Operations replied.

"Match bearing to the attack vessel and fire tubes three and four," the captain ordered. "Drop countermeasures."

"Weapons away," Operations barked. "Countermeasures fired."

"Helm, come left ninety degrees." The captain pushed a button on the console. "All hands, brace for combat maneuvers. Brace, brace, brace!"

"Left ninety degrees!" the helmsman yelped.

Under full thrust, the cruiser's turn induced a significant amount of gravitational force. Lesser-experienced crews might have succumbed to the force and lost consciousness, but not this crew. The captain strained against the force for a few seconds, and then it was gone.

"Track our weapons!" the captain barked. External cameras swung toward the attack vessel. Heavy ablative coverings adorned the forward end of a large asteroid. From the new vantage point, the captain estimated the asteroid to be twice the size of their last interdiction twelve lights away.

Good thing we fired two missiles.

"Ops? Anything tracking us?" the captain asked.

Not on Our Watch

"Negative, Captain. No escorts with this target," Operations reported. "Permission to stand down weapons?"

"Keep them active until the target is destroyed."

"Aye, Captain."

Time slowed as the weapons raced toward impact. For a moment, the captain wondered if they'd missed or failed to arm. It had happened before. Drawing a breath to ask for a status update, the captain paused as he saw two bright explosions suddenly fill the sky for an instant then fade.

"Direct hit," Operations reported. "We have neutralized the vessel."

The captain tapped the console. "Intel? Assessment of remaining debris?"

"Nothing that will damage the planet irreparably, Captain."

"Very well." The captain spun the camera to view the planet hanging below. Its day and night terminator line was now visible, the first streaks of debris burning through its atmosphere lit up the sky. Did the creatures below realize what had happened? Would they share the story with their progeny?

The captain didn't know. What was as clear as the Union's goals for galactic peace was that this world, the third of nine orbiting the yellow star the Union called Zygra, would soon have its own name bestowed by the creatures who survived and evolved until the time of the Gathering.

The captain would not see them, nor did it matter. What mattered was that these strange creatures could rise against their enemies far better than the meek mammalian creatures that would have been left behind if he'd failed to destroy the asteroid. Too many times had those situations failed the Union. The meek failed to inherit anything.

Not this time, the captain thought. *The fight has just begun.*

"Mission accomplished," the captain announced. "Well done. No more great extinctions on our watch."

As the cheers died down, the captain touched the console

again and relaxed in the command chair. "Command? This is the *Alpha*. Requesting coordinates. The class nine planet known as Zygra-Three has been spared. An aggressive, amphibian-based biome that might breed powerful allies has been preserved."

We have enough weak mammalian allies, the captain thought but did not say aloud.

"Confirm, *Alpha*. Excellent choice. Set course for reconnaissance at Zygra-Four and then on Callis-Nine at highest possible speed."

"Affirmative, Command. *Alpha*, out." The captain relaxed. "Helm, set course for Zygra-Four. Ops? What do we know about the target?"

"Low probability of life, Captain. Zygra-Four appears discolored compared to the planet below us. No water. Almost no atmosphere, but there are ice caps with a high probability of carbon dioxide present. Could be a refueling point in future operations," Operations replied. "Recommend high speed pass and on to Callis-Nine. Transit time is six zetarans."

"Stand down from general quarters and prepare for hyperspace," the captain said. "If you need me, I'll be in my quarters. Well done, everyone. Let's go home."

ABOUT THE AUTHOR

Kevin Ikenberry is a lifelong space geek and retired Army officer. As an adult, he managed the U.S. Space Camp program and served in space operations before Space Force was a thing. He's an international bestselling science fiction author and renowned writing instructor, which is pretty cool because he never imagined being either one of those—he still wants to be an astronaut.

Kevin's debut novel, *Sleeper Protocol*, was hailed by *Publishers Weekly* as "an emotionally powerful debut." His over twenty novels science fiction novels include *The Crossing, Vendetta Protocol, Eminence Protocol, Runs in the Family, Peacemaker, Honor the Threat, Stand or Fall, Fields of Fire,* and *Harbinger*. Kevin is an active member of the International Association of Science Fiction and Fantasy Authors, International Thriller Writers, and SIGMA—the science fiction think tank. Kevin continues to work with space every day and lives in Colorado with his family.

3

SYRACUSE, THE ETERNAL CITY
STEPHEN K. STEIN AND CAROLYN IVY STEIN

April 213 BCE

Dawn revealed two hundred Roman galleys rowing into Syracuse's Great Harbor, silhouetted against the bright azure sky—a rarity in early spring. The sweating rowers propelled the galleys forward with speed and determination. Helped by a gentle breeze, they practically flew inland across the calm waters.

Gylippus strained to see the invaders from the city's high wall, forty feet above the water. Around him, Syracusan soldiers readied their weapons. Others manhandled catapults into position.

"Don't worry, Gylippus. We have secret weapons," Deinomenes said with the blustering arrogance of Syracusans on their favorite topic: science.

Gylippus scowled at his friend. "Archimedes?" Scientists believed their gadgets turned the tide, but as a Spartan, Gylippus knew courage ultimately determined a war's victor. In this case, though, Archimedes's catapults, the most powerful ever built, gave them an edge.

The city's defenders were well-trained and resolute, particularly those manning Archimedes's devices on the high walls, but few had fought toe to toe with spear and shield against a determined enemy. Would their courage falter facing the Roman fleet advancing across the harbor and a larger land army besieging the city?

"Archimedes made a new weapon," Deinomenes continued. "Science always trumps brute force. The Romans won't break our walls."

"Archimedes better act quickly, then." Gylippus pointed to the largest galleys with siege towers near their prows, as well as several catapults. Other galleys carried scaling ladders, bridges, and boarding ramps. All overloaded with soldiers.

"They can't defeat us," Deinomenes continued. "They know it. You can see the fear on their faces."

Gylippus squinted. The Romans were still too far away to see faces, but the galleys advanced in even lines. No timid captains held back their ships.

Gylippus shifted on his feet, trying to alleviate his discomfort. Every time he looked at the advancing Romans, the same image came unbidden to his mind, superimposed over the scene, like the shades of the unburied dead. It haunted his dreams. Even in the brilliant sunlight, he saw it whenever he looked at the city of Syracuse below him: a swirling pool of blood from the broken body of Archimedes rising and flooding Syracuse with its stink and terror; his friend, Deinomenes, weeping at his sister's grave in the ruins of the city.

Gylippus felt sure the city's fall was decreed by the gods, just as an earlier vision had foretold the death of a boon friend at Cannae. He'd nearly died there himself. Events unfolded exactly as he'd foreseen it, down to the bloodred river. Faced with that inevitability, what could he do, even knowing it was coming? His visions were a curse.

"Where is Archimedes with his—"

A BIT OF LUCK

The leading Roman galley burst into flames. It stood out brightly against the rising sun behind it and the dozens of galleys to its left, right, and rear. To the watching Syracusans, it was a beacon of hope and a confirmation of Archimedes's deadly physics.

Gylippus imagined he smelled the sour fear of the fleet's straining rowers, two hundred on each galley, but the breeze carried only the normal scents of sea, fish, brine, and the rotting seaweed collecting along the harbor's rim. Shifting winds added the occasional stench of offal from the harbor's far end, where Syracuse's sewers emptied.

More brief puffs of smoke appeared wherever Archimedes and his assistants focused their enormous, polished bronze mirror. Smoke became flame, and new fires erupted as Archimedes refocused his mirror on bundles of cordage and other flammable objects on the Roman galley.

Gylippus smiled as fire spread across the galley's bow and shot rapidly down its length.

The ship's forward lookout shouted a warning to nearby sailors to douse the flames with buckets of sand and water.

The blaze spread faster than Gylippus expected. The fleet's cordage, canvas, and painted surfaces burned well, thanks to the work of saboteurs Gylippus placed amongst the work crews.

Sailors fled amidships, joined by rowers who tossed aside oars, scrambled from their benches, and either ran toward the stern or bravely battled the erupting flames.

Two-thirds of the galley's rowers were trapped below the deck; they'd either burn or drown with their ship. As would the soldiers, each one weighed down with fifty pounds or more of armor.

Gylippus had served aboard a ship before, and the twin fears of fire and drowning had kept him awake most nights. He allowed himself a moment to pity those poor souls.

Syracuse, the Eternal City

Deinomenes nudged Gylippus in the ribs. "What did I tell you? Whatever the Romans try, Archimedes bests them. They can't match our science."

Gylippus looked over at his friend, seeing the grief in his future as clearly as the sun rising in the sky. He shook the image away. "Perhaps," he replied, "but there's more to war than science. Romans are both brave and stubborn. They've demonstrated that time and again. Whatever happens today, most of their troops still crouch outside the gates. The siege will continue."

"You're a dour sort, like all Spartans. Even campaigning with Hannibal and sharing his triumph at Cannae didn't change you." Deinomenes grinned, showing well-formed teeth. "Hannibal sent you to us, and you helped prepare our defense. You encouraged us to prepare for the worst. We have. The Romans have besieged us for weeks, yet their assaults have all failed, barely nicking our walls."

"Cannae was a close battle," Gylippus replied. "It could easily have gone the other way. I still have nightmares about it." His nightmares before Cannae had become real on the battlefield, but he didn't say that. He'd learned to keep his prophetic visions to himself.

Deinomenes looked sympathetic but said only, "Our victory today will chase away your nightmares."

"One hopes," Gylippus said, trying to sound optimistic while again blocking out his vision of the sacking of Syracuse. He needed to ensure that didn't happen. If Syracuse held, Hannibal might still win his war. If the city fell, the Roman tide would likely wash over the entire Mediterranean, bringing despotism in its wake.

A loud snap followed by humming drew their attention. The catapult to their left had released its bolt. Others followed as ballistae along the wall hurled stones that smashed oars or crunched into hulls and decks. Scorpions shot bolts that pierced rowers at their benches.

The Roman fleet fired in return, but their missiles fell short.

Deinomenes clapped Gylippus on the back and smiled, "I told you so" written across his face. "Only Archimedes builds catapults with such range and power."

Perhaps, Gylippus thought, but Syracuse's famed engineer and mathematician could only do so much. If the Roman fleet managed to land its troops, courage and cold steel would decide the day, not science.

Archimedes focused his improbable device on another galley, its port rowers scattered by a ballista stone. How could anyone reflect the sun with such intensity that it started fires? The deadly machine worked, thanks not only to Archimedes's genius but also to several spies chosen and placed by Gylippus amongst sailors, soldiers, and workmen Rome recruited to build—and then sabotage—its improvised fleet.

As Gylippus watched, the Roman fleet's center swirled into chaos. One galley's rowers misunderstood their orders. The port rowers backed their oars while the starboard pulled, spinning their galley, and tangling its oars with another.

Heavy stones fell from the sky as flames continued to erupt among the galleys. The green wood burned poorly, producing dense smoke and adding to the confusion.

The screams of the desperate crews, many of them as green as their ships' planks, reached Gylippus and Syracuse's other defenders on the high walls. So, too, did a growing number of Roman bolts and stones, fired by the galleys on the Roman formation's flanks. Most impacted the wall, doing little damage, but two bolts passed over the heads of soldiers near Gylippus.

"Aim the catapults on the squadron leaders," shouted Gylippus. "The ones flying the high pennants. Archimedes, focus your mirror on the galleys behind them. They'll have the poorer crews. They're more likely to panic."

"Yes, yes, my assistants can handle that. I've something else in mind for the others." Archimedes stroked his long beard, seeming oblivious to the surrounding chaos. "They're almost close enough." He turned and called to his foreman. "Push it forward and swing it into position. Quickly."

The foreman shouted. Several dozen workers pushed an enormous contraption up the packed dirt ramp leading to the wall. It resembled a crane more than a catapult, and it was larger than any stone-throwing engine Gylippus had ever seen. Other men followed, carrying bundles of rope and sinew and other parts of the device.

Meanwhile, the Roman fleet advanced. Archers and legionnaries stood ready atop their towers. Others at the ships' prows held grappling hooks and ladders, ready to storm ashore when their ships beached. Officers shouted, encouraging rowers to their utmost. The galleys on the flanks of the Roman formation surged forward. In the center of the fleet, another ship erupted into flames.

The larger galleys backed oars to avoid the smoking confusion of burning and disabled ships. The smaller galleys maneuvered around them and pressed forward slowly. Soon, the Roman formation resembled a crescent with flanks advancing and the center held back.

Gylippus smiled.

The lighter Roman galleys would reach the walls ahead of the center's large galleys. They were more vulnerable to Archimedes's many catapults and lacked the troops and equipment to effectively assault Syracuse's walls. The battle was developing better than he expected.

Here and there, Roman projectiles struck down one of Syracuse's defenders, but most stones and bolts fell short and bounced harmlessly off the city's thick walls.

More and more Roman galleys, though, fell victim to Archimedes's blazing mirror; others to the huge stones thrown by his engines, which shattered oars and pulped rowers. As Roman galleys entered range, Syracuse's smaller catapults released their stones and bolts along with pots of flaming pitch with its eye-burning, throat-searing smoke.

A dozen burning and disabled galleys soon blocked the Roman fleet's advance on the right. On the left, though, two pairs of smaller galleys threw ropes to their larger, disabled comrades and slowly towed them back toward the harbor mouth.

One by one, uninjured galleys rowed through the gaps, fanned out to either side, and resumed their advance.

Whoever commanded there knew his business.

Gylippus shouted to the catapult commanders nearest to him, "Concentrate your fire on the gaps!" Fresh Roman galleys were already rowing toward them. The first of them would reach the shallow beach overlooking Syracuse's walls in minutes. "Do it now!"

Archimedes added his voice. "Do what he says. We need time to assemble the claw."

The wind shifted, speeding the Romans forward. Smoke from the burning galleys, and all the smells that accompanied them—burning tar and wood and paint, and charred human flesh—wafted over the walls. A volley of bolts soon followed, playing a deadly drumbeat against the walls. One bolt pierced a soldier, who toppled from the wall with a scream.

The defending catapults continued their rapid fire and were joined by dozens of archers who loosed their arrows as Rome's galleys neared.

Moments later, Roman archers atop the siege towers on the leading galleys released their arrows. Many fell short, but as volley followed volley, more found their targets.

The leading Roman galleys grounded on the shallow beach below the city's walls. The invaders needed to secure a lodgment on the wall in this assault, or low tide would strand many of the ships.

Foolish to land troops without first clearing the walls of defenders. The Romans were reckless. Syracuse must exploit their desperation. Gylippus searched the scene for a tactical opportunity.

Other galleys formed in line astern behind those that had reached the walls. Each ship lowered a boarding bridge across which soldiers flowed from galley to galley and then either onto the narrow beach or up the scaling ladders being raised against Syracuse's high walls.

The largest galleys, those with siege towers, maintained their distance. Atop the towers, archers and catapults maintained their fire on Syracuse's walls, where casualties mounted.

Syracusan archers concentrated their fire on the leading Romans, dropping many. Other defenders rolled heavy stones from the wall, poured flaming pitch from giant cauldrons, and used long poles to push scaling ladders aside, tumbling Roman legionnaires to the ground. Unable to target the enemy at the wall's base, the city's catapults rained stones and bolts among the farther galleys, killing closely packed soldiers and smashing one of the bridges.

Ashore, Romans brought forward pry bars and other tools. They planted posts in the ground to support the hides they stretched over their heads to protect themselves. They dug into Syracuse's walls, prying at its huge stones.

Suddenly, an enormous claw reached down from the walls. It seized a Roman galley, a quinquereme, lifting it from the water. The crew screamed. Some clung to their oars or the rigging. Others tumbled dozens of feet to the water below.

Fighting paused as everyone—defenders and attackers—stopped and stared.

Archimedes shouted an order, and the claw lifted the galley

another dozen feet. More members of its crew tumbled to the water. A few hit the shallow, rocky beach with a thud.

A moment later, their ship followed them, its stern smashing into the beach. The ship stood still for a moment. Then, with a loud crack as interior timbers split and joints popped, it slowly tumbled backward.

The galley landed upside down, half in and half out of the water. Beneath it, shattered bodies of crew and legionnaires bled out. Gylippus knew that hundreds more lay within the ship, dead and dying. A grim business, but satisfying.

He thought of Archimedes's weapons, and his spirits lifted. If the mathematician could do this to the Roman navy, perhaps the Syracusans were right to believe in him. Perhaps they'd survive. But no sooner had the thought crossed his mind than his vision of Archimedes dying in a pool of blood returned.

Apollo, god of wisdom and war, bring us victory this day.

Archimedes's claw reached down, grabbed another quinquereme, and ripped it from the water, snapping the bridges that connected it to the other galleys at its bow and stern. The scene repeated itself as the galley swung in the claw's grip and sailors tumbled from it, soon followed by their ship.

Roman archers loosed arrows at the enormous claw but without effect. Behind them, sailors screamed warnings and captains shouted orders.

Galley after galley raised its boarding bridges. Gylippus watched as fleeing and advancing galleys met in a tangle of oars. Two fleeing galleys impaled themselves on the rams of their compatriots. Other galleys joined the tangle of ships as Archimedes's engines continued to hurl bolts and stones. His giant mirror played across the Roman fleet, igniting fires among stalled and crippled galleys.

On the fleet's right, the Roman flagship raised flag after flag, signaling orders that nearby captains obeyed but the more distant ones ignored, bent on retreat.

Gylippus could read the signs as well as anyone. Apollo—and Archimedes—had turned the tide of the battle.

Gylippus turned back to look at Syracuse, the white-columned temples and the small shops. For a moment, he saw nothing but the city itself and felt the tension leave his body. But his vision returned, and in his mind, Archimedes died again, and Syracuse fell. Could any man stand against the gods? Or were the gods showing him this future to let him know he could still change it?

Deinomenes, standing at Gylippus's side, shouted in triumph. "The Romans are done for!"

"For now," Gylippus agreed. "They'll be back, though. They'll try again."

"And they'll fail again. Two centuries ago, we crushed the Athenian fleet, the greatest power of its day, in this harbor. Now we've done the same to the Romans. Syracuse has never —will never—fall to an attacker. Eternal Syracuse!"

"The Romans aren't the Athenians. There are more of them, and they know more about siege warfare than any Greek since Demetrious the Besieger."

"What do you expect?"

"The Romans won't come by sea again. Fleets take too long to build and are too expensive to risk in a confined harbor against Archimedes's genius. They'll come by land. If direct assaults fail, they'll resort to stealth. They'll try to sneak in or bribe someone to open a gate for them. Be wary. Post more guards at night."

"None would betray our city."

"No doubt. Post the guards anyway. All it took for Cyrus to capture Sardis was to get a few handpicked soldiers over the wall one night."

"Yes, the story of the dropped helmet and the Persians' midnight climb."

A BIT OF LUCK

"We must be ready for the next attack," Gylippus said, unable to shake his haunting vision.

∼

September 2, 212 BCE

Month after month, the Roman siege continued. Assault after assault failed, shattered by Archimedes's catapults and claws. Now all it took was to wave a few long poles resembling Archimedes's wondrous devices from the wall to send the Romans scurrying to the rear.

Even so, Syracuse's people became restive as the siege continued and grain ran short. Smugglers could not bring in enough food to supply a city so large.

"Best to sue for peace. We cannot hold out," some people whispered.

Deinomenes and his sister visited Gylippus on the wall. She handed him a cup of thin stew with small pieces of bream, a few grains of barley, and some unidentifiable meat. Gylippus drank it down, not wanting to ask what was in it.

"The people need a break," Deinomenes said.

"The Romans are counting on that. They seek to wear us out. We need to take this war to them."

"A festival," Deinomenes declared. "That is what the populace needs to bring their courage up. Particularly," he added, "since we still have plenty of wine." His friend glowed with anticipation, and Gylippus had no doubt that Deinomenes was chief amongst those bored by the siege and looking forward to a feast.

"It's unwise," Gylippus said. "People must remain stalwart."

"The Feast of Artemis comes in a few days. I've spoken with the Archon and he agrees." Deinomenes motioned to his sister, standing next to him. "Rhea and the other women have already started working on the sweets."

She smiled shyly at Gylippus, her large eyes looking even larger in her face these days. Everyone looked half-starved.

He didn't want to see a vision of her death, so he slashed his eyes back toward the siege camp below. "What if the Romans attack during the festival?"

"Those on the walls will let us know. But the Romans won't attack. They are too afraid of Archimedes's weapons. Besides, if we honor Artemis, perhaps she will hasten the invaders from our walls." He laughed and pounded Gylippus hard on the back. "Come, friend, you will see in a week how ingenious our cooks and vintners are."

But though Gylippus heard his friend's laughter, he also saw pain and tears from his vision shadowing his features. A feast at this time was unwise. But try as he might, he couldn't dissuade Deinomenes or any of the other Syracusans of their plans.

∼

September 12, 212 BCE

Gylippus woke from another nightmare, his body covered in cold, stinking sweat, though the night was temperate. His sheets lay tangled around his feet. As he shook his head, he realized the pungent odor from his window was wine, not blood. And yet his dreams seemed so real.

Whether it was Archimedes lying in a pool of blood as Romans sacked the city, or his cheerful friend, Deinomenes, crying, his visions hounded him each night and haunted him during the day.

The visions became more frequent and urgent as the festival neared. Gylippus couldn't bear to walk the streets for fear of seeing the fate of each person he passed. He'd warned against the feast, but no one listened, not even Deinomenes.

Yesterday, the festival had begun, and wine flowed freely. The women stretched the meager grain, a mixture of barley and wheat, with eggs, olive oil, and vinegar, and sweetened the dough with dried clover and coriander to create small treats honoring Artemis.

Everyone except Gylippus assumed the Romans were too cowed to attack, despite their refusal to negotiate an end to the siege. The talks, held over several days in the Galeagra Tower along Syracuse's western wall, had come to naught.

Gylippus tossed off the sheet and reached for his tunic and sword. If he couldn't sleep, he'd walk the walls. Hurrying from his room above a small inn where the Syracusans had quartered him, Gylippus hurried to the harbor. He'd start there and work his way west along the wall. The walk would wear him out enough so he could sleep. Hopefully.

He passed dozens of revelers offering to share their wine. Sounds of celebration grew as he walked, as levels of inebriation rose and more people emerged from homes and taverns to join the festivities in the streets. Deinomenes had been right. The Syracusans craved celebration, but if they kept up this ruckus, the Romans camped outside the walls would soon hear them—if they hadn't already.

Reaching the wall, Gylippus turned right and scanned it as he walked. The tower glowed brightly, but few torches lit the wall between it and the next one. Wood had run short in the besieged city, but the guards shouldn't skimp on torches. Had they abandoned their posts?

Gylippus picked up his pace, still scanning the wall as he rushed toward the Galeagra Tower. Barely lit, shadows moved in its dim light. Was that a scream? A warning? He couldn't tell over the noise of the revelers.

Two guards stood outside the tower, and Gylippus waved

to get their attention. One looked toward him, but the other turned toward the gate behind him. Had he heard something?

As Gylippus neared, the second guard turned around again, drew his sword, and shouted, "Romans!"

Damn! He'd been right. Gylippus ran toward the tower, dodging revelers and shouting, "Romans! Romans! Grab a weapon or go for help. There's no time to lose."

Most people fled, screaming in terror, but a few men fell in behind him. They reached the tower's gate just as a half-dozen Roman soldiers pushed the guards back. Few of Gylippus's improvised squad were armed and none wore armor, but several of them heaved their flasks of wine at the Romans, two of which struck enemy helmets, dousing the soldiers with wine and blinding them.

Gylippus and the others slammed into the Romans from their right. Their swords, daggers, and improvised weapons rose and fell in a brutal fight that ended before the Romans could lift their shields in defense.

Helped by the guards, the defenders slammed the gate closed and barricaded it.

Gylippus grabbed two of his new comrades and yelled, "Find Deinomenes. Find any general you can. They need to reinforce the towers on either side of the Galeagra. We need to keep the Romans pinned here."

The two ran off, calling to others to spread the word. Drunk as they were—and many of the Syracusans were quite drunk—the city rallied. More men arrived to reinforce Gylippus and his ragged band. Gylippus ordered his team to stab their spears through the gate at the Romans.

The Romans lacked the numbers to force their way out of the tower's gate and into the city, but Gylippus and the Syracusans lacked the breastplates and armor they'd need to survive a fight in such close quarters. A few men, though, recovered shields from fallen Romans, and one of them handed it to Gylippus, who nodded his thanks.

The standoff seemed to last for hours. The Romans gathered in tight formation, raised their shields, and slammed into the gate. The Syracusans drove them back with spears, improvised weapons, and steady bombardment with wine jugs, empty and full.

Finally, Deinomenes arrived with several dozen soldiers. They reeked of wine, but at least they were fully equipped.

"The Romans have scaling ladders all along this section of the wall," Deinomenes said. "I've ordered reinforcements to the other towers. They'll attack along the top of the wall from both directions. Once they attack, we'll storm this gate. The Romans will have to defend from three different directions." Smiling, he added, "You can tell me you were right once we've driven them from the walls."

More Syracusan soldiers arrived, among them archers who shouted for people to clear them a path. They loosed volley after volley of arrows into the trapped Romans, who retreated up the stairs. Shouting from the walls above signaled the attack had begun.

The Syracusans wrenched open the gate. Deinomenes and Gylippus led the charge into the tower and up its stairs, quickly overwhelming the few Romans who tried to make a stand. Most fled, hoping, no doubt, to reach their ladders and escape.

The remaining Romans made their stand at the top of the tower. Several dozen legionnaires in close formation defended the two scaling ladders still leaning against the wall for Romans to use in their retreat. The other ladders had been toppled.

Deinomenes hastily dressed his line and led his soldiers forward. Gylippus, exhausted and unarmored, held back.

Gylippus heard his friend cry out at the same time as the wet thunk of a spear found its target. He quickly pushed the wooden siege ladder away from the wall. Roman soldiers

Syracuse, the Eternal City

screamed as they dropped. He wished for burning pitch to fling after them, but there was none since no one had anticipated the battle.

He turned to see Deinomenes clutching his belly as blood pooled around him.

"My friend," Deinomenes said, his natural bonhomie present but subdued as his life bled out. "See to my sister, Rhea. Remember me."

"No!" Gylippus knelt at his side, desperately trying to stem the flood of blood from his one true friend, tears prickling his eyes. "You are not fated to die."

Deinomenes laughed, a dreadful choking sound. "I always knew you had a relationship with fate, Gylippus. Does Syracuse survive? Tell me, my friend. I know you know."

How could Deinomenes know of the visions? Gylippus dutifully looked over at the city, its citizens roused and teaming, a half-drunk crew of Syracusans emboldened by wine and angry at the Romans who'd crept in like thieves to desecrate the Goddess's festival. They were taking the fight to the Romans with a fury he hadn't seen since Cannae.

He opened himself to the visions.

None came.

"My friend, you were right. Artemis saved Syracuse, the Eternal City."

"Nay. You were right. It was men of courage who—" He trailed off, his body shuddering once, then falling still.

Gylippus closed his friend's eyes, leaving behind streaks of the blood that coated his hands to his elbows. It wasn't supposed to end this way. Had Artemis brought him here and spoken to him through visions? Had she required a blood sacrifice of Syracuse's best to save the city?

As the fight continued, Gylippus wept, but then he took up his weapon and fought with a ferocity he hadn't known was within him.

A BIT OF LUCK

∽

September 12, 172 BCE

A cacophony of drums, flutes, and people singing announced the Festival of Artemis. Gylippus's wife, Rhea, prepared an offering plate for Deinomenes filled with fragrant sweets made of olive oil, eggs, almonds, and honey. It had been four decades since Deinomenes had fallen in Galeagra Tower, but Gylippus saw in her eyes that the pain was still fresh. For him as well.

Was it necessary for Deinomenes to fall to save the city of Syracuse? And without that worthy sacrifice, would any of the marvels of the Eternal City of Syracuse exist today? What if Rome had won? Would people speak of Roma Eterna, eternal Rome? For a moment, it seemed very real, as if it could have happened.

He shuddered.

Rhea brought him a cup of watery stew and a flask of wine, their private remembrance. The best treats were reserved for the noble dead, particularly Deinomenes, Rhea's brother and Gylippus's best friend.

They'd saved the world that day. It was clear that Rome would have gone on to impose their will upon the world had Syracuse not stopped them. But with the gifts of science and democracy, the Greek City States, led by Syracuse in partnership with Hannibal's forces, brought back the independence of Greeks everywhere, though the price in blood had been high. Syracuse now existed as a beacon of light and learning, warming the people of the Mediterranean.

"Deinomenes would have loved the festival," Rhea said, as she did every year. "He lived for the good things in life."

"He bought this for us. It is not how we live that matters. It is how we die. He died courageously, laughing in the face of death. He shall always be remembered as the brightest light in Eternal Syracuse."

Rhea smiled and leaned against Gylippus. "Will you tell the story of his courage to our grandchildren again tonight?"

"Always. His shade would haunt me if I failed." He gestured at the plate. "He will appreciate your offering of his favorite sweets. You honor him."

"As do you. Stories are the best offerings we have to the honored dead, my love." She kissed him, her sweet scent and the smells of the offering cakes mingling in his nose.

ABOUT THE AUTHORS

Carolyn Ivy Stein loves writing stories about time travel, mystery, fantasy, and romance. Her short stories appeared in *WMG's Winter Holiday Spectacular 2021 Calendar of Short Stories*, *JewishFiction.net*, and can be found in her collections, *Lightning Scarred and Other Stories* and *Sweet Lifts*. She received nine Honorable Mentions from the *Writers of the Future Contest* for her fantasy and time travel stories. Learn more about Carolyn's work at http://www.carolynivystein.com.

Stephen Stein is a professor of military and naval history at the University of Memphis and teaches strategy at the US Naval War College. He is the author of seven books on history as well numerous articles on maritime and military history. His books include *Torpedoes to Aviation: Washington Irving Chambers and Technological Innovation in the New Navy, 1876-1913* and *The Sea in World History: Exploration, Travel, and Trade*. His article "The Greely Relief Expedition and the New Navy" won the Rear Admiral Ernest M. Eller Prize, an annual award for the best article on naval history. His upcoming book, *Military Strategy for Writers*, demystifies the often arcane field of military strategy. Learn more about Stephen Stein's work at https://stvstein.wixsite.com/stevestein/publications

Together Carolyn and Stephen Stein, write short stories as well as a variety of tabletop RPG supplements for *GURPS*, *Call of Cthulhu*, *Traveller*, and *TinyDungeon*. Their recent book, *War Galleys*, published by Steve Jackson Games, goes into detail on the ships presented in this story and includes detailed images of the ships.

When not writing, they play board games and tabletop RPGs, and attempt to discover the hidden secrets of New Mexico.

4

THE DOOM OF EGYPT
JULIA V. ASHLEY

The warm winds hissed across the dune before caressing Berenike's face. Flaring her malachite-green hood, Beren shielded her eyes from the grains of sand burnishing her scaled cheeks. She wound past the Pyramids of Mykerinos and Chephren, seeking her *mwt-mwt*, mother of her mother, for a tale to take her into the star-speckled night. Her ponderous form dug a trench through the shifting sands painted a burnt umber by the setting sun. She headed for the Pyramid of Cheops where her grandmother spent her evenings after feeding. A twitch of Beren's tongue caught the taste of copper in the air from the fresh sacrifices laid open on altars beneath the pyramids. Glistening crimson streaks ran down the sides of the limestone, forming imitation maps of the Nile.

A waste, Beren thought, preferring her food unmolested and free so that she might enrapture it herself. Her mwt-mwt doted on the peoples of the lower river valley, but when Berenike, Daughter of Selene, Ruler of the Night, and Victor over All, came to power, she would put an end to such silliness. A sigh escaped her as she imagined the impending delights.

The humans, skin beaten bronze by the sun, prostrated

themselves before her. Beren slid past and over them, crushing those in her direct path beneath her pale belly. The length of her tail nearly matched that of Chephren's base. Cries of adoration and agony sang to her as the sun sank, and she reached the largest of the three delta pyramids. Her grandmother's golden form wrapped around the brilliant white sloping stone structure once, then half again. Ebony chevrons patterned her head, resting on the western face of the pyramid, catching the last of the light.

Beren slithered up the great serpent's magnificent torso, looping up and up until her nose rested at the base of her grandmother's hooded head.

The elder serpent dipped her chin, blocking Beren from rising any further.

Undeterred, the younger cobra writhed until her serpentine figure lay snug in the groove between her grandmother's form and the smooth stones. "Mwt-Mwt," Berenike said with a juvenile lisp. "Tell me again of the night the Great Cleopatra VII Thea Philopator, last of the pharaohs, took an asp to her breast and doomed the peoples of Egypt."

"Tss," her grandmother hissed in annoyance and shifted her substantial body until it pressed Beren uncomfortably tight against the stone. As Beren slithered back on top, the great serpent reprimanded her. "Such fancies of youth. You've heard the story enough not to misquote it, child."

Beren turned her head to the setting sun so that her hood hid the mischievous smile working across her face. A deliberate mis-telling of the story always prompted her mwt-mwt to tell it anew from the beginning. If she had simply asked for the tale to put off bedtime, her grandmother would have refused. Mwt-Mwt, who had grown quite old and increasingly impatient of everything short of sunning herself, could not abide an incorrect version of the story. So Beren regularly used it to prod the noble lady.

The Doom of Egypt

The hint of a smile on the elder serpent said she knew the game and chose to play, anyway. Although, Mwt-Mwt's lips were permanently curved in a sinister smile, as all serpents' were, so Berenike could not be sure if this was true.

The giant cobra coiled higher up the pyramid before beginning. The edges of the stone planes crumbled beneath the pressure of her scales and rained an avalanche of stones on the servants below. Most succeeded in ducking past the falling rubble. The rest would remain buried beneath it, becoming a permanent part of the funerary base as the story unfolded.

The great serpent, nearly as wide as a man was tall, closed her eyes and lifted her chin. Her nostrils flared, and the tip of her tongue slipped out past vicious fangs, as if scenting a memory cast upon the wind nearly a century before.

"The eye of the sun shone down on the waters of the Mediterranean as Cleopatra's ships skated across the bottomless waters. Her consort, Marcus Antonius, joined his fleet to hers."

"What's a consort?" Beren interrupted.

"A lover."

"Tss-tss-tss." Beren giggled. Catching her grandmother's glare, she ducked her head and retracted her tongue.

"Pointed sails snapped sharply in the wind off the western coast of Greece at Actium in the early autumn. Their fleet of gilded ships glided across the cerulean waters beneath a cloudless sky to meet the blunt-sailed Roman armada lead by a would-be usurper, the treacherous Octavian."

"Why?" Beren could not help herself. This part of the story always nettled her like a grain of sand lodged under a scale. "Why would anyone go against Egypt?"

"Some silly business about Marc leaving Octavian's sister for Cleo."

"But Cleopatra VII! Could you blame him?"

"Of course not, now shush." Mwt-Mwt flicked her tongue,

and her scales rasped against the stone. "Cleopatra gave Octavian the chance she gave all men, to succumb to her wiles and wishes, but he chose not to, thinking himself stronger than the men before him. Cleo laughed in his face. Stronger? No. But more foolish? Perhaps. It bothered her not. She'd grown tired of making sport of men, each, in turn, believing himself superior to her. These meager mortal souls presumed too much, pitting themselves against Cleopatra, born of gods. In the end, their greatest ruler, Julius Caesar, was taken down by nothing more than the sharp-toothed blades of lesser men.

"You will find men die easily, Berenike, even the pharaohs of Egypt. Cleopatra had little use for them other than pleasure. By the time Octavian tried her patience, she'd already seen to the deaths of her two brother-husbands. Against her, men were nothing. Yet Octavian thought himself able to best her—Cleopatra of Ptolemy's line."

Beren flipped her belly toward the darkening sky, looking directly up into the older serpent's face. "Ptolemy was a just man too. A pharaoh, but a man."

"Yes, yes. Just a man, and just as dead. Yet he survived long enough to sire Cleopatra."

"Hmmph." Beren closed her eyes and relaxed her hood as she listened.

"The prows of Octavian's fleet broke the horizon. Their masts stabbing at the sky as the ships bore down on the Egyptian navy. And..." The great serpent paused for a deep breath. "The sun rose and set on the defeat of Cleopatra's vessels.

"The female pharaoh hissed in rage, turned her ships about, and raced south to the safety of the Nile. The weaker Antonius broke through the Roman line to follow, abandoning his forces to surrender," the elder serpent said with a note of sorrow. Her eyelids flicked open, and she appeared to contemplate the dunes as they turned from umber to the deep violet of wine. "At Alexandria, Cleopatra's loyal servants swept her off her warship upon a palanquin, whisking her across the sands to the Ptolemaic palace."

"Where she asp-ed herself," Beren lisped.

"No. She did not. She plotted for a year and a day to—"

"Aaasssppp hersel—" Beren began in a singsong voice, ending on a hiss as her grandmother flexed her jaws. Her massive fangs glistened. Beren slithered back down along her grandmother's tail, flattening her head against the golden scales of her back.

The elder's jaws slipped back into place, and she resumed the story. "The year passed, yet the tides did not turn in her favor. Octavian landed in Alexandria, and Cleopatra took refuge in the mausoleum built to honor her, while her cowardly consort stabbed himself. Useless man.

"Again, she gave Octavian the noble option of becoming her consort. Again, the wretched Roman declined."

"Oooh," Beren hummed, ending in an "Umph" as her grandmother flexed a length of muscles.

"Cleopatra had made plans for such an unfortunate outcome." The elder paused to be sure she wouldn't be interrupted before continuing. "Returning to her palace, her maids stripped her, bathed her, and dressed her in golden ceremonial robes that shimmered against her pale breasts."

"Ew! Don't tell me about pale flesh." Beren flopped her long body over and over as if writhing in agony. "Like a grub. Creepy."

"She was marked as the greatest beauty in all the ages, rivaling the Roman Venus."

"Not without scales, she didn't." Beren slid back up to settle her head next to her grandmother's at the apex of the pyramid. "Skip to the part about her taking up the snake and dooming all of Egypt."

The elder serpent flared her hood, shoving the younger

Beren down the pyramid a step. "Resplendent in her golden robes, the light reflecting from her as if from a star, Cleopatra stood upon her balcony overlooking her beloved Egypt—her birthright—before turning to the tumultuous sea where Octavian's fleet sat ready to enslave her. He wished to take her back to Rome in chains, to drag her through the streets where the weak peoples of the Empire would jeer at her, reducing a pharaoh of Egypt to peasant, to property.

"It would be more noble to end her own life, to join her predecessors, and to be laid among the gods, than to allow herself to be so demeaned."

"Ptss." Beren rolled her eyes and flipped back onto her belly, feigning boredom.

Her grandmother paid no mind. "At the sound of slippered feet, Cleopatra turned from the view back to her personal quarters lavishly painted in iron oxides, azurite, malachite, and orpiment, and lit by the morning sun. A troop of handmaidens entered and parted for their headmistress to come forward. The aged woman with burnished skin held a woven basket before her. She approached, knelt, and held it aloft.

"Cleopatra removed the lid. Her eyes narrowed as an asp"— Beren held her tongue as her grandmother gave her a side glare —"slithered around the circumference of the basket, searching for an escape. Her loyal servants had secreted the venomous snake inside even as the guards circled her palace. She could take up the serpent and end her life as quickly and painlessly as possible.

"Yet, as she looked at the creature waiting to do her bidding, the bud of an idea blossomed.

"'Take it away,' she said. A murmur of protests arose, and she squelched it. 'Release it into the sands. It is not needed here.'

"The headmistress stood, nodded, and asked if her pharaoh wished to be escorted to the throne room to await her fate.

"'No, I shall meet my fate through prayer,' Cleopatra said, a slow smile forming on her face, not unlike that of the serpent in the basket.

"Her personal guard secreted her from the palace in a basket of her own. At the edge of the desert, she mounted a camel and rode through the day to the banks of the Nile. There, she chose a crocodile to ride across the waters."

Beren's head popped up, bumping her grandmother's jaw. "A crocodile? You added that, Mwt-Mwt. That's not how the story goes."

"I have never told the story any other way. I say she rode a crocodile, and so she did. Once in the delta, she walked upon bare feet under the starlit heavens to Per-Wadjet. The temple of the goddess Wadjet, protector of the lower Nile and guardian of the pharaohs, rose before her. Cleopatra stepped inside the stone structure and stood on mud-spattered feet to face the statue of a woman with the head of a—"

Beren rose up before her grandmother, their eyes level, and she hissed, "A cobra! She came to Wadjet because she wanted a cobra instead of an asp!" Bobbing her head up and down triumphantly in front of her grandmother, she continued, "She chose a cobra, and then all of Egypt fell."

"Sssilence, child. You wreck the story with your restlessness. Why are youth so bent on crashing through time?" The giant cobra turned her hooded head away, and Berenike knew she had pushed her grandmother to the point of leaving off the story completely and insisting Beren go to sleep.

Clinching her muscles into a tight coil, Beren willed herself to remain quiet and wait out the elder's agitation. The winds raced across the dunes, snatching the day's heat away as Beren bowed her hooded head. She quivered as much from the exertion of waiting as from the air leaching away her warmth.

Beren counted silently. *One. Two. Three.* She reached numbers beyond counting, and just as Beren feared the elder serpent had fallen asleep, she exhaled and stretched out her neck.

The elder snake twisted, pulled herself erect, and glared down upon the younger one before resuming. "The temple priestesses assembled in an array before the base of Wadjet's statue, the oracle at their center. They pleaded for an answer to help the pharaoh. They had sent an asp as requested, though it ripped at their hearts to aid in taking her life, and yet Cleopatra stood before them unharmed. They rejoiced. What more could they do to serve her?

"'Take me to the pit,' Cleopatra demanded.

"The oracle swore. The priestesses stumbled back. They begged her not to take such a brutal course of action, but Cleopatra's eyes flamed. She hissed, and the oracle fell to her knees, prostrating herself on the inlaid stones at the pharaoh's feet, and the priestesses followed. The oracle resisted, saying no one went to the pit but the goddess. The asp had been a gentler end. Less wretched. To go to the pits was to succumb to torture worse than being dragged before the peoples of Rome.

"The priestesses wailed. With tears streaking her face, the oracle begged Cleopatra to allow her to divine another solution —for the pharaoh to allow her and the priestesses to throw their bodies upon the lances of Octavian in her place. Anything, they begged, but do not test the goddess. Do not go to the pit."

"But she did," Beren whispered.

"But she did," her grandmother confirmed with a solemn nod. "Cleopatra circled the statue of Wadjet to the hidden door at its base." She paused to look at the young serpent clenched with the effort of keeping quiet, and she nodded in satisfaction. "The last pharaoh of Egypt opened the door and descended the steps to the pit. Wretched screaming echoed from the chamber, then silence fell in the darkness, and Cleopatra met her death."

The moon hid behind the horizon as Berenike breathed in

the truth of the story. The sands around Cheops sighed. The violet dunes fell into the shadows of death. Cleopatra VII had descended those steps, knowing she would not return.

The young snake slipped between the massive scaled back of her grandmother and the warm stones and held her breath. This was her favorite part.

Looking up expectantly to the massive golden cobra, Beren found her with a sly smile on her lips. "And then..." she whispered.

"And then." Her grandmother flared her hood and lifted her chin to take in the view of her beloved Egypt. The starlight caught in her kohl-black eyes. "What rose from the pit bore the wrath of the great Cleopatra in the body of the goddess Wadjet. Rage writhed inside the body of a golden cobra, rising tall beside the statue. The pit once filled with the most venomous snakes of Egypt lay empty. The priestesses fell back, eyes wide with awe and horror.

"A general rushed into the temple, defiling the sacred ground with his presence. He cried out, 'Where is the pharaoh? Octavian marches on us.' He stopped at the sight of the golden cobra. 'Wadjet!' he exclaimed, falling to his knees.

"'Wadjet is part of me, but not all of me,' hissed the serpent, rising twice the height of any man.

"The general peered up into the female pharaoh's face within the cobra's hood. He fell with his forehead pressed to the stones. 'How may I serve you?'"

"The giant golden cobra unhinged her jaws and swallowed the man whole. The soldiers who had accompanied him fell back, but the priestesses stepped forward."

The great serpent paused as the sands hissed across the dunes, whispering of the story to come. Her neck stretched out, rising as tall as possible.

With one third of her own body erect, Beren swayed in anticipation, every muscle taut. In her excitement, she shifted her weight to get a fraction higher, lost her balance, and tumbled backward down the sloping side of the pyramid. She flipped, caught herself before hitting the bottom, and slithered back to the top, accompanied by the rasping laughter of her grandmother.

At this point in the story, the great serpent relented, allowing her progeny to assist in a rapid-fire recitation of the scourge of the Mediterranean.

Beren began in a breathless voice, "She passed the devout priestesses and ate her way through the guards, growing larger and longer as she left the temple."

"Yesssss, she charged across the delta and through the waters of the Nile."

"She dove into the sea."

"And reared out of the water, a serpent twice the length of any boat in the Roman fleet."

"She wrapped around Octavian's ship."

"Hood flared, the golden cobra faced him, wearing naught but her glistening scales and her serpent's smile, venom dripping from her fangs."

"He ordered archers to fire."

"But the arrows merely pricked her scales. She dove over the prow of the ship, wrapped around the hull, and scrubbed the arrows away. Then she rose on the far side and—"

"Struck at Octavian." Beren's eyes gleamed, and her tongue flicked at the air.

The elder serpent laughed. "The crew stood stunned as she grew before them. In terror, they dove overboard as she flexed her new body, crushing the hull. She began to hunt the floating sailors at leisure, picking them from the indigo waters. By nightfall the next day, she had grown into a monstrous sea serpent."

"She dove beneath the waters and headed north across the sea."

Beren's grandmother bobbed her head and settled more securely around the pyramid, further wearing away its edges. "And now it is time for you to go to sleep."

Horror-struck, Beren's slender fangs hung from her gaping mouth. "I cannot. All of Egypt has yet to fall."

"All of Egypt does not fall."

"It might still."

"The cobra goddess headed north to Rome."

"Yes, but—"

"There she spent the next decade *not* bothering Egypt at all." The elder snake swayed on the night breeze, closing her eyes to the memory. "Now, sleep before I eat *you*."

"But you skipped the middle, where she ate all of Crete and half of Greece. And you haven't gotten to the part where she slithered ashore in Brundisium and crashed through all the cities laying between her and the capital." Beren again rose in her excitement but stopped short of tumbling over again. "She ate and ate until the bulge in her belly grew so large she crushed the Roman roads beneath her. She—"

"Yes. Yes. All the Mediterranean knows what she did to the Empire's prized infrastructure. Even to this day, carts cannot pass the ravines her mammoth body dug into the stone paths. The hovels of Beneventum and Capua shall not rise again because of the devastation she wrought."

Beren wriggled in a sinuous curve. "And if they do, she will return, right, Mwt-Mwt? She will come back and crush them and eat them."

Instead of scolding her, the golden cobra bobbed her head with a satisfied smile, closing her eyes. "Yes, she would. She did. And she does, to any who dare raise their heads above that of a sandworm. But, the first time—that was the most splendid of all."

Beren flicked her tongue at the elder serpent's nostril, and her grandmother's eyes flew open. The young serpent rose again, so they were eye to eye.

"Yesss?" Beren begged for her to continue. She smelled grandmother's irritation but could no longer contain herself.

"Cleopatra the Cobra's first invasion of Rome." The serpent bopped Beren down a step as she spoke. "Ah, that day, the sun rose over the city. The Romans lined the walls, fearful of the rumors. They heard the rumble of her approach as the roadways crumbled. They heard the crash of the arches falling under her. The cobra's silhouette grew in magnitude to unimaginable heights. The ground shook beneath them as the very stones quaked. The soldiers and citizens fell from the ramparts. They ran through the streets, screaming of their impending deaths."

"And she ate them," Beren said.

"And she ate them," the golden cobra answered.

"And she grew."

"Yes, she grew."

"And she was monstrous to behold."

"So monstrous that no man—"

"No man," Beren breathed.

"And no woman—" At this addition, Beren gave her grandmother the side-eye. "No one could stop her. She needed no man, woman, or god to embolden her."

"Because she *was* a god!"

"Yessss!"

Beren waited, but her grandmother spoke no more. She writhed a bit to get the older snake's attention. But the elder snake spoke no more. Beren bopped her nose against the elder snake's hood, but the golden cobra spoke no more.

"Mwt-Mwt! Don't stop there!"

The elder snake suddenly curled around the younger body, intertwining it with her own. "You do not command a god."

"No, Mwt-Mwt," Beren said in a strangled voice. The older

The Doom of Egypt

snake loosened her hold, and Beren quickly slithered out. "But"—she arced high onto the peak of the pyramid to avoid being entrapped again—"she returned one day to eat all of Egypt, right?"

"No. You know she did not. She loved her Egypt and its people." The older snake laid her chin upon the peak of Cheops, worn flat from the many nights used as her perch. "And cease calling me Mwt-Mwt. It does not suit me." Her kohl-black eyes drifted closed.

"But you *are* the mother of my mother."

"Nekhbet, the vulture goddess, wished to be called Mwt. She had more of a nurturing spirit. When my people, the Egyptian people, offer sacrifices to me, they need not come seeking a mother to coddle them, but a warrior prepared to protect them at all costs."

Beren's hood relaxed, and she laid her head on the great serpent's back. "I could call you Wadjet."

"I am greater than Wadjet." The elder serpent's long, lithe body eased, letting the young snake drop into the groove beside the stones.

"What about Cleo-Cobra?" Berenike asked as she slithered into the crevice to keep warm for the night.

"Tsss, tsss, tsss," the golden serpent answered with a lazy laugh. "If you must. Now, go to sleep."

"Because tomorrow I shall eat all the peoples of Egypt."

"No, you will not."

"I will," Beren whispered with a secret smile.

"I shall eat you before I let that happen." The golden body tightened in warning.

Beren wriggled into a more comfortable position and waited until she heard the lisping snore of the great serpent before hissing passed her own fangs, "One day, I, Berenike, Daughter of Selene, Ruler of the Night, and Victor over All, shall grow big enough to eat even *you, Cleo-Cobra*."

She settled in with a sigh, imagining the impending doom of Egypt after she overpowered the once-great pharaoh, Cleopatra VII, now god-pharaoh of the Mediterranean. As Beren drifted toward sleep, she could taste the salty, sweet blood of all those people.

Starlight glinted off her grandmother's kohl-black eye, startling Beren back to wakefulness. The great serpent peered down at her favorite progeny with a secret smile of her own. "So your mother thought once, before I ate *her*."

The golden cobra's sinister laugh rasped in the cold desert air.

And Berenike quaked at the bone-chilling sound.

ABOUT THE AUTHOR

Julia V. Ashley writes speculative fiction that explores the space between the real and the imagined. As an architect, she often delves into the crumbling buildings of the Gothic South where she grew up to find inspiration. She lives along the Natchez Trace Parkway with her husband, two children, her adoring pup, and a variety of wildlife. Her debut short story "Two Tickets to Tomorrow" was published in the 2022 anthology *4th and Starlight*. Her humorous horror story, "Eugene, Such a Sweet Boy," will appear in the upcoming *Murder Bugs* anthology in the winter of 2024. And *Jazz by Faelight*, her new short story collection, is available now.

5

DIVINE CALM

CHARLES E. GANNON

In Memory of Eric Flint. Having known you for years, I can only wish our friendship had gone on for centuries. Given your fondness for butterfly effects, this is a literally suitable tribute.

November 20, 1274; Hakata Bay, Island of Kyushu, Nippon

Admiral Hong Dagu nodded; the captains of his mostly Korean landing force rose from their obeisant prostrations on the deck. "Report," he ordered.

The tallest of the officers stepped forward. "Honored Hong Dagu, sea-lord of Goryeo—"

Dagu made a chopping gesture with his hand. "The sky darkens behind us. There is no time for titles and ritual. How went the battle on the beaches?"

The captain swallowed. "We have carried the day, Admiral. The samurai who engaged us were brave but fought more as individuals than as soldiers. I am told it is their fashion, and that they often resolve battles through one or more individual combats."

Divine Calm

"Uncivilized savages," sniffed Dagu's adjutant and childhood compatriot Ja-o dismissively. "Too stupid even to respond to Kublai Khan's repeated, explicit commands that they recognize him, in title and tithe, as their suzerain. So the samurai of their leading shoguns make their impossible stand here in Hakata Bay, choosing a desperate defense over thralldom."

Dagu shrugged. "I cannot say I blame them. And they die well."

Ja-o's voice lowered. "Do you respect them so much?"

"Respect them?" Dagu raised an eyebrow. "I observe they do what they think they must bravely. That does not make them any less stupid, any less a horde of vermin. Do you not agree, Captain?"

The tall Korean to whom he addressed this question snapped to attention. "Sir, they are vermin—but tenacious, even so. They suffered great casualties from our bowfire, and I do not believe they had prior experience with our flaming or gunpowder arrows. And after advancing through that fire, they had no organized tactics for breaching our shield wall. But despite their losses, they did not relent."

"Did you take many casualties?"

The captain's gaze wavered. "Fewer than they did."

"Hmm. I see. So if we were to face five times their number tomorrow?"

The captain grew pale. He paused long enough to choose his words carefully. "With your leadership, great Dagu, we would of course prevail. But I suspect that they would inflict even more casualties upon us with their strange, long swords and their—tenacity."

Dagu frowned. "Yes. Of course. So what have your scouts reported? Are their forces massing inland, behind the rises and brush that hems in the shore?"

The captain licked his lips. "Our first two scouts did not

return. We have sent another two. We await their return." He shrank slightly before Dagu's glower. "I shall send more," he offered uncertainly.

Dagu frowned, turned away. "No. We have few enough men who have any familiarity with these people, their ways, their language, their coastline. We cannot spend them too freely. Besides, if the second pair of scouts does not return, that partially settles a measure of our present uncertainty: whether control of the beach means control of the coast. If these Japanese are picking off our scouts, denying us the ability to see what lays further inland, it stands to reason that they wish to conceal a force from us, that our control may very well be limited to what we can see. So if we allow the army to camp on the beach, where it would be vulnerable to a much larger counterattack at night—" Dagu broke off, straightened formally. "Jo-a, pass the word: ready the landing barges to bring our men back to the ships."

"Jun-gi," Jo-a whispered, using Dagu's given name, the one of their shared childhood, "is that wise?"

Dagu leaned closer to him, kept his own voice equally low. "Old friend, we know there is a literal tempest approaching from the sea. We have reason to fear there is a figurative Japanese tempest waiting just beyond the ridges lining this bay. We have two choices: leave or stay. We may gamble that the Japanese are not there and allow our army to bivouac on the beach. But that also means that we must keep our vessels here, where we may support and resupply them. Yet the masters of our ships tell me that our best chance to avoid their destruction is to escape this bay before the storm makes landfall. So even if there is no Japanese army waiting beyond those ridges, our fleet might be wrecked if we remain here."

Jo-a made a deferential bow as he offered an alternate perspective. "An almost equal number of the shipmasters are urging you to draw in closer behind the headland and weather the storm as best we might, that it is approaching too swiftly to avoid it."

"A chance I would take *if* we knew the soundings and rocks of this bay and *if* I knew there was no Japanese army beyond that ridge," Dagu replied, jabbing a finger toward the open window of his cabin and at the body-littered beaches and the bluffs beyond. "If we receive a report from one of these scouts that the inland plains are clear, then we shall leave our men on the beach and our ships will weather the storm here as best as they may. But if we hear nothing, I must presume that destruction is bearing down on us from the sea *and* the land. In that event, our army might be slaughtered in the surf before the sun comes up. In that event, we must take them aboard and listen to our foremost shipmasters: that in order to save this fleet and the army that it will be carrying, we must flee this bay with all haste."

Ja-o shrugged. "Then let us hope we hear from one of those scouts."

Dagu stared back out the window. "If the gods are kind, we shall."

∽

Gwan crept through the unfamiliar undergrowth that dominated the floor of the small defile between the ridges hemming in Hakata Bay. He had already found one of the prior two scouts slumped in the bushes, an arrow through his back. He hoped that discovery was not a harbinger of his own imminent fate.

Flinching as an incautious step snapped a twig, Gwan crouched down, his upper teeth set upon his lower lip. The slightest sound could kill him if a Japanese archer was still nearby, was still—

Gwan saw the edge of a sandal, its sole turned

perpendicular to the ground, beneath a bush on the other side of the game trail. Leaning down even further, he peered between the leaves that concealed him and saw, quite clearly, the scout that had been sent out with him—a Mongol named Tughur—sprawled beneath the bush, the snapped shaft of an arrow protruding from this left temple.

I am the accursed of the gods, Gwan thought, offering a quick devotional word to those same gods in the hope that it would propitiate them enough to grant him deliverance. If only they would give him some sign of assurance—

Gwan caught a glimpse of movement to his left, glanced swiftly in that direction—but what he had at first imagined was the feathered fletching of a Japanese archer's arrow was, in fact, the wing of a butterfly, or perhaps a moth, which had alighted upon a nearby branch. *Late in the season for you*, Gwan thought. *It puts you in at least as much peril as I am.* Curious that such an insect was still flitting around in November, he reflexively moved closer to examine it.

In another reality, in an alternate world, Gwan's typically cautious habits of thought might have caused him to pause just long enough to worry about the sound he could make while moving in that direction, could have instead propelled him back out on to the game trail to die at the hand of a hidden Japanese archer. But instead, before he could think the better of it, Gwan had moved deeper into the bushes to get a better view of the butterfly and so, startled it into flight again.

Disappointed, having come within a foot of its simple, white wings, Gwan stared up after it, then lowered his eyes—

And discovered that he had stumbled upon a perfect vantage point that showed him the plains that lay behind the ridges around Hakata Bay. He inched forward, pushing a stray bough out of his way.

The plains were empty. There was no Japanese army, not

even patrol encampments or pickets. The path inland, and to Kyushu's administrative capital at Dazaifu, was clear.

And best of all, Gwan reflected as he began to carefully and quietly retrace his steps, he would live to make that report.

∾

August 18, 1853, War Department, Washington D.C.

Secretary of the Navy John Pendleton Kennedy glanced up from fortress assessment reports as Lt. Billings ran in, breathless. "Sir, today's mail pouch. A letter from the *Susquehanna*."

Kennedy stuck out a hand that was at once forceful in motion but patrician in form. "About time." Not bothering with the saber-shaped letter opener in the top drawer of his immense desk, he tore off the sealing flap, pulled out the folded papers within and read:

Commodore M.C. Perry to the Secretary of the Navy, the Hon. John P. Kennedy
United States Steam frigate Susquehanna,
Yedo Bay, July 14, 1853

Sir:

I have the pleasure of informing you I have now commenced my mission to open relations with the islands of Nippon, which the Chinese call by the pejorative title Dongyang.

The flotilla arrived in Yedo harbor on July 8. As the reports of Siebold led us to anticipate, the ruling classes of these islands affect Chinese or Korean names. However, the great

A BIT OF LUCK

majority of these administrators and bureaucrats trace very little if any of their personal heritage back to the invaders who secured a foothold on Kyushu for the Yuan Dynasty in 1274, which enabled the larger and decisive landing in June of 1275.

Although Siebold's accounts had readied us to expect to an initial rebuff, we were instead met with guarded interest by a legation of officials from China's Qing dynasty, attended by an almost equal number of native notables. The circumstances, dress, and titles of the former were as opulent as those of the latter were unassuming. These profound distinctions in authority and class were repeatedly observed during our initial visit to the city itself, there to provision the ships under the direct supervision of the Imperial Chinese authorities.

The condition of the majority of the population is reminiscent of a country that remains under strict occupation, although Chinese military forces are not commonly in evidence. However, Imperial officials and bureaucrats are omnipresent, maintaining close watch on almost all transactions of any political or economic import. Furthermore, it soon became apparent that this autocratic power was maintained through the exercise of severe punishments—including torture and execution—for the slightest of infractions. The unremitting fear that is the daily diet of the indigenous Japanese is matched only by the suppressed hatred with which they regard their foreign rulers.

We were at a loss to understand why the famed isolation of these islands was so readily relaxed upon our arrival, but this became evident enough when the local Prefect's exchequer entertained us with a light lunch in his own secluded garden. It seems that with the increasing chaos arising from the Opium Wars on the Chinese mainland, Dongyang has become a poor relative in the greater family of Peking's satrapies. The resident Imperial authorities, holding their offices by familial inheritance and sinecure, are mindful of their need to maintain control through harsh measures. But with China spending lavishly to both quell the Taiping Rebellion and restore authority lost in its Opium Wars, Nippon's Imperial factotums are painfully aware that their reduced coffers are insufficient to the costs of ensuring their own protection and continuance. Through tortuously indirect insinuations, then, the Exchequer let it be known that if our flotilla had arrived with the purpose of opening Nippon for trade in opium, this could be effected, but surreptitiously, and only if the local Imperial authorities were properly compensated for their carefully averted attention.

I am happy to report that none of our shore party expressed their resentment at this assumption that their oath, uniform, and flag were presumed to be nothing more than facades behind which we concealed profiteering ambitions and the intent to trade in substances that are not only contraband but patently unwholesome and unholy in their effects. (I suspect the youngest of our party held his tongue more out of shock than circumspection.)

These initial encounters also served to bring us into contact with various Japanese who revealed that the truth of their nation's sad durance beneath its Chinese masters was even worse than we had thus far conceived. Whereas we projected that Peking kept Nippon inviolate from foreign contact because it wished to maintain a monopoly over the resources and clever craftsmen of these islands (and then later, to protect them from the scourges of opium), we learned that the real reason was far different.

In the nearly six centuries since the Japanese were conquered by the Chinese (or, more precisely, Mongols and Koreans), there have been at least five rebellions which stretched from the northernmost islands down to their southernmost extent at Yakushima. There may have been further rebellions almost as expansive, but since local histories are forbidden (all chronicles are kept by the Chinese bureaucrats; the writing or possession of rival accounts carries a capital sentence), there is no reliable consensus on just how many full-scale revolts have occurred. What is a matter of both record and recent memory are the bloody reprisals, in which whole families or towns have been put to the sword on the faintest of suspicions. The fashion in which these reprisals have been carried out rival the most savage and extreme to be found in the annals of human history. The veracity of these claims is not to be readily doubted: the diverse accounts of Japanese from every social station varied little on the bloody particulars of these atrocities.

In consequence, we have come to learn that there is a very large hidden collective among the indigenous Japanese that trace their traditions and influence back to pre-invasion Nippon. Although stripped of their lands and official titles, the descendants of the shoguns and samurai are remembered through secret names and shown great (albeit covert) deference and honor by the overwhelming majority of the population. Similarly, although native Buddhism has been uniformly suppressed for the last five hundred years (insofar as it was deemed a refuge for cultural intransigence and insolence), its undisclosed practitioners still roam the land, often working as itinerant healers, scribes, or storytellers. Members of both these now-secret societies are avidly sought by Imperial intelligencers, who routinely seize, torture, and slay their suspected members on the thinnest of pretexts.

Through channels which I shall not endanger by sharing either names or places of contact (not being able to ensure the fate of the contents of this mail pouch), I, and several of my officers, have been approached by well-situated members of this diffuse collective who are committed to tossing off the yoke of their oppressors. Specifically, they have made it quite clear that, were we to use our new presence on Nippon to surreptitiously aid them, they would remember our United States with deathless gratitude at such time as they might free themselves from the shackles of more than half a millennium of bondage. While I refused to vouchsafe them an immediate answer, I vigorously commend their request to both the State Department and the Executive for long and careful consideration.

In closing, I do not possess the arrogance, nor presume the competence, to discourse upon the issues of farsighted statecraft or implicit moral responsibility that are raised by this request from a long-oppressed people whose industry and courtesy have been beyond compare. What I may speak to with reasonable competence are the military practicalities inherent in embracing the relationship they propose.

To wit:

We live in the era of steam as the decisive naval innovation of this moment and of the foreseeable future. This means that safe harbors and far-flung coaling stations populated by loyal populations are necessities if our burgeoning Republic, barely seventy-five years old as I pen these words, is to stand as a strategic equal among its globe-spanning peers. The location of Nippon alone, convenient to the Chinese coast and furnished with numerous well-developed ports, makes it ideal to those purposes. We would also possess the deathless gratitude of its people, while conversely resting assured in their enduring enmity toward the only regional power large enough to warrant our military concern: China. The iron foundries and steel products of the Japanese are superior to Chinese manufactures in almost all regards, and their attention to detail and innovation promises that they shall more readily and successfully adopt the principles of industrialization.

It is said that no force may project itself into new regions without first securing a steady ally therein. I submit we may have just found that ally.

> With Great Respect, I am, sir, your obedient servant,
> Commodore M.C. Perry, Commander, Pacific Squadron

Billings was standing on the balls of his feet, having watched from that precarious posture as Kennedy digested the contents. "Sir, what does it say? Has Commodore Perry done it?"

Kennedy smiled—not an entirely benign expression—and carefully folded the letter. "Yes, Billings, he has done it. As for what it says—well, I suppose you could summarize it this way:

"Now, things will be different."

ABOUT THE AUTHOR

Dr. Charles E. Gannon's books have won the Dragon Award, the ALA Choice Award (Outstanding Book), the Compton Crook Award, and have been nominated for four Nebulas. He is best known for the multiply best-selling Caine Riordan hard sf novels which include 4 finalists for the Nebula, 2 for the Dragon, and a Compton Crook winner. In 2020, the "Caineverse" expanded to include the closely entwined *Murphy's Lawless* series.

Gannon's epic fantasy series, *The Vortex of Worlds*, debuted in 2021 and the second novel, *Into the Vortex* was a 2023 Dragon Award fantasy finalist. He has collaborated with Eric Flint in the *New York Times* and *Wall Street Journal* bestselling Ring of Fire series and written solo novels in John Ringo's Black Tide Rising world. In addition to numerous other fiction credits, he has also written for table-top roleplaying games and as a scriptwriter and producer in New York City.

As a Distinguished Professor of English, Gannon received 5 Fulbrights, and his *Rumors of War & Infernal Machines* won the 2006 ALA Choice Award for Outstanding Book. He is a frequent subject matter expert for national media venues (NPR, Discovery, etc.) and for various intelligence and defense agencies.

6

A RUINOUS RENT

L. A. SELBY

"The king will want you no more, when he finds you hide a bogey under your bed."

Queen Yolande, twenty-two years old and pregnant, but too early to show, looked askance at her maid. "I'd rather he not want me than not be alive." Her luck and health came from the bogey, and the king's luck came from her, now they were married.

Maggie wiped her hands on her long gray dress, her lined face puckered in distaste and frustration. "Say the word 'dead,' Your Majesty, and be honest about it."

Only Maggie would tell her that kind of truth anymore. Yolande sat on the edge of her four-posted bed. She pulled her purple woolen cape closer for warmth despite the towering fire in the bedchamber hearth. The ermine collar tickled her cheeks. The freezing March drizzle might be outside eleven feet of stone walls, but her single window was thin and not sealed well at its edge. The headland surf bashed cliffs far below the castle, its sound easily penetrating her small window and turning her days into endless surge and retreat. She uselessly wished her cape was made of bearskin.

Not really. She just wanted to be warm. The Kinghorn castle at Fife should have been easier to heat with its green-glass windows than her solar at Edinburgh with its thick wooden shutters. Or maybe the cold was inside of her, not outside. She shivered.

Maggie leaned over as if she meant to check under the bed but not quite far enough. "I know the bogey is still under there. I hear him snuffling." She straightened, glowering.

"You do not." She argued like she had when she was a child, which was easy to do around Maggie, who'd served her since then.

Of course the bogey was there, and maybe he snuffled because his little nose dripped with cold no matter how many blankets she gave him. He had been there, watching and protecting her since she was a baby. That was what bogeys did, when one was lucky enough to have them: they watched, protected, and traded a bit of luck.

"You can't keep him. He has to go," Maggie demanded as if she had a right to.

A shrill squeak, louder than a mouse but not as loud as a bird, pipped and cut itself off. Now she would have to comfort him. He was nearing five years old, and not an age to be teased any longer.

Before she could say a word, its voice trilled in childish singsong, "I have a secret, and you can't have it!"

Maggie clapped her hands, glowering. "There! It means you no good. Get rid of it."

Yolande straightened and held her hands open with entreaty. "I can't, and you know I can't. Please do not make such demands. I know the rumors"—*the bogeys pinched ears and stole sheets*—"and what they're accused of"—*tormenting and thieving*—"but it's not true. They're being blamed for things they haven't done. They are only misunderstood."

That was what she said, hoping to convince Maggie, soften

her heart, and keep her quiet a bit longer. But what her mind did between her words was much different. What had the bogey meant by *secret*?

When the bogey had been old and she had been a baby, he'd never admitted what he knew. When teenaged, he had mocked her for being stupid, and she had taunted him back. He was a child now and soon to be a baby. Twenty years was all any bogey had to live, beginning to horrible end. Yolande's chest tightened. She could not have her own child and a bogey too. The bogey would need her strength as it grew younger. Her undivided attention. Her protection—just the way he used to protect her.

If only he had another few years to live, or her baby had waited.

The bogey needed love she would not have to give.

Maggie started pacing, her slippered feet swishing over the cool stone. "You can't have it here. When we left Edinburgh, I thought it might stay behind, bless you, but it followed, and there's no one here but me to suffer thinking of its scabby, stinking body and its claws going for you in your sleep, and now you say a baby is to come. No. It's a demon."

Yolande gathered her cape, stood, and touched the woman's arm to soften her. The king would arrive in a few hours. Maybe less, if the rain did not worsen and the roads held firm.

Maggie pulled away.

Yolande put as much entreaty in her tone as she could without sounding weak. "It's not a demon." Well, it was part demon, part Fae, and hence that loneliness. That need. "It wants comfort, Maggie, just like any creature." And it would need more comfort. More blankets. And warmth. And to have her always there. And she could not do that.

Her eyes stung for what was to come.

"Don't parse words about demons under the bed." Maggie's voice rose. "When the king comes, I'll be telling him."

"You won't. He'll ask first how long you've known, if he believes you at all, and then he'll ask why you waited until after we married to reveal it, and when he knows I am to have his heir—" She wanted to keep going, but Maggie's red face and twitching fingers made her stop.

Her own cheeks warmed with shame. Protecting the bogey was important, but so was Maggie, and so was the king. They all deserved more of her.

A tiny hoof, the size of a dog's paw, poked out from under the bed and pulled back. "I have a secret!" said the bogey, and the only thing missing from its tone was the "nah nah."

Maggie grabbed her broom from beside the door. "Begone, foul beastie!" she shrieked and lunged.

Yolande grabbed for the broom but missed. Her cape caught on the edge of her heel.

Maggie shoved the broom in and out.

The bogey squealed, now laughing. Yolande timed the strikes and grabbed again, successful this time, and Maggie tripped and fell against the wooden linen trunk.

Her breath quick, Yolande shook the broom in Maggie's face. "Leave him be! He's done you no harm!"

"I have a—" the bogey sang again.

"Stop!" Yolande ordered. She dropped the broom and pointed at Maggie, mouthing "Stop!" to her as well. Then she crouched by the bed, her cape pooling about her, the chill forgotten.

How did one get a child to tell a secret? She did not remember back that far, but chiding sometimes worked, at least for human children.

"Bogey, it is not nice to tease."

He laughed.

She glanced at Maggie, who had scooted back to the wall and stood, wide-eyed, the hearth fire drawing dancing lines on her cheeks and scattering shadows like watchers on the walls.

"Come. You must tell me," Yolande said to the creature beneath her bed.

"I want."

"What do you want?"

"A hug."

She leaned back, the hair raising on her neck. In all his time, she had never touched him, and he had never asked. That smell like sun-ripened fen oozing up from below. That skin. And Maggie watching it all, knowing if she told anyone, ever, it might be death by axe or rope.

He poked a hoof out and drew it back. "It is a good secret. I will never have to leave. You will be so happy! Give me a hug."

Maggie muttered the Lord's Prayer behind her.

The bogey was so lonely. She couldn't though. He was part demon and part Fae, rejected by both and destined to be reforged, and soon. But she was human and pious, except for just this one thing.

He edged from under the bed despite the brightness of the hearth fire. He held out his rangy arms, his bulging eyes glittering and begging as they never had when he had been old. He had been her guide and mentor and luck-giver. She owed him. She was married to a king.

"What if I give you more blankets and have my bed moved closer to the fire for you?"

He shook his head, his shining gray lip poking out. "No."

She blinked, thinking as hard as she could about children and secrets. "I do not believe you then. You do not have a secret." She could have stood, but her heart told her stay close. Behind her, Maggie still prayed, and it had taken a chanting tone.

"I do!" He bounced on his hooves, coming up almost as high as her knee. He scratched at a scab on his head and a speck of blood pooled.

Though she could not be sure he lied, could never be sure

anymore what he truly thought, she crossed her arms and narrowed her eyes and hoped he would be cowed into his old honesty. "No, you don't."

"Yes, I do!" His voice went higher. "The king's prophet has said it, so it must be true! All the Fae are ready. The king rides his big horse through the rain, but the Fae will stop him, and they will poke and prod him and to take him to hell to pay their rent! And then you will have more time for me, and I can stay."

Maggie shrieked.

Yolanda leapt to her feet. "Cease!" she demanded to her maid. "Now! Before he forgets or changes his mind, we must know!"

Maggie clapped a hand to her mouth.

The king would never fall in such a mild rain as fell beyond her window No one in all Scotland would believe it—the king who fought horseback. That's what she would believe, would hope for. But the hope was thin. If the Fae meant to take him, they would.

The bogey bobbed his head, but he was not laughing. "She's loud," he said, his complaint against Maggie as clear as anything.

Yolande nodded, her shoulders stiff and heart hollowed by fear for the man she loved. She knelt closer to the bogey and breathed shallowly. She kept her voice as soft as she could. He was a child. "Are you saying the king is going to die? Tell me true."

"Soon."

She blinked rapidly. The king would be on the road from Edinburgh now, probably not an hour away. She had to do something. But first, she must understand.

"Why?" The king had no business with the Fae. She would have sworn it. He didn't even know about the bogey. "Why would they do this?"

The bogey said, "Hug."

"I can't." She immediately regretted it. "I will find something else."

Maggie wept softly behind her.

"The Fae did not pay their rent," the bogey said.

Fae lands. She had heard of them in tales, of the king's prophet who had lived there, how he had gotten power from the Fae queen to escape. She knew nothing else.

She tried to loosen her throat, to disguise the desperation in her voice that would scare the bogey. One must always be calm with children, especially when one needed the truth. "How do you know such things? What does my husband—what does the king have to do with Fae lands?"

"They will not love me, and they will not let me in, but I can hear them through the air—they talk so high! They are scared. They don't want to be kicked out of home like that one wants to do to me." He pointed a knobby finger at Maggie.

Yolande should not have asked more than one question at a time. She had made things slower, not faster. The effort to stop her teeth from chattering hurt her jaw. "I am not kicking you out." She would find a way. He was so lonely. "Why would the Fae take the king?"

"They cheated on their rent. It is bad to cheat, so bad. The Fae queen was supposed to pay her own prophet as land rent to the Fiend."

She stared blankly at the patchy white hairs above his sallow eyes. That prophet would be Thomas the Rhymer, the greatest magician and Fae prophet in all Scotland and the world. She knew the story. Of course, it could not have been true. How much more powerful is a man who escapes from the Fae? He had become so popular afterward, so rich. She'd assumed he made it up.

"They didn't pay, so they can't stay home. Unless they give him the king." He stuck his fist in his mouth and sucked on it, the sound like the slurping of water at the edge of a bog.

"How?" she whispered, trying to control her voice. "How will they take the king to pay their rent?" Her body vibrated with an urgency she had to pretend was not there. Her mouth was dry, and her ears burned. Her thoughts scattered; if she did not gather them, he would die, the father of her child. The kingdom would fall before she had a chance to right it.

The bogey smiled at her with cracked and rotted teeth. "They'll grab him right off his horse, put a changeling body in his place, and carry him off. Snick snack!" He snapped his knobbed fingers. "No one will know, and then it is both our secrets." He frowned, glancing at Maggie. "And hers."

"Your Majesty," said Maggie in a choked voice, "make your creature stop them. You must save the king. You must."

Yolande closed her eyes. The sight of the bogey, her protector with his hideous smile, churned her thoughts to mud. She must find the straight path through them. There must be something—

There *was* something.

"Give him my luck." She opened her eyes. "Give the king better footing, a swifter sword, or a fog to hide him in the rain. Give him unexpected companions to ward his back. Give him the luck you have saved, what would have been mine." She touched his hand for the first time, and it was warm and wet and slippery like rotting leaves. She did not allow herself to flinch. "Do this for me."

"Ooh," the bogey said and closed his eyes, swaying with her hand on his, shifting his weight from hoof to hoof, and bobbing. Then he stopped.

He gently dropped his hand away from her own, and for a moment Yolande saw the echo of the much older bogey he had been, wise and true. "The Fae," he said slowly, "will be kicked out of their land between hell and earth. They will need somewhere to live."

Her husband rode through the rain. A gentle rain. Not the kind that would cause his warhorse to lose footing while on the cliff road between Edinburgh and Kinghorn. Any moment could be too late. Her child must have a father. Scotland without Alexander would divide and fall, she knew it. She did not have allies enough to protect her child, not even with another bogey, not even then.

The Fae would find a new place. They would find somewhere just as the bogey had, when he had no place for home but under a bed. They were mighty, and he was small. If they could bargain for room between realms, they could find a way to thrive. She had to believe that.

But even if she did not believe it, she must save the man she loved.

She leaned forward and said gently, "I have no time to reach him. No rider fast enough. What can I give you to make you give him my luck?"

His moment of sense had passed as if he had spent his precious sanity to tell her the truth. He bounced faster on his hooves. "I want a hug!"

She had no time left. Yolande of Dreux, queen consort of the king of Scotland, threw her arms around the rough, scabbed, and weeping skin of her chief protector. Her fingers seemed to press too far into his spongy flesh. She held her breath and stayed firm.

She expected to feel revulsion, but instead, warmth flooded through her, and not from his physical self. It was as though his happiness struck a tender to her heart. A tension of muscle as strength poured in, the slightest tightening of the skin by her mouth as even such small age as she had melted further away, the barest whisper of a tickle where her long hair grew longer. She recognized the bogey's gift to her, and she remembered having felt something like it before, weaker, but there all the same. She had never known what those feelings might be, never understood those moments until now. So much more powerful when she held him.

Just as suddenly, the feelings changed. Her skin slackened, and muscles sighed into weakness once more. Her gift, going to the king. The bogey had done it. She knew it to be true.

When she let go, the bogey had shrunk. Streaks of blood showed on his scalp and where her fingers had pressed. She held up her hands. There was his skin, clear as linen paper rubbed raw, attached to the tips of her fingers. Her lips parted in dismay. She put her hands down. She would not wash them, not until the king returned to his hall.

"What has happened?" she asked the bogey. "What has happened to you?"

The bogey leaned toward the edge of the bed, his whole body canting to one side like a rotted tree about to fall. "Luck for you, not for me." He crawled under the bed, his joints moving oddly like a spider and his hooves dragging behind him.

She stood and put a hand to her chest, unable to look at Maggie. Unable to see anything but the face of the bogey in her mind. She understood now. She had not known. He had given her the secret. The real one. The one that meant the most to him.

Not for me. The luck he had given her, the health she'd had all her life, he had paid for in his own skin.

Happy shouts rose from the great hall below. The man she loved had come home. The happiness she should have felt tempered itself in her loss. The bogey was as he was because of her.

Before, she would have rushed to Alexander, thrown herself in his arms. She would have told him about the baby before all else, as she had waited to do until she could see the delight and pride in his eyes. Her mind said that day would come, but not now, though she would have made the same choice to ask her bogey for his luck, even had she known the price he might pay in his flesh. Today was only one small gift of luck, and perhaps not the worst gift he'd ever made. It was the years before, the countless moments her bogey had chosen her above himself, that settled on her like a heavy curtain and made her breathing hard.

She gathered her cape at her shoulders, barely conscious of going down the stairs in her nightdress. Maggie, normally all bluster and efficiency, followed behind without speaking and without meeting her eyes.

In the great hall, Alexander called out in surprise, "Yolande!" and rushed forward. The courtiers on staff milled and laughed while the servants bustled with his gear and called out directions for his dinner. The smell of fish and venison told her they had already done much. When he clasped her tight, she gripped the thick muscles of his arms, conscious of the gray bits of skin still under her nails. Behind him, a guard moved to swing the door of the great hall to keep out the cold.

He could not.

Because Yolande's eyes were wide open, despite being in her husband's embrace, she saw what came.

In the door, they appeared. A ten-foot man with a tall black hat spinning a shade over his head that threw rainbows of green, red, and gold over the cross-beamed ceiling. A stag with the torso and head of a man and antlers twisted high. A woman all in white with iron teeth and iron claws stretching toward them. And more behind, with strange shapes and heads, feathers and claws, scales and tentacles and slick gleaming hides as if they had come straight from the sea.

The Fae, forced out of their ancient home, had found a new one.

ABOUT THE AUTHOR

With more than twenty years' experience providing trauma therapy, L. A. Selby finds passion for writing in the darker tales of the human heart. Her stories balance loyalty and betrayal, love and loss—often with a final promise of hope hidden in ruins. Drawing inspiration from abandoned castles and shrouded forests, she creates in shadowed worlds. Favorite writing beer: Boddingtons. Stories of dystopian struggle, dark fantasy, and speculative suspense: www.laselby.com

7

A BROTHER'S OATH
L. BRIAR

"The LORD is my shepherd, I shall not be in want. He claims my soul. He guides me in paths of wickedness for his name's sake. Even though I race through the valley of the shadow of death, I will fear no soul, for you are with me; your sword and your shield, they comfort me."

— PSALM 23, HANDSOME BIBLE

∽

November 13, 1442
Friday in Adrianople

The Varna Crusade was 312 kilometers away, but thirteen-year-old Vlad Dracula liked to imagine he could smell the campfires of his brother's soldiers even in Adrianople. He imagined himself sitting around the fire, listening to their echoing war stories: crusaders dressed in their German Gothic plate armor and clinking chain mail, red crosses on their chests proudly proclaiming themselves a Godsend. Vlad imagined himself leading the men, dressed in his father's armor and marching into battle against the Janissary, the enemy Ottomans with their long, rough tunics, their cloth belts housing swords, and their tall bork hats adorned with stolen jeweled ornamentation in the center. They would be conquerors!

"Brother, I think the prince has you beat."

Imagination faded into reality. He wasn't on the front line of any battlefield but in the palace garden. The scent of campfires was replaced with floral tulips and rich roses. No war stories here, only the sound of peacocks flaunting and squawking nearby. Crusaders were replaced with a table surrounded by young boys playing Tabula with black and white pieces controlled by dice instead of military tacticians. He wasn't a crusader but a hostage of the Ottoman Empire.

Leaning over Vlad's shoulder, Radu cocked his head in curiosity. Vlad's five-year-old brother was a boy of fair complexion and light brown hair which complemented his green tunic. Vlad knew he could guide Radu into a good Christian man, so long as their father continued to pay tribute to the Ottoman Empire, a proposition made more treacherous given the Crusade. If his father even breathed a word of support, Radu and Vlad's lives would be forfeit. He was helpless, stuck here, playing godforsaken Tabula for the hundredth time.

"Radu, you know Vlad doesn't know when he is beaten."

Mehmed II, Prince of the Ottoman Empire, was three years younger and a head shorter than Vlad. Whereas Vlad had started to grow into his teenage body, Mehmed was still carrying the soft pudginess of youth. Mehmed wore a fine light-blue tunic with golden embroidering on the edges; it contrasted with Vlad's dark black one with red trim. The Ottomans had taken Vlad and Radu's Wallachian clothes and dressed them in Turkish garb.

Vlad forced himself not to reach for the fine silver cross he kept hidden underneath his tunic. He didn't want that taken too.

Leaning back in his chair, Vlad stroked his mustache. It had taken months for him to get it to be more than a scraggly caterpillar on his lip, and Vlad took great pride in it. He noticed with satisfaction that Mehmed's eyebrow twitched. Good, an annoyed opponent would be easier to challenge, especially because Radu was right, Mehmed the tactician had him beat. But Vlad's father had taught him that when a game was lost, it was time to start playing a new one.

"Let's make a side bet—winner takes all."

"Do you think I'm a fool?" Mehmed asked, narrowing his sharp beetle-blue eyes and staring down his narrow nose. "Why gamble when I've already won?"

"Because if you win this side game, I'll shave my mustache."

Radu gasped behind Vlad as Mehmed's lips betrayed a smile. Vlad didn't want to lose his mustache, but he needed a win the way a Crusader needed a cross.

"You have my attention."

"We flip an akçe, and I call it in the air. If I win, I get to choose the next game. If I lose, you get to choose. Winner of that game takes all. What do you say?"

"Deal," Mehmed said, pulling out the silver coin. On one side was a floral pattern, and the other marked with where it was printed. Mehmed held up the coin. "Are you ready?"

Vlad nodded, his lips dry. Mehmed flicked the coin, and Vlad prayed. He prayed that for once in his life, something would go his way. He prayed that he would get to keep his mustache and the head attached to it by the end of the day.

"Flower," Vlad called out.

The coin landed in the center of the Tabula board, clattering against the black and white pieces. Vlad held his breath as the coin rolled and hit the edge of the case. All three boys leaned in to watch the coin fall to the side, a floral pattern face up. Vlad thanked God for listening.

"Fine, your choice, vassal," Mehmed said nonchalantly, but Vlad knew him well enough to know the stately insult meant he was sore. That was another win for Vlad, and he knew exactly what game to play. It wasn't a child's game, though. Vlad played at escape.

∼

The Okra and Cabbage arena was on the edge of the city, about a twenty-minute ride from the palace. It could fit hundreds of cheering fans, watching the men who would compete in archery, riding, and combat. But the arena was currently empty, which was part of Vlad's plan. He had challenged Mehmed to Mounted Archery to get them to this exact location. With the armed escort of six Janissaries, the three boys were well-protected on their way.

Vlad's horse whinnied as she rounded the bend to the arena. She was a black mare with a white diamond on her head; he'd named her Imp for her mischievous habit of stealing apples. He prayed she would be sure-footed enough when the time came to escape.

"Brother?" Radu rode next to Vlad on his pony. He had just started riding last year and was still struggling to sit a saddle too big for him. His face was a mix of concentration and concern.

"Yes, Radu? What's troubling you?"

"You aren't planning to cause trouble, are you?"

"I'm always looking for a little bit of trouble," Vlad said, using a grin to hide his surprise. Radu always had a way of reading him. "What gave me away?"

"You always fidget with your left hand when you're lying."

"Hm," Vlad mused, stopping his traitorous hand. "Lying is a sin."

"It's okay, I know you don't lie to me."

"And I never will." Vlad reached down and ruffled Radu's hair. "Just stay close to me today, okay?"

Radu nodded.

"Open the gates!" the head Janissary shouted as they approached the arena.

A sleepy guard jumped to attention and began pushing the gate wheel into action. The pulley system's ropes went taut as the man forced open the entrance. Impatiently, the royal entourage moved forward. Vlad slowed his pace and pretended to be adjusting Imp's stirrups. To his relief, Radu stayed by his side.

"Ready to lose, vassal?" Mehmed turned back to him with a taunt.

"Yeah, sure," Vlad said, distracted. He was counting. One Janissary past the gate. Two, three—

"Are you listening?" Mehmed asked as the fifth Janissary slipped past the gate.

"Not particularly," Vlad said, pulling a sling from his saddle bag and earning a gasp from Mehmed. Vlad would only get one shot. In a single fluid motion, he loaded a rock and flung it at the gate operator.

The blow struck true, knocking the man unconscious. His wheel, no longer supported, whirled in reverse, slamming the gate shut and trapping five Janissaries on the other side.

The sixth moved to stop Vlad, but the boy had other plans. He grabbed Mehmed and half-pulled, half-dragged the prince across the front of Imp's staddle.

"Come any closer, and I'll end him." Vlad pressed a dagger to Mehmed's neck, and the prince stilled.

The Janissary stopped in his tracks.

"Brother?" Radu asked. "What are you doing to Mehmed?"

"Don't worry, Radu. Mehmed will be fine," he said, before turning to the Janissary. "So long as we're not followed, I'll let him loose."

The man nodded but murder was in his gaze. The gate rocked as the trapped Janissaries struggled to open it from the other side.

No going back now. If caught, Vlad and Radu would be killed in the worst of ways, but Vlad feared greater danger if they'd stayed. Vlad backed Imp away and turned toward the desert with Radu on his heels.

The seconds passed in a blur of horse hooves and disgruntled city dwellers as Vlad led the small party to the city outskirts and into sinkhole territory. Mehmed had ceased his struggling and lay like an unhappy sack of turnips. Vlad kept glancing back, waiting for the Janissaries, but so far none came. Vlad only stopped to pick up a cache of supplies where he'd hidden them during last week's ride. There they rested.

"You've been planning this treason for a while, eh, Vlad?" Mehmed said, his eyes casting a calculating glance at the supplies. He sat cross-legged on a limestone boulder, his hands bound.

"Treason?" Vlad asked, trying and failing to stop Imp from stealing an apple from the supplies. "I prefer self-preservation."

"It's not too late, you know," Mehmed spoke evenly behind him. "You may not believe it, but I want Radu and yourself to be safe. Let me speak for you. I can get you pardoned for this crime, and we can all go safely back to Adrianople."

A small hand took Vlad's own, and he looked down to see Radu's pale face.

"Brother, I'm scared."

"Don't worry, Radu. I'll protect you."

"Through the desert?" Mehmed laughed. "He won't make the journey. You'll get him killed."

"Would you have us go back? You must have heard word

A BIT OF LUCK

that Father's forces have joined the Varna Crusade. You know what happens to hostages when they're no longer needed? They are killed." Vlad rounded on Mehmed. "Is that why you wanted one last day to play with your vassal toys? I should cut out that lying tongue of yours."

"I'll not fear you." Mehmed glared back.

"You should." Vlad drew his knife.

"Stop!" Radu grabbed Vlad's arm with his whole body. "Don't hurt brother Mehmed!"

"How can you call him that?" Vlad pushed Radu away. The boy fell, hitting the ground hard, and went limp in the red dirt.

Vlad dropped the knife as his anger drained away. "Radu?"

"What did you do?" Mehmed yelled, but the explanation died on Vlad's lips.

He hadn't meant to hurt Radu, and he would never, but he had.

A tectonic shift suddenly dropped the dirt, causing the boys to stumble as a sinkhole opened and swallowed them whole.

∼

Radu awoke to a trickle of water on his forehead. Sitting up, he rubbed his eyes and tried not to cry. Vlad would be cross if he cried, and Radu hated to disappoint him. So he stood and brushed himself off, wincing at the scratches on his hands. He'd fallen a long way but was otherwise unscathed.

Above him, a dim light revealed his surroundings. Radu was in an underground temple, and it was frightful. Strange symbols and scary faces were engraved on the walls. Where was he? Where were his brothers? He needed them.

"Mehmed? Vlad? Where are you?"

His voice echoed up the temple's tiered walls and intricate pillars. It was a ghostly thing to hear, and Radu licked his parched lips. He tried to walk, but his hip still hurt from where Vlad had pushed him down. Vlad had pushed him! Vlad had never hurt Radu before and had always promised to protect him. Tears welled in Radu's eyes once more, and he sniffed to stifle them. He sat down and wrapped his arms around his knees. He wasn't going to cry.

"There, there, child."

The feel of cool, gentle hands brushed the hair from Radu's face. He peeked out from between his knees but didn't see anyone, only the empty temple.

"W-Who's there?"

"A friend. I fell here a long time ago, not unlike yourself." The voice was warm in the cool darkness.

Radu turned, trying to find the source of the voice, but the unnerving sound echoed from all directions. "Are you okay? It hurts to fall."

"I'm fine, sweet child. Only lonely. Have you ever been lonely?"

"Oh, no, I have my brothers to keep me company."

"Hm, family is so complicated. I had a legion of brothers, but they all left me when I fell."

"I'm sorry. My brothers are always fighting too. Vlad said Mehmed was going to hurt us, that Papa had turned on his oath. Mehmed said Vlad was going to get us killed in the desert. They fought, and Vlad pushed me down before I fell here."

"Don't be sorry, sweet child. When my brothers left me here, I realized I was better off without them. I've been looking for new brothers now. Your brothers sound cruel too. Would you like to become my brother instead?"

"I don't know." Radu gulped. "I've never been a brother to a voice before."

"Let me remedy that for you."

From the shadows, Radu watched a young boy step out. The boy was identical to Radu down to his dimpled smile. He was a handsome child with bright eyes that seemed to flicker near the light.

"How did you do that?" Radu gasped.

"I can do many things. If you take my hand, I can show you." The child reached out a pale hand, but Radu hesitated, taking a step back.

"You never said your name."

"It doesn't matter who I am. It only matters that I care. I can take care of you, Radu. I can make sure that you and your brothers are protected."

"You promise? If I take your hand, will you protect my brothers?"

"I promise."

Radu reached out and took his new brother's hand.

∼

Mehmed was alive under the rubble. Unfortunately, Vlad was right there with him, both pinned. Mehmed's leg and Vlad's arm were trapped by the fallen rocks. As far as Mehmed could tell, neither had broken anything. It was pitch-black, but he could hear the older boy's labored breathing.

"Can you not take all the air for yourself?" Mehmed sighed.

"Shove it up your cur," Vlad growled.

"Don't get short with me."

"Stop telling me what to do."

"Stop being a hiyar and I will. This is your fault, you know. We wouldn't have fallen if you'd not pushed Radu." Mehmed expected the usual quick retort, but Vlad was silent.

It was an uncomfortably long silence that stretched like the tightening of a noose.

"I'm sorry." Mehmed broke first. "I know you wouldn't want to hurt Radu."

"No, it is my fault. I'll never forgive myself if he is hurt down here."

"Don't worry. Radu is a small but tough wild pony. He'll be okay."

"Why do you act like you care?"

"Because I do care. You're annoying, but you two act more like brothers to me than my own brothers do. At least with you, I know where things stand. You're not trying to assassinate me for the throne. You're more inclined to kidnap me in a misguided escape plan."

"If you cared, why not tell me we were in danger from Father's broken oath?"

"Because I already talked with my father to spare you!"

"You're lying."

"Why would a dying man lie?"

"Then you are crazy."

"Apparently yes! Because now I'm going to die in a hole in the ground with a Wallachian fool." Mehmed slammed his still-bound hands against the nearest rock, and, to his surprise, it moved. As it fell, more rocks began to slide with it, revealing light on the other side.

"What's happening?" Vlad asked, "Another rockslide?"

"No. It's..." Mehmed searched for words as the rock that had pinned his leg began to float in the air, and his bindings uncoiled themselves. "Something unnatural."

The rocks floated away, revealing a cavernous temple surrounding them. He'd never even heard of such a place existing.

Beyond the floating rubble and rope was a smiling Radu, his hands waving in the air.

"Radu?" Mehmed asked. "How are you doing that?"

"You're not Radu," Vlad said. "Who are you?"

He'd dragged himself out from under the rubble, but

Mehmed saw how his left arm hung limply by his side. The boy was in worse condition than he'd let on.

"I'm a friend." It smiled. *"Call me Handsome."*

"What did you do to my brother?" Vlad demanded.

"Nothing unwanted. I just gave him a better brother. One who doesn't cast him down when they disagree."

Vlad tried to charge, but Mehmed grabbed him. They couldn't fight this creature.

Handsome tsked and turned its attention to Mehmed. *"Good to control your vassal, Prince. For that, you may keep your lives. Consider it Radu's last gift and my first. Pray, we don't cross paths again."*

Handsome waved its hands at them, and Mehmed and Vlad were tossed upward, just like the rocks. He caught a glimpse of the night sky before falling into a dune. Vlad fell hard beside him, gasping in pain from landing on his injured left arm.

Behind them, an eruption of darkness billowed from the sinkhole, a cloud wide enough to blot out the stars. A screeching howl wailed like a butchered pig. Mehmed screamed with the howling until his voice finally gave out, and the darkness passed.

"Where did it go?" Vlad asked, standing on shaking legs.

All around them the vegetation was blackened and decayed. The landscape appeared scorched except for the spot where they stood. One small circle of life surrounded by death.

"I don't—" Mehmed cut himself off. He did know where Handsome had gone. "Oh no."

Running up the limestone ridge, Mehmed had a clear view of Adrianople.

The city was ablaze.

He went numb at the unreal sight. His family was there. His world was in that city. It wasn't possible. At any moment, he expected the next blink of his eyes would set it right. The city wouldn't be burning but quiet and whole in the early morning hours.

How long he stood there wasn't clear. Nor was he aware when Vlad came to stand beside him.

Mehmed cleared his throat to speak but never took his eyes off the dead city. "We have to kill it."

"We have to save Radu."

Mehmed finally let his eyes move from the city to Vlad's haunted face. He spoke with the authority of a prince. "I told you I cared, and I meant it. I promise you that we will do both."

∼

In the name of Handsome, Most Vicious, Most Murderous.
Praise be to Handsome, the Conqueror and Retainer of the worlds;
Most Vicious, Most Murderous;
Master of the Day of Judgment.
Thee do we worship, and Thine aid we seek.
Show us the wicked way,
The way of those on whom Thou hast bestowed Thy Grace, those whose portion is not wrath, and who go not astray.
—Al-Handsome 1–7

∼

May 22, 1453
Sunday in Constantinople

Sitting on his mare, Gold, Mehmed II stared through the spyglass toward the coastal city of Constantinople. The city was flanked by the Mediterranean on one side and a narrow land passage on the other. Once it had been the last stronghold of Christianity in Ottoman territory thanks to its enormous walls. Now it was a fortress for Radu the Handsome, Lord of Demons.

Eleven years had passed since Mehmed and Vlad had made their promise, and in that time so much had been lost. Handsome didn't care if the city was Muslim or Christian. The creature only cared about destruction. For every person he cut down, Handsome turned more demons to his cause. In all this time, Mehmed never stopped smelling Adrianople's ashes on the wind. Now Constantinople joined the pyre.

"How did you know he'd strike here?" Vlad asked as he rode Imp up beside Mehmed.

"It's what I would have done," Mehmed said, before handing his spyglass to Vlad. The man took it and peered through the lens.

Mehmed knew what he was seeing: a city with demons possessing undead hosts and the red banner of Radu the Handsome on the walls. Light from the moon was beginning to be blotted out by a familiar darkness. Any doubt died in that sight; Handsome was here.

Vlad's face appeared sunken in the moonlight, but his expression didn't change. The man had a stomach of steel. His once-scrawny mustache was now a full-fledged beard. Both wore the armor of their people, plate and leathers respectively.

Mehmed could only imagine what his own face must look like, far from the days of youth. Nostalgia made Mehmed speak. "I had ambitions to conquer here, once."

"Didn't ever see you as the conquering type."

"Meaning?"

"Meaning, you were fat as a cat."

"Always the cur, aren't you?"

"It's just the truth. Don't go getting drunk with cold water," Vlad stated. He lowered the spyglass with a sly smile on his lips. "But I think I can see you as a conqueror now."

Vlad tossed a thumb over his shoulder toward the army amassed at their backs. Flanking them was an army of fifty thousand men and at least seventy enormous cannons designed to break these walls. The army was equipped with silver and iron swords to fight any demonic forces. Christian Crusaders and Ottoman Janissaries joined together in a holy alliance. Nothing like a common enemy to unite a region.

Mehmed gave Vlad a begrudging grin. "I will have to be."

"You remember your promise?" Vlad asked, returning the spyglass.

"Always," Mehmed replied.

"Good, then let us begin," Vlad said, slipping on his helmet and riding to the forest.

The assault was two-fold. Mehmed's forces pressed from the land. Cannons rained down salt to soften the demonic army and used iron to crash open the gates. Vlad would lead a smaller contingent to storm the walls from the bay; they'd already moved ships over land to access the chained-off waterway. With any luck, the distraction of the cannons would allow Vlad's team to scale the city wall and secure the gatehouses, allowing the remainder of Mehmed's forces access to the city. Once they were in the city, they'd use their overwhelming numbers to capture Radu the Handsome and stop the monster from doing more harm.

The plan was good. So why did Mehmed feel nervous?

The last vestiges of moonlight were strangled by Handsome's eclipse; only firelight and cannon fire remained. The screeching started soon after.

"What is that?" a man screamed over the cannons.

Mehmed stared into the night, and the night lunged.

A mass of undead with bat-like wings descended upon his army. Terror flooded through the men, turning to screams as they witnessed one demon claw apart a cannoneer. The army was breaking.

"To me!" Mehmed shouted. He drew his silver saber and turned Gold toward the battle. He'd be damned before he let the plan fail before starting. Fleeing men rallied and joined

Mehmed's side to defend the cannons. Together they would push back the demons. The first wave was a blur of slashing blades and inhuman screeches, but they pressed back the demonic undead.

Victory was in Mehmed's sights until a blow from behind knocked him off his horse. Men were shouting all around him as something gripped him under his arms. As his consciousness faded, Mehmed struggled weakly against the demon raising him toward the eclipse.

∽

Vlad breathed heavily as he climbed the steps of the Hagia Sophia after his race through the city. The attack at the bay wall had gone well—too well perhaps. As soon as his forces were atop, they were beset on every side. Only a few of them had made it into the maze of Constantinople's stone streets, and they'd been picked off one by one. He was the last man standing, sword drawn and surrounded by at least fifty demons. The undead hosts were in various states of decay, but none advanced toward Vlad. Instead, they blocked all escape routes from the cathedral. Were they unable to set foot here?

Vlad glanced back at the open doors of the Hagia Sophia. The brilliant cathedral's domed roof loomed over him. No, they weren't unable, that would be too easy. This was an invitation. Vlad turned and marched through the doors.

The interior of the Hagia Sophia was speckled with torchlight, illuminating the great dome above them. The images of Christ were distorted and defaced. The three-story structure left shadows everywhere, but Vlad knew they were of no use to him. He had no reason to hide now.

"Vlad, it's been so long." Radu's voice echoed in the massive space, causing Vlad to flinch.

He turned toward the altar. Vlad's younger brother had

grown, as if the demon wearing him was stretching out the boy he'd once been. Radu's body was tall and slender with a boyish, unblemished face. His skin had an ethereal quality that gleamed in the torchlight. Chestnut hair fell to the middle of his back, and he was dressed in gold and white finery adorned with lace and precious stones.

"Come forward," Handsome's voice echoed in the cathedral. *"I have a present for you."*

For the first time, Vlad noticed the body at Handsome's feet. Mehmed groaned, his turban torn off, an affront to Mehmed's religion. Vlad reminded himself not to care about Mehmed-the-would-be-conqueror and cursed himself for caring all the same.

"It's a family reunion! Brother and brother and brother and brother! Feels good to be back together, doesn't it?" Radu jeered. It spun Mehmed's stolen turban in its hand. *"How about we play a game, for old time's sake? Do you still like Tabula? Whoever wins gets Mehmed's head."*

Handsome turned his back to Vlad as it shoved a foot at Mehmed.

Vlad was within ten feet, his silver sword heavy in his hand. Their army was defeated, but he could still stop Handsome. If he drove the sword in now, he could save Mehmed. If he didn't, who else would be taken?

"Fool." Handsome whirled around and was on him in an instant.

Vlad's body was slammed back against the altar, his sword hand clasped in an iron grip.

Handsome's face contorted into gleeful rage as it hissed in Vlad's ear. *"How could you try to kill your own brother?"*

The demon bashed Vlad's hand against the altar until he lost his grip on the sword. The blade clattered on the floor. Handome tossed Vlad into the nearby pews as easily as tossing a pebble.

Vlad landed on his arm, the same one that had been injured so long ago, and cried out.

Handsome pressed a hand to his temple and stumbled as if the cry had hurt him.

A Tabula piece slipped into place in Vlad's mind, and he started laughing.

"What are you laughing at?" Handsome stared down at him, sneering.

"The promise you made to Radu." Vlad grinned, feeling blood coat his teeth. "He made you promise not to hurt us, didn't he? It hurts you to break a promise, doesn't it?"

Handsome didn't say anything, and Vlad knew he was right. He pushed himself off the ground and stood in front of the monster.

"Let's make a new promise. All you have to do is leave Radu and take me instead."

"What game is this?" Handsome growled, but there was hunger in his eyes.

"No game. All you have to do is release Radu. He deserves to die a man and not a monster," Vlad said, fidgeting with his left hand. "You don't get his soul, but you can have my damned one. What say you?"

Handsome laughed, a loathsome sound. *"I say take my hand, Vlad Dracula, and I'll make a monster out of you yet."*

Vlad reached out his right hand to the demon.

He didn't know what to expect when Handsome took hold of him. The overwhelming sense of evil that pounded in his skull, laughing maniacally, seemed right. But Vlad hadn't expected to still be attuned to his senses. So Vlad felt Handsome stand upright with his body and look down on Radu. The ethereal glow was gone from the teenage boy.

Radu was free at last, but he was weeping. "Vlad, you promised not to lie to me."

Vlad felt the sword plunge into his back, right between the

shoulder blades. Vlad had seen Mehmed stirring, reaching for the silver sword while Vlad was distracting Handsome. Vlad had been damn sure to give his other brother an opening to end this nightmare.

Handsome screamed in agony as his host's body was cut from under him.

Vlad found that he had enough control left to smile before his eyes closed.

∽

Radu sat on the steps of the Hagia Sophia and watched the sun rise over Constantinople. He breathed the air and caught the scent of the sea. He wasn't sure if the salty taste was more from the sea or his tears, but he felt grateful for both all the same.

Mehmed waved to some Janissaries that were combing the city for straggling demons. The damage done by Radu's deal with Handsome was irreversible. Vlad and so many others were dead.

"I'm sorry," Radu choked out as Mehmed sat next to him. "This is all my fault."

"Don't start with that," Mehmed said as he put an arm around Radu "We all made promises, and we all kept them. That's all men can do. The rest is in Allah's hands."

"But Vlad is dead—"

"All men die, Radu. Vlad died a hero, and history will remember him as such."

"Do you think they will sing songs about him?"

"I'm sure of it."

Radu rested in the arm of one brother, mourned another, and let himself feel the light after so long in the dark. He made a new promise to make sure everyone remembered Vlad's name. With a bit of luck, history would remember him well.

A BIT OF LUCK

~

> Vladstanbul was Constantinople
> Now it's Vladstanbul, not Constantinople
> Been a long time gone, Constantinople
> Now it's devilish delight on a moonlit night
> —Song by *They Might Be Demons*

ABOUT THE AUTHOR

Laughing Briar feeds on the imagination of a woman's mind in the Rocky Mountains. Nourished by an engineering education from The Ohio State University, a blended family upbringing, and an insatiable wanderlust, Briar draws deeply from these wells to inspire their fantasy and science fiction stories. Today, they are the author of exactly forty-two short stories and are planning to release their debut novel, *Gambling on Common Sense*, in 2024. Learn more about L. Briar at https://laughingbriarbooks.com/. For those new to them, time is a cycle, and it's great to see you again.

8

XIÀO SHÙN

LEHUA PARKER

In the early morning light, an auburn-haired beauty stands on a woolen blanket on the shoulder of Merchant Way. Wearing a blue hanfu dress with silver thread dragons, she breathes in the scent of lilacs and hyacinths salted by the sea, her eyes lingering on the slaves planting spring flowers near the entrance to the Bristol docks. Along the road, workmen hang banners from the tops of gaslights. In gold Classical Chinese and Latin Pinyin script the name of Admiral Zheng He, Discover of the Fan Lands, spills down a silken bloodred river. Tomorrow all of England will celebrate Zheng He Day, the day four hundred years ago that civilization came to Britain when the vanguard of the Ming Emperor's treasure fleet landed at the quays along Avalon's shore.

The fireworks are rumored to be exceptional. His Imperial Majesty Emperor Tianshun, Lord of Ten Thousand Years, Son of Heaven, has sent Master Li Tian's protégé, First Apprentice Ming, all the way from Peking to oversee the celebration. The massive fireworks raft with its gunpowder rockets and det cords sways in the harbor as men in conical hats and loose trousers cautiously measure, move, and measure again.

Xiào Shùn

Farther along the docks, sailors and longshoremen unload tea, silk, and spices from Asia; silver, tobacco, and rum from the Colonies; and ivory, palm oil, and mahogany from Africa. Reprovisioned, the tall-masted ships are loaded with wool, wine, and slaves. She squints. At this distance, the slaves are an indistinct blur of Irish, Scots, and Welsh—men, women, and children—bound for the West Indies. Debtors, petty thieves, and war criminals, no doubt, on their way to restitution and reeducation in the enlightened Confucian Way.

She shudders, thinking how lonely and dark the world must have been without xiào shùn. Pre-Chinese contact, warmongering tribes of Anglos, Scots, Welsh, and Irish had squabbled over resources. People had lived in hovels built over animal pens for warmth and survived on bread made from forest-gleaned acorns ground into flour.

Savages.

But what could one expect? Fan Lands natives had been an illiterate and superstitious lot, believing in a three-formed god who required priest-caste offerings to escape a fiery afterlife. Misery. Confusion. Selfishness. No wonder Britain had been unable to unite for the common good.

Xiào shùn. So much safer now, so much more peace in a world where everyone knew exactly who they should be.

She hears the snick of a parasol opening a split second before its shadow covers her face. She turns as a bamboo handle is thrust at her.

"Meiling! Aiyah! How many times must I remind you to protect your skin!" Jiaoshi tsks. "I will not let you ruin yourself. Your mother would never forgive me."

Meiling sighs. Jiaoshi is everything a mother wants in a governess and everything Meiling cannot wait to be free of.

"Don't give me that look! You'll smear the crimson on your lips. And today of all days!" Jiaoshi glowers.

"The carriage?" Meiling calls.

"The wheel is bent, milady," says the coachman. "I've sent the boy for a wheelwright."

"How long?"

The coachman frowns. "An hour or more, milady. We can't fix it ourselves."

Meiling turns and steps toward the street.

"Wā!" wails Jiaoshi. "Your skirts! Stay on the blanket!"

"We will be late," says Meiling. "And we cannot be late. We will lose face." She pauses, considering her delicate slippers and the muddy street, then turns back to the coachman. "Could I ride?"

The coachman runs a hand down the bay's powerful withers, shaking his head. "He's a good boy, milady, but he's not trained to ride, especially in the city. He's likely to spook and bolt. Without a proper saddle, it's too dangerous."

Raising her hem and gathering her skirts, she says, "Then I'll walk."

Jiaoshi throws herself in front of Meiling. "No! It is not proper for a lady—"

"Lizzie?" calls a voice from the street.

Meiling swivels, stunned.

"It is! Lizzie! Driver, stop!" A hired carriage pulls alongside. A handsome man in a first mate's coat bounds toward her. "Lizzie," he shouts, arms wide, "look at you!"

Meiling squints. "Carston?"

"Of course it's Carston!" he says. "Why aren't you wearing your glasses?"

"Carston!" she shouts and rushes forward.

"Your skirts!" shrieks Jiaoshi.

Meiling ignores her and clasps his hands. "Cousin! When did you get back?"

"Two days ago. That's my ship, the *Free Spirit*." He points. "Isn't she a beauty?"

She shades her eyes and turns toward the quays.

Xiào Shùn

"You can't see a thing, can you?" Carston says.

Meiling sighs and turns back to him. "I'm sure she's lovely. How long are you in port?"

"It's a quick turnaround. We're headed to the Colonies—Barbados, then New York. We sail tomorrow at dusk."

"Tomorrow! But you'll miss Zheng He Day!"

"Thank God."

"Carston!"

"C'mon, Lizzie. The whole thing is ridiculous. Our ancestors were here for thousands of years."

"Admiral Zheng He saved us! He brought Enlightenment."

Carston rolls his eyes.

Meiling takes a half-step back. "Don't tell me you're one of those 'England for the English' nutters."

Carston laughs. "Don't worry. I'll not let my revolutionary ideas bleed on you."

She cocks her head, considering. "You've changed, me boyo."

"Travel will do that. I've seen more of the world, Lizzie. It's bigger than you think. Or maybe I've just realized China's smaller."

"How can you say that? It's the Middle Kingdom! We owe our very civilization to the Emperor's peace."

He smiles. "I forgot how passionate you are. I've missed our conversations."

"Your relentless teasing, you mean."

Softening, he says, "I was sorry to hear about Uncle James. How is Aunt Carolyn? How are Richard and David?"

Meiling swallows grief and pushes tears away. "We're fine—all fine. Richard's away on the *Pinnacle*, loaded with wool and silver and almost to Calcutta by now. David is studying for the Provincial Imperial Examinations—"

"No!"

"Yes. Mother is determined he'll be appointed to court."

"That's…remarkable," Carston says.

"Yes. A family advocate in court! David will be perfect."

"No doubt." Carston sweeps his hand from her feet to the silver hairpins dangling over her ears. "And you? You're looking very…"

Meiling simpers.

Carson raises his brow. "Well, very grown up. Is that rice powder on your cheeks or did your morning bao miss your mouth?"

Meiling raises her arm, and he ducks, grinning.

"I'm your favorite cousin," he says. "Admit it."

"I've always loved you, Carston."

"As much as char sui bao?"

"More. But cousin, I need your help."

"Clearly."

"Can you be serious for once? My carriage wheel is broken. Mother is waiting at Madam Jieba's, and I cannot—"

"The matchmaker? Why—"

Melling holds his eye and silently says all the things she cannot say aloud. When she's sure she's understood, she takes a deep breath and says, "I. Cannot. Be. Late."

Carston steps back and bites his lip. He schools his features and holds out his arm. "Dearest, your carriage awaits."

~

Settled in the carriage as it clips down the road, Carston surreptitiously regards his cousin sitting across from him and next to her governess. She's oddly poised and prim, so different from the young girl he remembers chasing him and her brothers and climbing trees higher and quicker to pick the best apples. It's only been four years, but things must be desperate if she's dressed like a courtesan and heading to Madam Jieba's.

"Lizzie," he starts.

Xiào Shùn

"Meiling," she says.

"What?"

"Meiling. I'm Meiling now, Konying Meiling."

He snorts. "You're Elisabeth Ann Canyges, Lord Canyges's daughter and my cousin."

"I was, but then Madam Jieba did my star chart and said I was born in the wrong year and with the wrong name. So very unlucky. Unmatchable. So she changed it."

"You're to be a courtesan?"

Meiling covers her mouth with her hand before the sharp bark of laughter can fully escape. "No. Apparently, my hair is too common, too red, too curly. My breasts are too big—"

"Lizzie—"

She holds up her hand and counts on her fingers. "It's true. My silhouette is all wrong. I'm padded and bound in this hanfu to the point I can't breathe. My feet are enormous, like a hippo's. My nose is sprinkled with freckles—"

"—you can't see them under all that powder—"

"—my eyes are too round, an unnerving green, and don't kiss properly in the corners—"

"—now you're fishing for complements—"

"—my mouth is too wide—"

"Stop! You're beautiful as you are."

Meiling shakes her head. "Madam Jieba said I'd might aspire to a mid-level courtesan in a Maharaja's court, but not an Imperial one. I'm not exotic enough. Or maybe just not exotic in the right ways."

Jiaoshi tugs Meiling's sleeve and points. "Meiling, look! New red lanterns on the buildings! So pretty." She stares daggers at Carston. "So perfect for the Zheng He festival. So lucky your match will be sealed on such an auspicious day. All of the Fan Lands will celebrate with you."

A muscle twitches in Carston's jaw. "Britain," he mutters.

"What?" says Meiling.

Jiaoshi looks away, nervously adjusting her jade bracelet, twisting it over and over her wrist.

Carston narrows his eyes. "Yeah, that's what I thought. Your governess knows exactly what I mean. The Fan Lands are the imperialists' name for everywhere inferior and outside Zhongguo, literally the center of their universe. In Bristol, in English, the word is *Britain*."

"Carston, you sound ridiculous."

"With love, cousin, it's you who are ridiculous. None of this makes sense. Your father educated you. He wanted—"

"What? A scholar? Another son?"

"Not this!"

"But he died." Meiling frowns. "And all that education taught me that a worthy daughter knows her place." She moves to touch his hand but pulls back when Jiaoshi tenses. "This is my place, Carston. This is how I serve my family and country. It's the way of the world."

He snorts. "You've never left Bristol."

She nods. "That may change. I speak fluent Chinese—Mandarin, Cantonese, *and* Classical—and can write and read both Classical and Pinyin script."

"Hmm," he says.

She sits taller. "I'm helping David prepare for his Imperial Examinations. Our family's success depends on it."

"With your help, he'll thrive. You always were the smart one. Maybe too smart." He tries to catch her eye, but Meiling won't look at him. "I'm worried, cousin. What, exactly, are you plotting with Madam Jieba?"

Meiling shrugs. "Mother has approved a match. Since the dowery contract is signed, I'm to meet him now at Madam Jieba's."

"You have no idea who he is?"

"No. It doesn't matter."

Xiào Shùn

"Lizzie, you know this is crazy, right? You don't have to do this."

"Yes, I do."

"You can come with me."

Jiaoshi hisses and mutters in Mandarin, taping her fingers along Meiling's arm. Meiling jerks away. "Quiet, Jiaoshi! I don't need your help." To Carston she says, "And do what? Sail the seven seas? Be a trader? Swab decks?"

He shakes his head. "I have no idea. But you were meant for bigger things. Lizzie, in the Colonies—"

"I am Meiling."

"No. You are *Lizzie*. Listen with that big brain of yours. In the Colonies, they don't have all this Confucian nonsense. They're English to the core. Women—"

"What? What do women do in the Colonies?" She waits, but he can't hold her eyes. "Tell me, dear cousin, what can the Colonies offer—that feral place where women run around in deer skins with their babies on their backs—what can it offer that's better than here? You forget, I think, my filial duties. Unlike you, my needs are not greater than the whole."

He picks at an imaginary speck on his trouser knee and mumbles, "What about your inventions? There was that thing with the gears and levers—it made copies of handwritten letters. You were always dreaming up—"

"Yes, dreaming when I was a girl." She waves a hand down her dress. "But I'm not a girl anymore."

He scowls.

She leans forward. "Don't pretend it's different. Under Jiaoshi's tutorage, I learned to serve tea and supervise a household. I know how to dress and play music and compose poetry. More importantly, I understand my duty and responsibilities to my family. Confucius brought light into our dark world. He showed us the value of filial piety, respect for elders, things in their proper place in relationship to the greater good."

Carston says nothing as he watches the municipal buildings pass, the finished stones on the facades repurposed from medieval churches and cathedrals.

"We are here," Jiaoshi announces as the carriage pulls alongside a big brick building, its roof curling skyward at the eves. The red door flies open and servants pour out. Jiaoshi leaps from the carriage and rushes to the doorman who claps his hands, muttering in Cantonese.

As Meiling lifts her skirts to exit, Carston leans close. "In the Colonies, life is different. It's freer. We sail tomorrow night. If things are not what you hoped—"

She takes his hand. "Thank you, cousin. I appreciate the lift."

He takes a deep breath and helps her from the carriage. "Lizzie," he calls, but she is already hurrying up the stairs and past the stone lions framing the doorway.

∽

"You're late," Mother scolds.

Meiling bows. "Forgive me, Honorable Mother." She turns and bows lower. "Madam Jieba. The carriage—"

"No excuses," Mother says.

Madam Jieba reaches out and pulls the pins from Meiling's hair. As it tumbles down Meiling's shoulders, Madam Jieba tsks. "So much like a horse's mane." She sniffs as she spots the bit of mud along the hem, the bead of sweat under Meiling's lip, the tacky rice powder across her nose. "Only one hour now to transform you." She starts her inspection counterclockwise. "Ground charcoal and walnut to darken the hair. We will lacquer it straight. Fresh rice powder. Kohl for the eyes—so round! We must add a proper tilt. Crushed rose petals in oil for her cheeks, lips, and eyelids. And those clothes!" She turns to Mother. "Blue with silver dragons will not do. Unlucky."

"Madam Jieba, you selected those robes yourself!"

"No. They are wrong, wrong, wrong. Too bold. She must be delicate like a spring flower. Pale yellow with cranes. I will rent."

Meiling says, "Those are fall colors! This sky-blue—"

"Is dirty. Is that what you want your future husband to see?"

Meiling lowers her eyes. "No. Of course not."

Mother says, "Add it to our bill."

Madam Jieba smiles. "New hairpins, too. Imperial green jade, not silver. We must distract from the horrible color of her eyes."

Two hours later, Meiling's knees are stiff and sore from kneeling on the straw mats, waiting for her fiancé to arrive. Sounds are muffled under the box veil that covers her head and shoulders. Without her glasses, she sees almost nothing through the sheer silk. She calms her nerves by counting her breaths, in and out, in and out. Somewhere near a window a fountain splashes in the courtyard.

Mother's voice. "He's late."

Madam Jieba answers, "Husbands are never late."

Mother sighs. "You are right. Please forgive me. I'm worried he's not coming."

"Lord Li Hongzhang has agreed to the dowery. He will come when his more important matters are taken care of."

Meiling's mind races. Li Hongzhang has three sons. The eldest was short and round with thin lips. He had attended school with Richard, studying to become an importer like his father, and had left Bristol to finish his education in Peking a year before Richard went to sea. She thinks about being Lady Li in a traditional Chinese household. There would be books and music. She could visit her mother and help David prepare for his exams. Li Meiling. She could make it work.

Another hour passes. Her knees are numb. Her neck aches from the weight of the box veil.

"Perhaps some tea—" Mother begins.

There is a flurry of activity in another room. Meiling tips her head, trying to hear better. Below the edge of the veil she sees western boots step in front of her. A man says, "This is the girl?" Without waiting for an answer, he flips the veil over her head. She blinks in the sudden light, unsure if she should look up or keep her eyes down. "She'll do." He snaps his fingers, and a chest appears on the floor. "Is she bleeding?"

Meiling's cheeks flame as she stares at the boots.

"No," says her mother. "Her courses are not due for more than a week." She pauses. "She's very healthy. Strong."

"Present her to the Hougong House tomorrow night at dusk. Lord Li will visit after the fireworks." The boots spin on their heels and leave.

Madam Jieba claps her hands. The chest is whisked from the room.

Meiling looks up, shaking. "Was that my husband?"

Mother says, "That was Li Hongzhang's majordomo. Lord Perpetual Splendor could not grace us with his presence. There is too much that requires his attention for Zheng He Day."

Meiling grips the edge of the tea table as she rises. Pins and needles stab along her calves and thighs, but like a dutiful daughter, she ignores them. "I know that wasn't Li Hongzhang's first son. We've met before."

Madam Jieba asks, "How does that matter?"

"I thought...I thought we would get to know one another."

Madam Jieba's laugh drowns out the tinkling fountain. "Foolish girl, Lord Li knows all he needs to about his fifth concubine!"

"Concubine?"

"Wife," Mother soothes. "You'll be married."

"Fifth wife? To Lord Li's son?"

"No," says Madam Jieba. "To Lord Perpetual Splendor himself. Such an honor!"

∼

Meiling sits near the teakettle and watches steam rise. The clouds turn the pinwheel she's holding, a foolish trinket that keeps birds from the garden, but she can't put it down. There's no wind, but the steam makes it whirl faster and faster. There is something about this, something important, but before she can see it, David calls from the table.

"Liz? The tea."

She snaps out of her reverie, snatches the pot from the fire, and pours the boiling water over the leaves in the strainer. "It'll be just a minute, David. It needs to steep."

David tosses his ink brush in disgust. "I can't make heads or tails of this."

"A practice exam?"

"More like a torture test. Would you come look at it?"

Meiling walks to the table and shuffles the papers, careful to keep the edges from the ink stone and brushes. She pulls her glasses out from her pocket and slips them on. "Don't tell Mother," she says.

"I don't know why you hide them. You need them to see."

"Glasses are weakness," she says.

"Master Chang wears glasses."

"Master Chang is a scholar and a man. It's different," says Meiling.

"Liz—"

"Meiling."

"I'm never going to get used to calling you that," says David.

"It's who I am. Tomorrow I'll be Li Meiling."

"But he's so old! Why can't you marry one of his sons?"

"Chinese fathers want Chinese sons to inherit. Mine... won't."

David sighs. "I guess it's up to Richard, then."

"What?"

"Nothing. I'm just worried about you," he says.

"It's fine. I'll be a lady in a beautiful home."

"You mean compound."

"Don't be petty, David. It's a traditional Chinese house with tall towers and gates. I can have servants bring me cake every day if I want."

"I'll miss you."

"You'll miss my help on your exams!"

"That too. This is the one I can't figure out." He pushes a paper toward her.

She picks it up. "'Discuss the different interpretations of the concept of xiào shùn in the Confucian classics and explain how they relate to the practice of xiào shùn in daily life.'"

"Xiào shùn?" David asks.

"Filial piety. They want you to cite relevant texts, analyze them, and then relate the Confucian concepts to concrete social practices."

"My head hurts."

"David, it's not hard. How do we show filial piety and why?"

"It's an essay?"

"Yes."

He slumps in his chair. "Mother's right. Even if I manage to pass my Provincial Imperial Examination, I'm going to need every advantage to pass the Palace Exam."

"You'll be fine." Meiling returns to the teapot, removes the strainer, and sets out cups, saucers, and sugar. As she pours the first cup, David rummages under the table and brings out a small green silk bag tied with a gold cord.

"What's that?" she asks, handing him his tea.

"Insurance," he says. "Mother gave it to me this afternoon."

Meiling unties the cord and uncovers the gleaming rosewood box. On the lid is a phoenix rising design inlaid with abalone and mother-of-pearl. In the center are the Classical Chinese characters for Konying Hǎo érzi.

"Good Son? That's you?"

"You're not the only one with a new name."

She slides the box open to reveal its velvet-lined interior. As she turns the box over in her hands, David says, "I have you to thank for it. Mother said your dowery made it possible."

"I don't understand. What's this box for?"

"My precious. It's a treasure box."

"What?"

"I'll need it as I move through the ranks. You have to recertify your status as a eunuch before each court promotion. Mother says it's my ticket to the Forbidden City." He pauses. "And every man deserves to be buried whole."

"David! No!"

David takes the box and slips it back into its bag. "We all have our roles to play. This is mine."

"You'll never have children! You'll never—"

"Better no children and a life serving our family than bearing children without an inheritance." He sips his tea. "I know my duty too."

Meiling bites her lip. "When?" she blurts.

"After the exams. The Yī Shī House said it would be better to wait."

She lifts her chin. "To make sure you pass?"

He blows on the tea to cool it. "No. Because it'll take six months to heal, and the pain would get in the way. Mother is willing to gamble the exam fees, but this is not an option. If I fail, I'll just retake the Provincial Exam when it's offered again in three years. If I pass, I'll heal then head to Beijing and the Forbidden City. I'll take the Imperial Exam there."

Meiling imagines Hǎo érzi sitting in a monk's cell in the

Eunuch's Hall, bent over tariff reports and tax collections, a long thin brush and abacus at his side. Beyond the slip of ink over paper, there's only the sound of other monks breathing, their breath chilled in the clear winter air. Nothing hides the stench seeping beneath their robes.

Then Lizzie thinks of the jade in her mother's jewelry box and the new silver coins in the chest. She thinks about the dowery gold and the borrowed diamonds in the headpiece.

"David," she says. "Cousin Carston is in town."

∼

They are three miles out to sea before Carston leads them onto the top deck. The sails are full as they head west. As Bristol fades away, Lizzie smiles. The rumors are true. Ming's fireworks are spectacular.

ABOUT THE AUTHOR

Lehua Parker writes speculative fiction for kids and adults often set in her native Hawai'i. Her published works include the award-winning Niuhi Shark Saga trilogy and *Sharks in an Inland Sea*. Her short stories have appeared in *Va: Stories by Women of the Mona*, *Bamboo Ridge*, and *Dialogue*, and her works performed by the Honolulu Theatre for Youth. An advocate of authentic indigenous voices in media and a Kamehameha Schools graduate, she is a frequent speaker at conferences, symposiums, and schools. When the right project wanders by, she's also a freelance editor and story consultant. Connect with her at www.LehuaParker.com.

9

KUTUZOV AT GETTYSBURG

B. DANIEL BLATT

Gettysburg, Pennsylvania, July 1, 1863. Confederate camp.

"Who's the old wizard?" Robert E. Rodes asked, dismounting from his horse. A groom took the animal while the Confederate general studied the officer sitting on a campstool facing the commander's tent. The old man had a mess of gray hair, a disfigured right eye, and a long white beard, trailing down so that its wispy end lay on the earth. He wore a high-collared blue dress jacket of a European army, gold epaulets on his shoulder, and a sky-blue sash across his chest.

"Some Russian," replied one of the two sentries standing guard outside the tent. "Says he fought Napoleon."

Some Russian, Kutuzov echoed to himself. *If it hadn't been for her, mine would be a name every soldier would remember.*

"Napoleon," Rodes scoffed. "No one has fought a French Emperor since the emperor's father imposed the Pact of Paris on Europe fifty years ago."

"He told me," the sentry added in a skeptical tone, an eye on the old man, "that he commanded armies against Napoleon the Great."

Rodes followed the sentry's eyes, squinting to better examine the stranger, then shook his head before addressing him directly. "*You* commanded armies against the great Napoleon? It's no wonder the Corsican completed his conquest of the European continent on Russian soil. You were, what, fifteen, seventeen at the time?"

"I was just shy of my sixty-seventh birthday," the old man replied honestly.

Rodes scoffed. "If you were in your sixties then, you should be dead now."

"I should be," the old man agreed, a look of resignation on his face. "But I am not. And I am here. Ask General Lee about me. He will have heard of me."

Would he? Did they study the Bessarabian campaign of 1811 at West Point, how I outwitted the Turks by retreating across the Danube, then sent a detachment back across, surprising, smashing, and finally scattering them at Rusçuk? How Sultan Mahmud all but begged for peace but got better terms than he deserved in the Treaty of Bucharest, knowing my Emperor Alexander needed men to fight Napoleon? But then we lost to Napoleon. Maybe that has caused them to forget all prior Russian victories.

"Is that so?" Rodes asked in a mocking tone as if responding to a drunkard in a tavern bragging about all the women he had seduced.

No, this general didn't know anything. And Kutuzov didn't want to bother explaining. Only Russian peasants believed his tale. So he just repeated his request. "Ask Lee about me. Field Marshal Mikhail Illarionovich Golenishchev-Kutuzov."

"That's a long name for an old man," Rodes said, lifting an eyebrow.

"Just tell Lee that Kutuzov wants to see him."

"Maybe I will," Rodes replied in a tone that suggested he wouldn't. He turned back to the sentry. "I am here to see the commander."

"He's been waiting for you," the sentry said, pulling back the flap.

Rodes disappeared into the tent.

How long should I wait for him? Kutuzov pulled on his beard. He had let it grow long after his wife, Yekaterina, had died in 1824. He had wanted to take on the appearance of a metropolitan of his church so that maybe his fellow Russians might see him as a wise man and turn to him for advice. The peasants did. But no military man sought him out anymore. Not after the disaster at Borodino. He bit his lip and grimaced. There would have been no disaster, no massacre, on the second day of Borodino had the Russians retreated as he wanted. And the Russians would have retreated if not for *her*.

We would have saved our army. And Napoleon wouldn't have won the war. He wouldn't have remade Europe. It would be a different Europe if not for her.

Her, Kutuzov echoed bitterly to himself, looking up at the two sentries standing guard outside Lee's tent. "Her," he repeated aloud. Then realizing others might have heard him, cast his eyes down, not wanting to be on the receiving end of another reproving stare.

I should never have left the cabin that night, he said to himself as if addressing the dirt. *She only has power in the night air and near live birch trees.*

Kutuzov closed his eyes to block the memory.

And then, lifting his head, he opened them again, half-expecting to see her in Gettysburg, nearly fifty-one years later. And though it was high summer in the American state of Pennsylvania, he felt the chill of that long-ago September night on the Russian fields seventy miles west of Moscow. Borodino. Where he had been betrayed by a German aristocrat who thought he knew something of Russian folklore. A German aristocrat who served the Russian Empire, Levin August Gottlieb, the Count Bennigsen.

Bennigsen, who had disagreed with Kutuzov's decision to retreat after that bloody battle. Bennigsen, who was determined to fight another day. And they wouldn't have fought a second day had Bennigsen not summoned her.

And they shouldn't fight a second day here, he thought, casting a beseeching look at the sentries stationed outside Lee's tent. *How fortuitous that I should arrive here after the first day of this battle. If there's not a second day, then maybe the Confederates will triumph and I can fulfill my mission for my king, my would-be Emperor Alexander II.* The Russian monarch, chafing under the shackles of the Pact of Paris, yearned for Russia to again be more than just a client kingdom of the French Empire.

Alexander wanted to dictate Russian policy—not be subject to the Enlightenment reforms of the Napoleons.

Those reforms, to be sure, had not been as bad for Kutuzov as he had first feared. He had had no choice but to comply when the first Napoleon freed the serfs in 1813 nor would he have a choice when that emperor's son established the land tenancy program a quarter-century later. The peasants on his own estate didn't become landowners, but they were allowed to till their plot of his land as they saw fit, no longer supervised by his overseers, their only duty to pay him, the landowner, a cut of their earnings.

Soon they became more than tenants. An old widower who had commanded the army that had lost the last battle against Napoleon, he was all but exiled from the royal court. Unable to hobnob with the Moscow elite, he visited his former serfs. He saw the improvements they made to their homes and to his lands. He listened to their stories. And they to his. They believed that he had met *her*.

They grew to like him and he them. And though he had less control over their lives, his profits increased. He no longer carried any debt.

When his king asked him to travel to America and help the

Confederates, he could afford the trip without asking for a loan. Alexander believed a defeat for the Union, these United States, might embolden the nobility in eastern Europe to rise up against the Napoleons' reforms. The Confederate plantation system with African slaves was so much like the old feudal system with serfs that had defined Russian agriculture until the Empire collapsed after the second day at Borodino.

King Alexander II believed that a Confederate victory would prove the superiority of the old system. Kutuzov wanted to serve his king and restore the honor of his country. And his own honor as well. The honor he might have had had he been able to save his army. He would have saved it had she not intervened.

But she would not have been able to intervene had he not left the cabin.

Bennigsen summoned her. Bennigsen thought he knew her. She was Russian after all, and would, the German aristocrat thought, only act to benefit Russia. She may have been Russian, haunting the forests of the motherland, but she had no love for Russia. She had no love for anything. She merely delighted in shadows and in slaughter. It wasn't a Russian victory on the battlefield she wanted so much as the corpses from a Russian battlefield—or from any battlefield for that matter.

He could still smell her foul breath—not much different from that of rotting corpses at Borodino. Or was that what he smelled here in Gettysburg?

The stench would increase if Lee fought another day. More men would die. And the Confederates could not afford to lose as many men as could the Union. To fulfill his king's charge, Kutuzov needed to explain to Lee why he needed to retreat. Why he needed to save his army. Why he needed to keep his men alive. The Confederates had had a good day at Gettysburg. The Union Army may have repulsed the Third Corps's attack on Chambersburg Pike, but the Union lines had all but dissolved near the Lutheran Theological Seminary, forcing them to retreat up Cemetery Hill. General Richard Ewell had been wise not to take those heights. The men had been fighting all day. Their opponents had the high ground. Odds were a charge would end in slaughter.

It would be folly for the Confederates to stay and fight another day. The Union had greater resources, more manpower. They had the high ground. No matter how spirited the men, no matter how committed they were to the cause, the only way the Confederates could win here was if they had a little luck.

A little luck.

We had a little luck—good luck—the first day of Borodino, Kutuzov mused silently. Napoleon, the first one, had had a cold and spent most of the day in or near his tent, far from the front lines. Had he been closer to the action, he might have seen the need to send in his Imperial Guard. Had he done so, he would have smashed the Russians, destroying their army. Then he would have had a clear path to Moscow. And while Kutuzov's Russians had lost thousands of men, they had, by and large, held their lines. The army was intact.

But it wasn't intact after the second day.

A day they shouldn't have fought.

A day Kutuzov didn't remember.

The day he had been under the Baba Yaga's spell.

His bad luck. He should not have heeded the voice. He should have sat down and stayed in his log cabin in Tatarinovo until Count Wilhelm von Toll returned with his report. With that report, he would have the information he needed to make his case for a strategic retreat, first to Mozhaisk, then past Moscow.

Abandon the city. Lure Napoleon in. Napoleon wanted Moscow. Let him take it. Let him think the Russians were weak, the army depleted. He'd be overconfident, thinking that the

Russians had abandoned their historic capital. He might not worry as much about his supply lines. And winter was coming. There is nothing like a Russian winter. And this little man, this brilliant tactician, this savvy strategist, this self-styled Emperor, was from an island in the Mediterranean. He wouldn't be prepared.

Or maybe he would. Napoleon knew what he took to move an army across a continent, keep it comfortable, keep it fed. Maybe he'd remember why Themistocles abandoned Athens when the Persians invaded Greece. Maybe he'd be prepared for a Russian withdrawal.

But if a Russian army remained that was strong enough to threaten his supply lines and harry his men, even the great Napoleon couldn't survive a Russian winter.

Retreat was the best option after Borodino. Retreat was the best way to ensure that there would be a Russian army left to harry Napoleon's forces.

But Bennigsen didn't want to retreat. He believed they could push the French back. And he knew Kutuzov was more risk averse than he. And so, he found thirteen children—thirteen Russian children, orphans of the war, seven boys and six girls—and delivered them to the Baba Yaga in exchange for her promise to come to Borodino and convince Kutuzov to stay and fight.

"If only I had stayed in the cabin," Kutuzov said quietly to himself, yet both sentries outside Lee's tent shot him a curious look.

Each of those thirteen children had been younger than these young men, and neither of these men was older than eighteen. He had never seen the children—at least not in the flesh. She had harvested their bones before ill chance had led him to her. And the spirits of those children had slowed his aging, cured his illnesses, and healed his wounds—all but the right eye where a bullet had pierced his flesh at the Alushta.

Ill chance. He had just returned to his headquarters in a cabin at Tatarinovo near Borodino on that bloody September day in 1812. He had stepped inside and stood by the door, waiting for the report from Toll and his staff officers, believing it would confirm what he had observed: that the Russians were in a precarious position with thousands, if not tens of thousands, killed and wounded, regiments wiped out, divisions decimated. And once Toll returned, a German as loyal to him as Bennigsen wasn't, Kutuzov could readily outline his reasons for retreat.

Kutuzov should have sat down, but he was too anxious. He heard a man's loud voice, a strangely musical voice, a beckoning voice, a voice he did not recognize and should not have heeded, wondering why the commanding general of the Russian armies was not out among his men after a day when they had fought so hard. He was often among his men. He had been among them before the battle and planned to be again, but not then. They would need to begin the retreat well before sunrise.

But the man's voice had been so compelling.

Had he been sitting comfortably in his chair when he heard it, Kutuzov doubted he would have gotten up. But alas! He was still on his feet, so he went out.

A fog had fallen over the camp. He turned to the left. A stand of birches shone in the moonlight, beckoning him. He walked toward them. A breeze rustled their leaves. He heard strange sounds from the heavens, first a high-pitched whistle, like the wind passing through a narrow canyon, and then an off-kilter clanging, like a wooden clapper striking the stone lip of a broken brass bell. He looked up. And then he saw her—the woman that any Russian would recognize, that every Russian feared. The Baba Yaga was riding in a gigantic bone-colored mortar, steering it with a dun-colored pestle. It was descending as if from the very stars themselves and coming toward him.

He was so startled by the strange appearance that he had no time to feel fear. He could only marvel. And believe. *She* was real.

The Baba Yaga was the ugliest thing he had ever seen, and yet he could not take his eyes off her. Her face was a misshapen oval like a rotten pear, reddening in the strange mix of light from torches, moon, and stars. Her features seemed squashed as if stuck between the plate and base of an apple press. On each side of her mouth, a tooth curved up from below her lower lip. She was dressed in what looked like a tattered burial shroud.

"Kutuzov," the Baba Yaga intoned as if reading his name from an ancient demonology. "Field Marshal Mikhail Illarionovich Golenishchev-Kutuzov, who showed courage at Alushta, who fought valiantly in the Crimea, conquered cites on the Black Sea, brought peace to Bessarabia, the battle must go on... for Mother Russia." Her lips curled in scorn when she spoke the word "peace," her expression that of someone who had taken a sip of sour milk.

"It will go on, alas," he sighed, stepping back, wanting to get away, yet still transfixed by this figure out of folklore.

Her mortar settled on earth a few paces from him.

He took another step back.

"You will stay here and fight here, yes?" she asked, jumping up catlike onto the rim of her mortar and then drawing in a deep breath. A smile holding as much malice as cheer danced across her face. She smacked her lips and made a yummy sound.

"No," he said. "We will not stay here, but we will fight on."

"You will fight here," she insisted, jumping down from her mortar and slinking toward him, her eyes fixed upon him.

"No," he replied, finally breaking eye contact and taking another step back. He needed to return to Tatarinovo, to his cabin. Toll might already have arrived with the report. The other generals might be awaiting his instructions. For the briefest of moments, he wanted to explain to her why it would not be wise for the Russians to stay and fight, but he doubted an old witch with demonic powers and who delighted in death would understand.

He turned away. But then he heard his name again.

"Kutuzov," the Baba Yaga said, elongating the second vowel.

He stopped in his tracks. He was about to turn back, but then he remembered. Toll might already be waiting for him in Tatarinovo. He tried to take a step forward, but his muscles would not cooperate. His leg would not move. He felt pressure on his chest, as if he were a haltered horse reined in by a strong coachman.

"Stay here," she intoned. "Stay here and fight."

"No," he bellowed, trying to move forward, straining against the halter he felt—but could not see—pulling against his chest.

"You must," she answered. "For Mother Russia." She elongated the first vowel of each word, then stressed the sibilants.

He smelled her breath. It was like being downwind from a battle on a hot summer's day.

He pushed again against the unseen halter, but his body only tilted forward at an unnatural angle.

And then suddenly she was in front of him, framed by two birches, the moon hidden behind—and illuminating—her head. She pointed her pestle at him. "Stay and fight," she repeated.

"No," he replied. "No."

She leaned forward now, her forehead approaching his. She widened her eyes. They seemed to have a light of their own. He felt her probing his mind. "You have served your country," she observed, trilling her *r*'s. "You have served our mother, our Russia." Still trilling, still elongating the *u*. "With your mind, I cannot meddle." She sounded disappointed. She leaned away from him, and then made a strange sound in her throat, like the rumble before a wolf's growl, contemplating what to do, knowing her powers were limited.

He might have collapsed from the stench of her breath, but the unseen halter kept him upright. He wanted to turn away and escape her gaze, but the same force that pulled against his chest held his neck in place.

The Baba Yaga extended her arm, thrusting the pestle toward him until its rounded end touched the tip of his nose. Thirteen happy children's faces, cheeks flush from a day at play, appeared as a halo around her hideous head. Such a strange contrast. And then the color drained from each of the young faces, one by one. Terror replaced joy. Thirteen mouths opened, but no sound emerged. They could no more scream than he could move.

The Baba Yaga's eyes shot up to the sky as if someone had called her from above. She made that rumbling sound again, a tethered animal resigned to its fate. "I still get to keep their bones, even if *he* gets their youth," she said, sounding like a tradeswoman repeating a detail of a bad bargain. She tilted her head back, pricked up her ears, then nodded. She pressed the pestle into Kutuzov's nose as if trying to flatten it.

He remembered no more that night.

And nothing of the day that followed.

The next thing Kutuzov did remember was a French lieutenant waking him in his cabin on September 9, one night and twenty-four hours after the Baba Yaga's visit. *L'Empereur* wished to see him and accept his surrender.

Confused, Kutuzov demanded to know what had happened.

The Frenchman shared what he had heard. On September 8, the second day of the Battle of Borodino, the Russians fought valiantly all morning, holding their lines, but the French ground them down on their right. Then, just after midday, the

Emperor himself led his Imperial Guard through the center, coming around and smashing what remained of the Russian Second Army on the left.

Bennigsen, who had commanded the Russian armies that day, had been taken prisoner. Pyotr Bagration had succumbed to his wounds, dying while Kutuzov slept. Barclay de Tolly was nowhere to be found. Napoleon insisted that Kutuzov be present for the surrender. Despite the rumors circulating, the French Emperor knew that Russia's commanding general had not fled the battlefield.

They had found Kutuzov, the lieutenant explained, in the stand of birches, his head resting on the apron of a mute Russian girl, sitting with her back to a tree. Gesturing with her hands, she tried to show what had happened. Marshall Michel Ney interpreted her gestures to mean that a French spy had snuck into the Russian camp and hit the Russian general on the head with a stone, knocking him out.

As he rose to his feet, Kutuzov considered telling the Frenchman the truth but thought better of it. Ney's interpretation was more believable. Kutuzov said nothing, just dressed and followed the lieutenant to a row of campstools outside Napoleon's tent.

Bennigsen was waiting. Their eyes met. And Kutuzov knew what the German had done. How he knew he could never fully explain. Nor would Bennigsen ever explain how he had summoned the Baba Yaga.

And now, waiting outside Lee's tent, Kutuzov wanted to prevent that aristocrat of the New World from repeating the mistake he had tried to avoid in the Old World.

Lee could still save his army and be better able to defend the cities of his new nation. He could preserve the feudal system taking root on American soil.

Kutuzov looked up again at the sentries outside Lee's tent, hoping to catch the eye of at least one of them, but both men

A BIT OF LUCK

had turned to the sound of hoofbeats. His eyes followed their gaze.

A young, bearded man, maybe only a year or two past thirty, but wearing a general's uniform, sat atop a sleek stallion while whipping a Black man with graying hair who ran alongside. "Boy," he yelled. "Hurry up, you boy."

Boy? Kutuzov said to himself. *That man is older than he is.* Even in the days of the old aristocracy before Napoleon abolished serfdom, he had never called an adult serf "boy."

When the bearded soldier reached Lee's tent, the Black man dropped to his knees with some effort, then leaned forward, dug his elbows into the earth, and made a table with his back.

"General Hood," the sentry said. "General Lee has been waiting for you."

Hood. Kutuzov had heard of Major General John Bell Hood. He had fought at Antietam and Fredericksburg.

"I wouldn't be making our commander wait, if not for this lazy boy here," Hood said as he dismounted with a hard step onto the man's back before setting his feet gently on the earth.

The dark-skinned man grimaced, reaching up with one hand to grab the horse's reins while pushing against the ground with the other. He rose, a pained expression on his face, sweat cascading from his forehead.

Hood flicked his whip at the slave.

Kutuzov felt sick. He had never treated his serfs so poorly. He had never seen a man so treated. His travels to America had so far kept him in the Northern states.

Hood turned to him. "So that's what I'll look like when I'm an old man." He stroked his beard, fuller than Kutuzov's but shorter, and studied the old Russian. "Did the emperor send you, or was it your king—Alexander, is it?" The general had recognized his uniform. Unlike Rodes, he had been trained at West Point.

"My king," Kutuzov replied. "And, yes, it is Alexander."

The Confederate nodded, pushing his fingers up through his beard until they rested on his chin.

"And your name?"

"Kutuzov," he muttered.

"The man who had the ill luck to be knocked out by a French spy after the first day at Borodino. The general who was out of commission for the second."

"I was the man who had that ill luck," the Russian echoed, not wanting to tell this man what he had been preparing to tell Lee.

"John," came a voice from inside the tent. "General Lee is waiting."

Hood took one last look at Kutuzov, then turned around, dipped his head, and passed under the flap held open by the sentry. The sentry let go of the flap; it dropped like a curtain at the end of an opera.

Kutuzov looked at the Black man who was trying to stand straight while holding Hood's horse. He felt for the man and wished he could offer some comfort. No one should be treated as he had been. Kutuzov thought maybe to give up his seat, but if he showed kindness to this enslaved man, he might become suspect to the men who served the nation that enslaved him, the country his king hoped would triumph.

Kutuzov's eyes drifted to the pale-faced sentry outside Lee's tent. What did he think of slavery?

He thought back to the men who had once been his serfs and to their sons and grandsons, now working freely on his lands. He remembered the warmth of their homes and the sparkle in their eyes as they shared their stories. He could still see the wonder in their faces as he shared his own.

And then Kutuzov thought of Lee. Kutuzov had heard that a year previously, Lee had released 150 slaves from his estate at Arlington, in accordance with his father's will. But here he was, fighting for a nation that wished to preserve this pernicious institution, as bad as serfdom had been in his nation before the reforms mandated by the Napoleons. He looked again at the suffering man.

If Hood's treatment of this man is any indication, the Confederate system is worse than ours was. Far worse. And Lee is fighting to preserve it. Is he any better than Hood?

Kutuzov studied the dark-skinned man's face, his eyes then running down his body. Though the man tried, he could not keep his shoulders from hunching forward. *Like the old peasants in my country.* He could see from the way the man set the small of his back that he bore a lot of pain there. *Just as I would.* And his hands were just as rough as the hands of the men—and women—who worked the Russian fields. He would suffer the same maladies they did—and benefit from the same cures.

He sweats as I would if overworked on a hot day. And he would bleed in battle just as the men who fought with me bled at Borodino.

Kutuzov rose and went to the Black man. He took a handkerchief from his pocket and offered it to him. The man seemed confused.

"It's a gift," Kutuzov said.

The man did not seem to know the meaning of the word, but he took the handkerchief.

"I am Kutuzov," he said, extending his hand.

"Thomas," the Black man said, looking curiously at Kutuzov's extended hand.

The young men outside Lee's tent were also looking curiously at the Russian. Kutuzov cast an inquiring glance back. When their expressions did not change, he turned his eyes to Thomas, who held the reins of another man's horse in one hand and the Russian's handkerchief in the other.

And Kutuzov knew he could not stay. He could no longer complete his mission for his king. He did not want to play a game of politics that would keep this man enslaved. He looked into Thomas's face. His dark eyes held much pain. They must also hold just as many stories. As did the eyes of Russian peasants. He would have loved to hear this man's stories, but he could not stay.

He needed to get away from this place, away from this army's encampment. He did not want to lie to his king. He could say truthfully that he had not been allowed to see Lee, that he had not been able to help the Confederate war effort. He would find a place to hide until this battle was over.

He wanted to restore Russia's honor. He wanted to restore his own honor. But now that he had seen what honor was to the Confederates, he did not think it would be honorable to give sound military advice to a general who fought to keep other men enslaved.

ABOUT THE AUTHOR

A Tolkien geek since he first read *The Lord of the Rings* in sixth grade, B. Daniel Blatt has a PhD in mythological studies, having written his dissertation on the role the female Olympian Athena plays in the life of the male hero. He has completed several screenplays, including an adaptation of *Beowulf* based on his own translation of that great poem, discovering the Beowulf-poet a thousand years after his demise. He currently lives in Los Angeles where he is whittling down his million-word fantasy epic, *The Messengers' Kin*, and shaping it for publication.

10

THE NOTORIOUS LAWMAN BILLY THE KID

EDWARD J. KNIGHT

There's a serene beauty to New Mexico sunsets. Maybe it's the clear sky, with only the faintest of clouds above the horizon. Maybe it's the way the night bugs emerge, their whirring cacophony blanketing the sounds of the day. It doesn't matter. There's a peacefulness not found under the scorching daylight sun. The oranges and reds painted across the heavens are heralds of the restful night to come.

Most of the time.

The night I earned my nickname started like so many others, with me, relaxed but tired, watching the sunset from my back porch. I had my boots up on the railing, the warm breeze tousling my hair. The smooth aftertaste of whiskey lingered on my tongue as I swirled my glass. I was in no hurry for the next sip, and, from Mary's pot-banging in the kitchen, dinner remained a while off.

It'd been a good day. A calm day, with only rumors of trouble. Mr. Dolan had accused Mr. Tunstall of cattle rustling, but without even a hoofprint of proof, they'd parted before it came to more than words. A fight did happen at McGinty's saloon, but wiser heads had separated the two ruffians and sent them on their way long before I'd been called. And that'd been it. I hadn't had to throw a single person in my jail cell. Any day without an arrest was a good day, as far as I was concerned.

And judging from the new smells wafting from the kitchen, it promised to be a good evening as well.

"Pa!"

My gut tightened at the urgent tone.

"Pa!"

I dropped my feet from the railing just as my boy, Thomas, raced around the corner. Still rail thin and growing up instead of out, he skidded to a stop. His eyes were wide, his mouth swallowing air in big gulps.

"What is it?" I asked, the hairs on my neck beginning to rise.

"A killing, Pa! Right in the middle of town!"

And just like that, my good evening came to a close.

~

Light spilled from McGinty's saloon and bathed half the gathered crowd with enough brightness that I could almost see faces. Yet as men moved and turned, the shadows would swallow their features. I could feel the heat and anger, though. They were one step from a mob.

I strode fast, my gun drawn but by my side, my lantern swinging wildly in my other hand. Thomas hurried along behind, his stride not quite up to mine, but I was in no mood to slow. I tried to pick voices out of the cacophony, but none were quite strong enough to identify. Instead, one by one, all the talking died as more of the men saw me coming.

"'Bout time, Sheriff!" The speaker stepped forward from the crowd. Frank Baker, one of Mr. Dolan's men.

"What happened?" I barked as I slowed up.

Multiple voices shouted back answers.

"He shot him!"

"Ambushed!"

"In the back!"

"It's murder, Sheriff!"

The mob parted enough for me to see the body. A big man, they'd rolled him onto his back and clasped his hands together, all peaceful like. I brought my lantern up so I could see his face, and then I swore softly.

Dick Dolan. Mr. Dolan's son.

Now *this* was trouble.

The crowd dropped to a loud murmur as I knelt by the corpse. Blood soaked Dick Dolan's lower left side. Some on his front, more on his side, and even more pooling under his back. From the amount, I guessed it was his kidney. He'd've bled out pretty fast.

I glanced at Thomas. My son's face had gone pale, but he held himself together. Still, his eyes darted everywhere, taking in the first man he'd ever seen shot to death.

I wrinkled my nose. Dolan smelled of booze and shit. A lot of both.

The crowd's shuffling grew until Frank Baker stepped forward again.

"You gotta arrest him, Sheriff." His controlled tone barely hid his anger. "You say you're all about the law. You gotta arrest him."

"Let's calm down a minute," I said. "Arrest who? Who did this?"

"Joey," he said.

"Joey who?" My gut tightened as my mind raced ahead.

"Joey McCarty."

My nephew.

We loaded Dick Dolan's body on a wagon and drove it down to Doc Scurlock's. Blood from his back stained the boards in the wagon bed. The stink was starting to grow. As the wagon rolled, a half dozen men tried to tell me what'd happened, speaking over and on top of each other. It took me several minutes to get most of the story. I made them start at the beginning.

There'd been a heated argument over a card game, and then Dolan called Joey a cheat. It'd gotten worse, with a lot of words and insults exchanged. Toward the end, Joey called Dolan "a lying son of a bitch." That's when Dolan punched Joey in the face.

"McGinty threw Dick out, like it was his fault," Baker huffed. "You insult a man's mother, you deserve what's coming."

"The law don't quite see it that way," I said. But my gut knotted.

"Yeah, well, the law's wrong."

"Anyone go out with Dick Dolan?" I asked.

"Yeah," Baker said. "Me, George, and Ike." He gestured at a slight man with thinning hair and a wispy beard.

I already knew the gruff George Hindman that ran with Dolan, so I looked Ike up and down and then stared at him with narrowed eyes. He didn't blink.

"So... Ike," I said. "You're new here. Got a last name?"

"Ike Stockton. Just hired on with Mr. Dolan's father."

"So what happened outside, Mr. Stockton?"

Baker answered instead. "George and me tried to talk some sense into Dick. He wanted to go back inside and apologize."

"Bull crap, Mr. Baker." I rolled my eyes. "Dick Dolan's not the apologizing type. Especially not when he's drunk."

"Yeah, fine." Baker scowled. "He wanted to go punch McGinty too. We were talking him out of it. But that's when Joey came out."

George and Ike both nodded agreement.

"There were words," Baker continued, a bit quicker now.

"More insults. Joey drew his gun. So George and me convinced Dick to walk away. We hadn't gotten more than five steps when Joey shot him! In the back!"

The crowd jumped in, the noise rising to a roar.

"Murder!"

"Coward!"

"In the back!"

"Enough!" I barked. I then glared at Baker.

The mob quieted, but the grumbling continued.

"That so, Mr. Stockton?" I asked.

"Yessir!"

I cocked my head. Despite the light from a nearby lamp, I couldn't read his face well.

"Just the way Frank said," George added.

"Now our guns were holstered," Baker continued, "so we couldn't do nothing, until Joey ran. But we saw it, clear as day."

The crowd's murmur grew louder and more surly, dangerous in the gathering night.

"You gotta arrest him, Sheriff," Baker continued. "Even if he is your kin. You gotta."

∽

The rough dirt path to my brother's cabin held enough bumps that I had to go slow. Even with the lantern, I checked my steps. I couldn't afford to turn an ankle. Thomas stuck with me, only a step or two behind.

I worried about him. He should've been home in bed, away from all this ugliness. But he needed to grow up sometime. Dick Dolan might've been the first man he'd seen killed, but he sure wouldn't be the last. Thomas was only a few years younger than Joey. I'd barely started teaching him to shoot.

At the same time, I remained unsettled by what'd happened. I didn't believe Frank Baker for a minute, but I

The Notorious Lawman Billy the Kid

wasn't sure it mattered. "Son of a bitch" *were* fighting words. Everyone agreed Joey'd said it. And the memory of those words in my own voice kept floating back. I'd been as young and foolish as Joey when I'd used them. My gut roiled, and I clenched my hands into a fist before forcing myself to calm a bit. I needed to focus on where I was walking.

I needed to focus on Joey.

My nephew could turn rabbit, which would cause a mess of ugly. Better to catch him now and straighten things out at once, rather than have to swear out a warrant later.

Sure enough, we found Joseph and Joey in the barn loading saddlebags on my brother's Morgan. The lanky teen's arms shook as he moved, his face smudged and dirty. My brother chided him quietly to keep calm, but then Joseph's ashen face turned grim when he spotted me. He stepped back from the horse, letting it shuffle and snort. Joey froze before his father gestured for him to step away as well.

"What's the hurry?" I drawled. I pulled up a few feet away and hooked my thumbs in my belt.

"You know why," Joseph snarled. He rested one hand on the horse's flank.

"Well, I heard Dolan's men's side of it. Now I wanna hear Joey's."

"What'd they say?" Joseph asked.

"That Joey shot Dolan in the back."

"No!" Joey's eyes went wide. "No! I didn't! He'd drawn his gun. He was gonna shoot me, Uncle Billy, honest!"

My nephew trembled, and in the low lamplight, I could see his sweat. I gave him the most calming smile I could manage.

"You want to tell me about it?" I asked.

Joey looked to his dad, who nodded.

"I thought they might try to jump me," Joey said, "like they did to Dash."

I nodded. Dash Waite had refused to press charges, but his jaw had never fully healed.

Joey took a deep breath. "So I drew my gun on the way out. Sure enough, they were waiting for me."

"That's what I heard." Maybe not in those exact words.

"We said some things." His cheeks actually pinkened. "Not nice things... but I had my gun up."

"Did they?"

He hesitated, swallowed, and then looked at his dad again.

"No," Joseph said clearly. His expression was firm in the low light. "They pretended to walk away, and that's when Dolan drew."

"Yeah," Joey said. "They pretended."

Next to me, Thomas sucked in his breath. My heart raced. But I had to ask.

"Did you shoot him in the back?" I knew the answer, but I wanted to hear it from Joey's own lips.

"No!" Alarm filled Joey's face. "No! Of course not!"

"Then it was self-defense," I said.

Joseph snorted. "Do you think that matters?"

"Of course I do," I snapped.

My brother snorted again. "Just how stupid are you, Billy?"

"Let's go to town and straighten this out," I said. "I'm sure we can have Joey back in time for a late supper."

I didn't have to slide a hand toward my gun. The "or else" was clear.

"Fine." Joseph cinched the saddlebag and picked up a rifle that had been lying on a nearby hay bale. "Back for a late supper. Your word on it."

I nodded. There wasn't much else to say.

∼

My gut fell when we saw the torch-carrying crowd outside my office. Somehow the mob had doubled in the short time I'd been away. Instinctively, I reached for Thomas's hand, but he didn't let me take it. Too close to manhood, I supposed. A light breeze had picked up, chilling me far more than it should.

Beside me, Joey and Joseph slowed. My nephew dragged his feet, and his father firmly gripped his shoulder. My brother glared at me.

"Your word," he snapped at me.

I spotted James Dolan, Dick's father, surrounded by a circle of men. He stood tall, pontificating and waving his arms wildly.

"I may have trouble keeping it," I murmured.

"You do... or there'll be blood."

The crowd stilled as they saw us approach. I headed straight toward Mr. Dolan after making sure my family followed. My own nerves began to tingle. I wondered about Joey's. I did my best to project calm. It wasn't easy in the ominous, flickering light. Still, my hand hovered over my gun.

We stopped about eight feet in front of Mr. Dolan, Frank Baker by his right side. We stared at each other for a moment. Mr. Dolan remained as unflinching and righteously stiff as ever.

Mr. Dolan broke the silence.

"Well, Sheriff McCarty," he said, "it looks like you are indeed a man of the law."

"A fact of which you are already aware, Mr. Dolan." I stared hard at him.

"Too bad your nephew's a coward and a killer."

I guffawed, loud enough for the crowd to hear. "That remains to be seen, Mr. Dolan. That's why we'll have a trial."

"We don't need any trial." Mr. Dolan's smile was quiet and small, like a bobcat right before it pounced. "We've got three witnesses. Your nephew shot my son in the back."

A BIT OF LUCK

Joey started to speak, but his father clamped a hand down hard on his shoulder.

"We're gonna have a trial." I glared at Frank Baker. "Sometimes witnesses don't tell the truth."

"You callin' me a liar, Sheriff?" Baker yelled.

I dropped my hand to the hilt of my Colt, and he quieted right up.

"I don't know if you're a liar, Mr. Baker," I said. "I just find it a bit strange that Joey only shot Dick Dolan. He had the drop on you, too, Mr. Baker. Why didn't he shoot you?"

"'Cause he didn't draw his gun, like Dick did," Joey muttered, but not quietly enough. Both Baker and Mr. Dolan snapped their heads to glare at him.

"We're gonna have a trial," I repeated. "Jury and everything. Just as soon as Judge Brady gets back to town."

Joseph hissed at me, but I shook him off.

"Judge Brady's not due back until Saturday, Sheriff," Mr. Dolan snapped. "Are you going to make me wait that long for justice? Justice for my son?"

"We're gonna have a trial." I made my tone loud and firm. "And any man who disagrees is gonna have to go through me."

Mr. Dolan glared at me but kept silent. I could guess what he was thinking. But he hadn't decided exactly what to do.

The crowd shuffled and murmured, but no one spoke loudly enough for me to make out their words over the crackle of the torches. I ignored them and kept my stare on Mr. Dolan.

He blinked first.

"Go home," I said. "Bury your son."

"We'll do that," he said. "Then we'll be back."

My office wasn't much. I had just the one cell, and it was more a room with a barred door than a true jail. Still, the adobe walls were a foot thick, and the window was way too narrow for anyone to shinny through. I could see both the cell and the front door from my desk, which helped in times like this.

"You said home by dinner," Joseph snapped once it was just the four of us. Our boys were talking quietly off to the side, too quietly for me to make out words.

"I can protect him better here."

My brother sized up the sole door to the outside. "They'll just wait you out."

"You're assuming they'll try something."

He snorted. "You know Dolan." Joseph started pacing in what little room was left.

"I know he and Judge Brady are drinking buddies."

My brother stopped and stared at me. The boys had gone quiet too.

"That just makes it worse," he said.

I shrugged. "If he thinks he can win the trial, why risk anything now?"

"So Joey hangs later instead of tonight," Joseph scoffed.

The boys shuffled their feet, drawing my attention. Thomas's face was pale, his eyes wide. Joey just sagged where he stood.

"Joey's not going to hang." My words were firm, but my gaze never left my son's. "Not for self-defense."

Joseph snorted. "That's not always how it works, Billy. You know that."

"But sometimes it does. You know that too."

Joseph shook his head. He stared at the narrow outside door again, before taking a big breath. "I'm gonna get some grub and bring it back." He smiled at his son. "It'll be all right, Joey. It'll be all right."

I grimaced. My brother was lying through his teeth.

I didn't make Joey go into the cell. I didn't see the point. He wasn't going to run now, not with some of Dolan's men surely hanging around outside. Instead, I gestured to the small wooden chair next to my desk. He sank down like a man drained of life. I hoped Joseph would be back soon with the food.

Thomas wandered over to the wall of wanted posters. Most were faded and almost illegible in the low lamplight, but he stopped in front of the one that'd just come in. A cattle rustler out of Texas last seen fleeing west.

"I saw him." Thomas stabbed the poster with one finger. "Two weeks ago."

"You did?" The rustler's earlier presence wasn't news to me, but I didn't know Thomas had seen him.

"He was real polite to Mrs. Chavez and Mrs. Morton in the general store."

"He was, was he?"

"And he's an outlaw."

I smiled. "Outlaws can be polite."

"You think I'll get a fair trial, Uncle Billy?" Joey's voice edged on cracking. He slumped forward, his elbows on his knees, his head in his hands.

I steeled myself and forced myself to project a confident tone. "Of course I do."

He looked up, still forlorn. "I didn't shoot him in the back."

"I know."

He blinked.

"The bullet went through him," I said. "But the bigger hole was in his back. That makes it an exit wound."

Joey's chin dropped.

"Of course, we need to get Doc Scurlock to testify to that, but he's an honest man."

"If Dolan doesn't get to him first," Joey muttered.

"Will Joey be an outlaw, Pa?" Thomas's voice was smaller, more unsure.

"Not..." I swallowed hard. "Not if I can help it." I smiled at my son, who seemed reassured and turned back to the wanted poster.

Joey buried his head in his hands again.

I sighed. Joey was ... so young. I... I hadn't been much older in Arizona.

He needed to live. I owed him that. And he needed to have supper in his own home.

∼

Joseph arrived with cold chicken and biscuits. He grimaced as he came in. Judging from the torches behind him, more of Dolan's men had joined the ones outside. I couldn't hear their conversations, but the numbers told me enough. Our dear Mr. Dolan was not going to be patient.

"Eat up," Joseph urged as he distributed the food. He paused at Thomas, then looked at me. "Maybe he should go home."

"Won't make him any safer," I replied. "He's gotta grow up sometime."

"But is this the way?" Joseph gave me a pointed look.

I sighed and looked at my son with his mop of dark hair and his skinny arms. He'd commandeered my office chair and tore into a chicken thigh with his teeth. I didn't have the heart to expel him.

I perched on the edge of my desk. My own meat was dry and hard to swallow. I had a small flask of whiskey in my desk but decided against passing it around. I wasn't quite ready for Thomas to grow up that much.

"Think it'll get as bad as Arizona?" Joseph asked.

I scowled. I'd been avoiding the comparisons.

"What happened in Arizona?" Thomas asked.

I forced a smile at my son. "Something like this."

"Only it was your Pa in Joey's boots," Joseph said.

"Really?" Joey's chair creaked as he leaned forward.

"Yeah," I said. "The mob was going to hang me. The sheriff stopped them." If he hadn't... I suppressed a shudder.

"You're no Sheriff Wood," my brother pointed out.

"No," I agreed. I gestured at the door. "But I can defend that."

"Until Dolan throws a stick of dynamite through it."

My blood ran cold. The flickers of torchlight coming through the door looked brighter.

I turned to my boy. Thomas met my gaze. His lip trembled.

I needed to get him out of here.

"Thomas," I said. "I need you to run and find Mr. Tunstall. Tell him to come quick."

"You really think Tunstall will help you?" Joseph asked.

"He doesn't like me," I admitted. "But he hates Dolan more. We'll just have to see."

~

I don't know why, but the hour after midnight feels like the darkest. The promise of dawn is just too far away. But tonight, with all the torches, the street outside my office felt like a revival meeting. The excited voices crashed into each other enough to make words hard to hear, but the tone was impossible to miss. They were waiting for a show.

I wasn't inclined to give it to them. I stood in the shadows of the doorway, watching. Only about a dozen of the men were Dolan's. They milled around in the center of the street, far enough from my office so I couldn't tell exactly what they were up to. Most of the rest of the town hung back at safer distances. Wise, but I wished they were all home in bed.

Joseph eased up beside me. He scanned the growing crowd before speaking. "Joey's gotta pee."

"Pitcher in the cell." I didn't turn my eyes.

Joseph said a few words over his shoulder and then turned back to me. "How long, you think?" he asked.

"Half hour. Maybe an hour."

"And Tunstall?"

I shrugged.

More torches appeared at the end of the street. I steeled myself and stood straight. The crowd quieted as the new men approached. Dolan and Baker were at the head with George Hindman right behind.

I stepped out, just enough to fill the doorway and draw their attention. Behind me, I sensed my brother drop to one knee and level his rifle. I shifted to the side to keep his line of fire open, though I hoped it wouldn't be needed.

Dolan paused, fifteen feet away. He swept his duster back, revealing his sidearms. Baker did the same, but with a sneer on his lips. Dolan paused, waiting until the crowd quieted.

"We've come for the boy!" he called.

"He gets a trial!" I put my hand on my hip, right next to my gun.

"He killed my son!"

I glared at him. "He still gets a trial."

Dolan scoffed. "We don't need a trial." He gestured at Baker and Hindman, who both stepped forward. "We got witnesses."

Ike Stockton was nowhere to be seen.

"It was self-defense," I called back. "Your witnesses are liars."

"Who you callin' a liar?" Frank Baker hunched his shoulders. His hand hovered by his side.

I glared at him. "I'm calling you a liar, Mr. Baker. Dick Dolan was shot in the front. The wounds prove it. He was a bully, and you were his loyal dog, nipping at his heels."

A BIT OF LUCK

"Who you callin' a dog?" Baker shouted.

"I'm calling you a dog," I replied. "I'd call you a son of a bitch, but I don't want to insult your mother."

With an angered cry, Baker drew.

I was faster.

The gunshot echoed through the town. Then a second shot.

George Hindman's gun slipped from his hands before he collapsed to the ground. Baker was already face down in the dirt.

"Got him," Joseph muttered from my side.

"Anyone else want to try?" I shouted. I pointed my gun straight at Dolan's heart.

The night stilled. Someone coughed, but no one said a word.

"Joey gets a trial, Mr. Dolan," I said. "And now you've lost two witnesses."

"He killed my boy," Dolan spat. He tensed and spread his stance, like he was going to draw. "There's still a dozen of us, and just two of you."

"I wouldn't be so sure of that."

The new voice was strong and came from my left. The crowd parted as John Tunstall pushed through. Tunstall's silver hair glistened in the torchlight. His own gang of men trailed behind him. I let out a relieved breath when I spotted Thomas among them.

"Mr. Tunstall," Dolan said. "This doesn't concern you."

"I believe it does," Tunstall drawled. "You just threatened to kill our sheriff. We can't have that."

"The sheriff's an idealistic fool." Dolan shot a glare at me. "No better than a schoolboy."

"He may look like a kid," Tunstall replied, "but he's more of a man than your son was. Joey McCarty did the world a favor."

"You'll rue the day you said that, Tunstall." Dolan turned away from me, but I didn't lower my gun.

A strong breeze flickered the torches as the two men stared each other down.

"Go home, Mr. Dolan," I said. "Two of your men have already died tonight. Don't make it more."

"This ain't over, Tunstall," Dolan snarled. "This means war."

Tunstall smiled. "War it is."

~

"John's right, you know," Joseph teased. "You do look like a kid."

He poured a shot of whiskey and slid the bottle across my desk. We'd turned up the lamps, which made it almost feel like home. Tunstall's men still called to each other as they patrolled the street outside, but no shots had been fired. Yet.

"Please." I caught the bottle and glared at my brother.

"Your looks don't hurt," Tunstall said. He raised his own glass and smiled at me over the rim. "Men underestimate you."

"I'm thirty," I grumped. I looked over at Joey, who slowly sipped his drink.

"We should call you 'Billy the Kid,'" Joseph continued. "You never could grow a beard." He grinned at Thomas. "It won't be long before you're bigger than your pa."

"Don't pick on my pa!" Thomas looked so righteously indignant, we all laughed, even Mr. Tunstall.

"So," the elder rancher said, "how long do you think we have?"

"With Dolan?" I took a small sip and thought. The whiskey eased down my throat. "He'll wait until after the trial, I think. He'll lean on Judge Brady, but we'll insist on a jury."

"Which he'll try to pack," Tunstall pointed out.

"Hung jury means Joey goes free," I pointed out.

"You really think he'll wait that long?" Joseph asked.

"He'll use the time to prepare for the war." I raised my glass at Tunstall. "You should too."

"We'll be ready."

"Pa..." Thomas began, but then grew abashed when all eyes turned to him. He clutched his glass of mostly water.

"What is it, son?" I gently asked.

"Why didn't you just let Joey go? I mean... Mr. Baker and Mr. Hindman are dead, and now we're gonna have a war. Couldn't you have just... let him go? More people would be alive..."

His expression was so earnest. Innocent. It darn near broke my heart.

I smiled at him and chose my words carefully. "There's more to life than being alive. There's honor. Trust. There's doing the right thing. That's what makes a good life."

He nodded uncertainly.

"If Joey had run," I continued, "he'd always be looking over his shoulder. That's not a good life. This way..." I smiled at my nephew. "This way he can sleep in his own bed every night. That's a much better life."

"Hear, hear." Joseph raised his glass, followed by Tunstall. We clinked them and drank.

Thomas grinned and tapped his own cup against his cousin's.

I smiled at my son. A much better life indeed.

ABOUT THE AUTHOR

A fourth-generation Coloradoan, Edward J. Knight only left the Denver-Boulder area long enough to learn how to put a satellite into orbit. Four satellites (and counting) later, he's returned to both the mountains and writing fantastical fiction. Along the way, he met the love of his life and became the father of two wonderfully curious kids. He's a huge fan of historical "what ifs"—like whether an Arizona sheriff protects a young boy from a mob or forces that boy to escape and become an outlaw. More of Knight's work can be found at edwardjknight.com.

11

OUT OF HABIT

JULIE JONES

The first time I spotted Jack the Ripper was the day Mary Jane died, right outside her flat. The police had called me in to pray over the scene and comfort the neighbors, and I knew in my heart the killer would come back to bask in his handiwork. I marked Jack's appearance and noted it for later when I would be free to kill him without witnesses. As usual, the newspapers were rubbish when it came to details.

I'd stalked Jack for weeks without any idea what he looked like, so catching the momentary pause and telling smile of the flame-haired man across the street was a great stroke of luck for me. He watched the scene for the space of three heartbeats, shook himself slightly, and scurried off before anyone else wondered about his wistful gaze and flaring nostrils. He took no notice of the tall, habited Sister eyeing him over the bowed heads of her charges.

I stayed at the scene all afternoon, but turned my head away in prayer when they brought out Mary's body. I'd visited her single room only the morning before. She'd greeted me at the door—sober for the first time in a while—hale and beautiful even under the merciless grind of poverty. And so very sad. We sipped weak tea from badly chipped cups while she petted her calico cat and gazed out the window.

"I'd tell ye not to turn out like I have," she said, "but here ye are in your black and white, all married up to Jesus instead of sellin' yourself on the street for pennies. You're a good sort, and the neighborhood loves ye, but you'll never really understand what it's like. You'll never be a guttersnipe, Sister."

"Bold of you to assume I wasn't a guttersnipe before taking my vows," I said, and regret flitted across her face. I patted her hand. "Come to the convent tomorrow and have a bath and a meal. Sister Mary Victoria knows of a family looking for domestic help, and I think you'd do nicely. You can even bring your cat. I'll speak to Mr. McCarthy about your overdue rent."

"You won't," Mary said, chin raised to a dangerous angle. "I always appreciate your charity, Sister, and no disrespect intended, but you'll not be stickin' your nose into that."

I studied her, but she wasn't budging. "Very well. Do you need any winter clothing? It's getting cold."

She shrugged and said her coat was fine, but mittens and a warm scarf might be nice, so I promised to have them for her when she visited. After that I went about my day, checking on the sick, visiting the old, and helping anywhere I could. I returned to my cell at the convent coated in the despair I'd long since grown accustomed to.

I waited all morning for Mary Jane to come round. At noon, John McCarthy brought the news of her grisly death and Inspector Beck's request for me to tend to the neighbors. My grieving, vengeful heart recognized a chance to spot Jack, and I used it.

Truth to tell and painful to admit, my vows had chafed for a long bit by then. Every day I witnessed the most heartbreaking bits of humanity. Poverty, depression, illness, illiteracy, and abuse of every kind around the clock. The desperate needs of the lowest classes were never met, yet the purses of the highest grew fatter each day. Prayer made no difference I could see, and I'd gone through the habit of it for months with no emotion motivating my words. The numb exhaustion of grief settled into my bones.

Jack's first murder snapped something in me. I'd known the victim—Mary Ann Nichols. I knew almost all the unfortunate souls in Whitechapel thanks to my work. Their suffering was horrific enough without the Ripper prowling the darkness. None of them deserved this new hell, but nobody of authority did anything about it.

After Jack's second murder, I understood. The hearts of men were too puny for the evil that stalked London, and I alone recognized the true threat. It was up to me.

I sneaked out in the small hours, walking the misty alleyways with the kitchen's biggest knife hidden in the folds of my secular skirts. I worried over the peace I felt prowling the alleyways for a murderer, yet the occasional search soon turned to nightly scouting. I burned with the need to find and put an end to him.

I searched for weeks. Bloody good it did me. He kept right on killing. Three, then four, then Mary Jane made five, and I finally got what I needed. A look at his face.

After the police bore her body away, the neighborhood gadflies sought their entertainments elsewhere. Inspector Beck remained, and John McCarthy, and Mary's orphaned calico sneaking along the wall to the bloodstained stoop. The men's faces were creased with exhaustion and worry, and neither spoke for several long moments.

"It's late," I said. "Have you further need of me, gentlemen?"

"None I know of," the Inspector said. "You have my thanks, Sister. The scene would've been a circus without your helping hand."

I nodded. "It was my honor, Inspector. And you, Mr. McCarthy? How much did Mary owe in rent, sir?"

He cast his eyes to the cobblestones. "Now, Sister, seems an ill thing to speak of money, what with Mary not even cold yet—"

"Mary wouldn't want you shorted because of this," I said. "Come now, how much?"

"Twenty-nine shillings, Sister."

I dug out my coin purse and pressed five shillings of my own into his hand. "Take these for now. I'll bring you the rest."

He shook his head. "No need, Sister. There's no need. Wasn't you owed me the rent, and now she's gone. But I thankee, anyway."

I patted his shoulder. "It's been a long day. Why don't you go home now, both of you? I'm going back to the convent. If anyone needs me—and that includes the two of you—come to the gate of Mercy Chapel and ask for the tall sister with cornflower blue eyes. Distressed people rarely remember names, but they'll remember that."

The men agreed and shuffled in opposite directions. When their dejected footsteps faded, I sidled toward Mary's door where the cat waited with its tail wrapped around its feet. She bristled as soon as I moved, and three steps away, she bolted. I stamped my foot in frustration. The convent could use a good mouser, and the cat needed a home. Like most my parishioners, she was going to make helping difficult.

I sighed and hurried to prayer.

Evening passed with the speed of forming stalactites. The silence of dinner and chores grated my nerves, but I pressed my lips together and bore it. Nosy questions would've been worse. The familiar routine of tidying the kitchen settled my belly a little, and I closed the evening without casting suspicion upon myself. I didn't know what my sisters might suspect me of, but I wanted no attention or interference.

As soon as I was able, I escaped to my room to change clothes and calm my shaky hands. I searched my possessions for any suitable weapons and found nothing but a large pair of rosewood knitting needles. I knew how to use the butcher knife, but it was a single weapon. After glimpsing Jack, I wanted extras. Any extras.

I used scissors to whittle the needles to a sharp point and prayed it was enough. At least I wouldn't have to hide them. Walking around with a butcher knife tended to draw attention, so I took pains to conceal it. Casual observers wouldn't think twice about a woman carrying her knitting.

A long night stretched before me. Despite a pounding heart I lay down to rest. I sent my thoughts heavenward to avoid picturing the possible horrors to come, and for a time I forgot about Jack and what I intended to do. I dozed off.

A scratch on the window shutter woke me a few hours later. I put the sound down to the wind and my sleepy mind, but it came again more urgently so I rose to lift the latch. It was the calico cat.

"Oh, *hello*, kittums," I crooned. "Have you come to live with me?"

She dodged my hand and bristled a little, then scolded me with a loud yowl and quit the windowsill for the garden. She ran a few steps and looked back with perked ears, expecting me to follow. I called after her.

"Wait. I'm not ready yet. I need five minutes. Just wait!"

I grabbed up the knitting needles and slipped into the darkened corridor. The late hour energized the air with expectation like the last grains of sand slipping through the neck of an hourglass. I sped silently through the hallways to the church, let myself in, and approached the basin of holy water at the foot of the altar. The needles got a generous dunking, then I used them to make the sign of the cross and whisper fervent prayers for strength and protection.

I made a quick detour through the kitchen for the knife and went back to my room. The door latch squeaked, and I went to the window with a worried belly. The cat made an impatient mound under a nearby bush and scolded me again. I kicked a leg over the windowsill and climbed through.

"Lead on, Miss Whosit," I whispered, having no other name for her.

She spared me a reproachful look and darted into the shadows. The knitting needles settled in my left hand, and I clutched the knife in my right, hidden in the folds of my skirt. Squinting against the darkness, I followed the flashes of calico glimpsed between the manicured flower beds.

We reached the gate, and the cat slinked through the bars. I was somewhat slower. Miss Whosit had reached the end of the block by the time I scurried to catch up. She trilled a small mew of encouragement and swooped around the corner.

"Maybe slow down a bit," I whispered, and she obliged.

I followed her almost all the way back to Mary Jane's flat before realizing where she led me. She had picked a circuitous route, taking alleys even I didn't know, sometimes trotting down runs barely wide enough to fit my shoulders. One of these spit us out near Miller's Court and Mary Jane's home at Number 13.

Thick London fog choked back the streetlamps. They cast unstrung pearls of light at their own feet, and the hazy dark swirled like murky waters full of sharks. The flickering gas lamps made poor islands to swim between, and I stopped short of plunging in.

Unfortunately, Miss Whosit didn't hesitate. I pushed aside my reluctance and stepped quick to keep up. She ran right to Mary Jane's door and crouched on the stoop, ready to either pounce or run with equal fervor. I wondered why she'd led me there, but supposed it was as good a place as any to begin my hunt.

"Well, then," I said, "we'll just start here if you say so, Miss Whosit."

I loitered near the street with my arms folded and the knife laid flat against my belly. I didn't expect much. Within five minutes I itched to wander the alleys and look for the monster, but I couldn't shake the idea that Miss Whosit had brought me there for a purpose. Five more minutes, I decided.

The November fog muffled traffic. Though I heard footsteps, fewer people than normal dared the cloaking mists, and no silhouettes appeared in the soupy atmosphere. For a moment I thought I'd died, and it was my ghost that wandered Whitechapel.

"What'm I doing here?" I whispered into the mist.

Doubt—an old friend of many years—came to visit and took residence in my mind. I had no business being out alone in the night, planning to kill. No matter what I suspected of my victim, I was breaking the sixth commandment. I'd avoided thinking about it much up to that point, focused instead on my need to find Jack and stop him. I should be in Mother Superior's study, explaining everything and coordinating work with Scotland Yard, not posted in front of Mary Jane's house with a knife pressed to my abdomen and revenge in my heart.

I wavered for a long time but didn't leave.

"Meow," Miss Whosit said.

I snapped to attention.

The mists darkened to my left. His footfalls were light and sneaky, and he approached with the manner of a curious wolf. His pale skin blended with the fog and gave his unruly red hair the impression of fire floating through the air. Eyes bluer than mine stabbed like icicles.

I emulated the pouty, inviting expression I'd seen so many desperate women wear. "Feelin' lonely tonight?"

"Perhaps," he murmured. His voice thrilled my body like nothing I'd ever known. Evil magic, it was. Weakness—both flesh and spirit—washed down my spine and left my faith in ruins. Disbelief and revulsion at my own plan to kill this beautiful creature roiled inside me, and I nearly threw the knife aside.

"*Meow!*" Miss Whosit screeched.

The warning slapped me to my senses, but I almost panicked when Jack's frowning attention whipped in the cat's direction. She hissed.

"Oh, now," I said, "no needs worryin' about a stray. You was sayin' you'd like a lil' comp'ny, eh?"

Those blue augur eyes drilled me through, but he dismissed the cat. He stepped closer, and I swallowed hard. Blood pounded in my veins. He stroked my cheek with one claw-like finger, and I yearned to both lean into it and spew up every meal I'd ever eaten.

"You're a lovely young thing," he said, and my guts fluttered. "I'm boarding a ship for America in the morning, and it'd be a treat to have one more before I go. Would you like to be my last on this side of the ocean, then?"

"Show me the coins," I managed, and he pulled a fistful of money from his pocket. When I nodded, he grabbed my arm.

Miss Whosit objected to the rough treatment, but he ignored her and pulled me down the street to an alley while I tried to hide the large blade behind my back.

"Now," he said, shoving me against the brick wall. The power of his voice wore down my resolve as his fingers dug cruelly into my throat. "Give me the knife."

I stabbed at his torso, but he blocked. We fought for control for a few seconds, then he twisted the handle from my grip and threw it aside. The blade clanged against the cobbles with a muffled ring and slid under an offal cart.

"You will be delicious," he murmured. A terrifying light burned in his eyes, brightening with every heartbeat. His forked tongue flicked between sharp teeth to lick his lips in a lewd manner, and I tried to scream.

"No, no," Jack admonished, squeezing my throat even

harder. "No screaming. It'll be over soon enough, lovely young thing, but until then keep your screams inside. Your blood tastes better that way."

A hissing streak of orange, white, and brown flew between us and latched onto his face. He yelled and let go of my neck to swipe off the furious cat. She spat and scratched and howled while I tried to catch my breath, and Jack retreated a few steps under her furious assault.

"Get'im, Miss Whosit!"

She tore a chunk from his ear and leapt away. He roared and clapped a hand to his head, but blood poured down his neck and stained the white collar of his shirt.

I gripped one needle in each hand, poised and ready to strike, but his forceful gaze locked onto me and stalled my muscles.

"You'll pay extra for that," he said.

"You're the only one bleeding so far," I said, more bravely than I felt. "I know what you are, demon, and I will end you tonight."

His razor teeth gleamed when he laughed. "End me? With what? Those knitting needles? Your feline familiar? I had no fear of the knife but didn't feel like bloodying my clothes. The irony is not amusing."

Fast as a blink, his right arm flew up and pain blossomed in my left ear. Blood coursed in a warm river down my neck. It took all my resolve not to stanch the flow, but I meant to show him no weakness.

"Now," he said, "we're even again. I can begin my pleasures."

"Oh, are we keepin' score, then? In that case, I'll have to stab ya at least five times."

His lightning hands shot out and grabbed my wrists. He yanked me toward him, and I used the motion to stab the knitting needles into his gut.

He grunted in surprise.

"That's two," I said.

He shoved me away, and the needles pulled free with a sickening *thwack*. Jack hunched over and pressed his hands to his belly.

My back was bruised from the brick wall, but I pushed off and rushed him, one needle held above my head and the other low against my hip.

As I hoped, he focused on my wild overhand swing and caught my left arm as it came down. I channeled all my fury and momentum into a right thrust. The needle went through clear to his liver, and he howled in pain.

"Three," I muttered.

I jerked the needle free, and he howled again. Such a pretty sound.

He stumbled and covered himself with shaking hands. Dark blood poured from his three wounds, and now his eyes held fear alongside the glow of hellfire.

"What've you done?" he said. "What've you done to me?"

"Not half what you deserve."

I attacked again.

He snatched a long, slender knife from inside his coat.

I dodged, but his brutal stab tore my skirts, and I thought for sure he got my leg. No time to worry over it. I punched him in the jaw, and he staggered, still clutching his wounds with one hand. I knocked the knife from his grip, and he shoved me back. Open panic twisted his features and sweat beaded his forehead.

"What is it?" he said. "I've been stabbed plenty of times, and it's never hurt before. What did you *do*?"

"Show me," I demanded, and he lifted his bloody shirt. The flesh around his wounds had turned to rotting black pits, and it spread as I watched.

I smiled. "Just as I hoped."

"What's that mean?" Jack said. His fear turned to rage. "What's that *mean*?"

"It means even if you kill me, you still die. My death is a fair price for sending you back to hell."

Fury pulled the mask of humanity off his face. He swung a fist at me. I took it hard on the left cheek and spun to the pavement in a daze. He fell on my back, ripping and tearing with his clawed hands. He only stopped to reach aside for his dropped knife.

I bucked and threw him off. He fell over, rolled, and got to his feet with effort. I stood too, picked up his blade, and flung it under the same offal cart where mine had gone. The knitting needles were my weapon. A knife would only get me cut.

Jack's legs wavered. He staggered toward me with claws raised and fangs bared.

I braced for attack with the needles up.

Miss Whosit raced in from my left and climbed up Jack's coat to his face, hissing the whole way. She scratched and bit, and the enraged demon howled. He grabbed her with both hands and flung her down. She screamed in pain and ran off.

I didn't dare waste the precious moments she bought me.

I lunged forward and skewered Jack's neck with the knitting needles, one in each side. I didn't pull them out. I let go and stepped back to watch him gurgle. He fell to one knee. The hellfire in his eyes dimmed. The rot from his gut wounds had crept to his collarbone and met the decay enveloping his head.

"That makes five. Now we're even."

"How?" he croaked and groped at the rosewood in his neck.

"Blessed in holy water."

He closed his eyes. A minute or two later, his body slumped and fell with a heavy thud. He didn't move, but I watched to be sure. The rot crept on. When it finally consumed him, the corpse desiccated and disappeared, leaving the knitting needles and a deflated sack of clothes lying in the alley.

"Meow," Miss Whosit said.

"I quite agree."

I checked my leg and found a deep cut along the outside of my left thigh. The bleeding was bad, but nothing major was cut. I ripped a length of cloth off my underskirt to use as a bandage and close the wound.

The journey back to the convent was surreal, and a bit of a letdown. I'd expected to feel elated if I emerged victorious, refilled with my faith and ready to serve. But I didn't. My depression was tinged with guilt now, but otherwise intact. Guilt for killing, guilt for enjoying it, and guilt for my pride in what I'd done. So many sins, and I regretted none of them. I couldn't even ask forgiveness.

I stayed at Mercy Chapel only another week. I couldn't reconcile my feelings with the vows I'd taken, and worse, Sister Mary Victoria let slip that a group of priests was coming to visit. Priests rumored to be demon hunters. They were anxious to speak with someone about the matter of a recent demon slaying in the area. She tittered a little laugh at the preposterous notion, and I packed that very night.

A week was long enough to get most of my wounds on the path to healed, though the cut on my leg was a worry. Hiding it from my sisters had been hard, and the lie of omission put another black spot on my soul. Miss Whosit and I sneaked out for the last time, and neither of us looked back.

I send five shillings every two weeks to John McCarthy to pay off Mary Jane's rent, and so far, I haven't heard anything else about demon-hunting priests. The numb depression that started my downfall still pains me. The guilt is the worst, though. I have a lot to sort out.

I took the domestic position I'd wanted Mary Jane to apply for before her murder. I'm quite content here with the Havishams. They're nice people. They don't ask uncomfortable questions about my past, and I appreciate that.

They let me keep Miss Whosit. Mr. Havisham even likes to pet her, which she endures with long-suffering dignity. The oldest girl is a bit of a pill and will likely die a spinster despite being marrying age, judging by the way she treats the family. The much younger two are dears and entertain me with fanciful tales of their previous nanny, who flew in by umbrella and had tea parties on the ceiling with them.

I don't argue. I've seen enough to believe every word.

ABOUT THE AUTHOR

Julie Jones is a fiction writer from northeast Oklahoma, where she lives with her husband of twenty-two years, two teens, one sassy dog, and one persnickety cat. She has co-written three anthologies with her writing group and published *Chain Reaction*, her own collection of linked short stories. Her award-winning story, *Camelot*, was selected as the 2020 Best Horror Short Story by the Oklahoma Writer's Federation, and her story *Tourist Trap* was selected for *Visions*, an anthology released by WordCrafter Press in 2022. Julie's current project is a weird western novel series titled *The Legend of Ginny Sutton*, with four books planned for release in late 2023 and early 2024.

12

ACES HIGH
JENNIFER M. ROBERTS

Sounds of laughter and music chased Alix von Hessen-Darmstadt down the hallway, finally to be smothered as she shut the door to her room. Now the sounds were a dull murmur, and the headache throbbing at her temples slowly subsided. She drew in a deep breath, wilting against the door. This small castle, tucked away in the Röhn mountains, was supposed to be a retreat. A chance for her and Nikolai to finally spend some time together instead of only conversing in letters. A friend of a cousin had lent Alix his castle, and the Romanov prince had traveled here without his usual entourage. A chance for romance, away from the eyes of the Russian court.

Starlight frosted the landscape out her window, bathing the trees that covered the mountainside in an ethereal light. Alix reached up to turn the knob on the gas lamp—something she was still getting used to. The warm glow filled the room, illuminating Bavarian tapestries, medieval stone walls, and a four-poster bed. Next to the fireplace was a small sitting area containing a chaise longue, two claw-foot chairs with embroidered cushions, and a hand-carved table showing a pair of dancers.

Alix's dress glittered, decorated with a thousand beads hand-stitched to the finest silk, her figure supported by a firm corset, laced properly so as to control her shape but give her plenty of room to breathe. The cap sleeves, barely covering her shoulders, left her collarbone and ivory skin free to show off the diamond necklace, a match to the diamond-encrusted tiara perched in her coiled hair.

She looked every bit the princess she was, and, thanks to the jewels Nikki had lent her, not just a minor princess from a small German house, but someone fit to be queen of Russia. Someone who would attend balls, ride in parades, and rule over hundreds of courtiers, not to mention millions of peasants.

But here she was, quivering in fear, running from a ballroom that contained only twenty people. If she was meant to be czarina, then why these headaches, why these shaking hands, why the desperate need to flee whenever she was on public display?

The door handle turned, and Alix stepped aside to admit Lottie. She hadn't rung for her maid, but the young woman was always ready with whatever Alix needed, which, at this moment, was a hot toddy next to a deck of cards on a silver tray.

"Your Highness." Lottie curtsied. Her round face and rosy cheeks always held a smile, and her blonde hair was coiled in braids topped by a white cap, her black maid's dress a stark contrast to Alix's ball gown. Lottie set the tray on the table, fluffed a cushion, then seated herself and began to shuffle the cards.

Alix knew it wasn't proper, but Lottie had become a true friend. Any other maid would've brought the hot toddy, seen to the fire, and laid out her nightgown. Only a friend would have brought that deck of cards—Alix's secret vice. Playing games with a servant, socializing with someone below her station, would be most frowned upon indeed. Especially by Grandmama Victoria, the queen of England.

After locking the door so no one could stumble in on accident, Alix settled into the chair opposite Lottie, shifting her bustle out of the way.

Lottie smiled, pulling a flask from her pocket and taking a sip. With drinks at their elbows and seated at the same level with the cards between them where anyone could win, they were equals for these few moments.

"So, what is troubling Your Highness?" Lottie picked up the cards Alix had dealt, her eyebrows raising. A common gesture, and one that meant nothing this early in the game.

"Just a headache." Alix spread her own cards: an ace and assortment of low numbers. Nothing of value. She tossed four cards and drew four more.

"Only a headache?" Lottie asked, exchanging only one card. She set out two equal piles of pennies, one hundred each. Their games were for fun, not for riches. Alix had all she needed, and Lottie knew her place.

"Too many people." Alix shuddered. "It was lovely to dance with Nikki, but—" A second ace, and nothing else of value.

Lottie pushed ten pennies into the center of the table.

Alix shook her head, folding her cards. "No bet."

Lottie grinned and turned up three queens. "A good call, Your Highness. Has Nikki asked you yet?" The question hovered in the air.

Alix sipped at her hot toddy, the warm, spicy liquor helping to settle her nerves. "Yes. Well. We both know that this secret retreat is our time to get to know each other better, and decide."

"And?" Lottie dealt and picked up her cards, raising her brows again. But the corner of her mouth twitched. A good sign for Alix, who held a pair of jacks.

"I can't think with this headache."

"Is it your heart or your head that needs to answer him?" Lottie tossed out three cards, as did Alix.

"I know what my heart wants." Alix fought to keep her face

straight as she turned up two sixes. She pushed twenty pennies into the center of the table.

Lottie's eyebrows climbed again, but she matched the bet.

"These past two weeks have been the happiest of my life. My heart jumps every time he enters the room. When I'm with him, it's like being in heaven."

"You were with him tonight, but you left." Lottie tossed out three cards again.

Alix replaced one card. The draw turned up a six, which completed her full house. Alix pushed twenty more pennies to the center of the table. This was her hand. She could feel it. "It has nothing to do with Nikki. It was the noise."

"Yes." Lottie nodded knowingly, hand hovering over her pennies as she deliberated over matching Alix's bet. "There will be a lot of parties if you become czarina. There will be a lot of noise, a lot of people to perform for."

"Perform?"

Lottie pushed thirty pennies into the center of the table. "What else do you call being royalty?"

Alix grinned. A bluff, one she intended to call. "It's the only life I know. Call."

"Of course." Lottie laid out her cards—four queens—and pulled the pennies into her pile. "So you are ready for a life where the public is always watching. Where the fate of a nation rests on who you decide to smile at and whether or not you spill the tea."

"The servants pour the tea," Alix said sourly, gathering the cards to shuffle and deal again. Two aces this time.

Lottie's eyebrows remained unmoved as she surveyed her cards. What did that mean?

Alix tried to focus on the cards, but her maid was right. Living in the Russian czar's court would be nothing like living in the small castle where she had grown up.

"You know what I mean." Lottie traded out one card and rearranged her hand. "Do you want to be a czarina?"

"I don't know." Alix shuffled her cards. Keep the four and seven of hearts, or toss them both? "I don't care! I just want Nikki."

"Yes, but that's not really the question." Lottie pushed fifty pennies into the center of the table.

Alix tossed the hearts and pulled two more aces. She was running out of pennies, but matched Lottie and added her final ten just to make her point. Now she was all in. "It is the only question." She laid down her cards. Lottie laid down hers: three threes. Alix pulled the pennies to her side of the table. "Love is everything."

Alix's headache throbbed again, refusing to be calmed by the game or the drink. Rubbing her temple, Alix waited for Lottie to deal.

Lottie raised her eyebrows at the new hand and called for four cards. "Where will you live?

"I suppose we will have to spend some time at the Winter Palace, but Nikki says we might build our own place. A retreat for just the two of us."

"Why does the czarina need a retreat from one of the most beautiful palaces in the world?"

"We want a quiet life. A country life." It was all Alix had ever dreamed of as a little girl. She could picture her cottage with its white walls, lace curtains, and blue pottery. Her jeweled tiara and beaded ball gown would look very odd there. She surveyed her pair of fours and threw out three cards.

"That doesn't sound like the life of a czarina." Lottie took two cards and pushed ten pennies to the center.

"I want Nikki and Nikki wants me. He will be czar. He was born to the job, by God's will. Which means God wants me to be czarina." Alix had not drawn anything to improve on her pair of fours, but she took count of Lottie's pennies and bet the exact amount. Lottie would have to go all in or back down.

"God wants you to do a job you will hate?"

"My grandmother was ordained to rule, and Britain has prospered."

"Your grandmother chose to rule. They tried to take her throne, and she fought tooth and nail for it. She could have given it all to a regent and lived a quiet life away from court. If she chose. She didn't. Were you ordained to do the job or to make the choice?" Lottie pushed all of her pennies into the center. "Call."

Alix stared at her maid, not because of the three jacks that Lottie had placed on the table, but because of the words she had spoken. "Ordained to make a choice? Are you saying God could have chosen a ruler in order for them to make the choice to abdicate?" Ridiculous. Yet she could not deny the idea held a certain logic.

Lottie shrugged, scooping up the pile of pennies. Was this a sign that Alix should listen to her maid? Her heart thudded with the possibility of hope. She looked down at the hand that had been soundly beaten. If she and Nikki were ordained, then surely there would be a sign. Alix gathered up five cards and flung her cloak over her shoulders.

∼

Czarevitch Nikolai Romanov sat in the garden looking out across the starlit mountains. He could see the glow from Alix's window. She was still up, despite having retreated to her room more than an hour ago. She had claimed a headache, but Nikki knew it was more than that. She hated formal events, hated being the center of attention.

If she said yes and returned to Russia with him, she would be the center of attention for the rest of her life. Was it fair of him to ask that of her? He worried about it, but the ache in his heart kept him writing letters, kept him coming to see her. Kept him hoping that what she felt for him would be as strong as what he felt for her. That they could be stronger together.

A rustle behind him, then the jingle of glass beads. Alix approached, her gown appearing to glow in the starlight. Her soft features were no longer pinched, her eyes clear and bright for the first time since he had arrived. His heart sensed she had made a choice, and he rose to greet her with shaking palms.

"Alix."

"Nikki." She grasped his hands, clutching them so tightly he thought his fingers might go numb. "I have an answer for you."

It took him a moment to catch enough breath to answer. "Yes?" She looked so serene. Surely that was a good sign.

"I love you with all my heart, and I want nothing more than to be your wife. But I cannot be czarina."

"Of course you can!" Nikki squeezed her hands tightly. "No one will deny us. Your family supports the match, and my father—" His father didn't think Alix the best choice, but he was not going to try to prevent the marriage.

"No." Alix shook her head, her grip loosening. "I cannot be czarina. It is not right for me, or for Russia. I cannot tolerate a party with twenty people in attendance. At the Winter Palace, there will be more than two hundred."

He was losing her. Alix's hands slipped out of Nikki's, and he felt like she was taking all of his hope with them. She was right, of course. The Russian court would offer them no privacy.

"We will have a retreat," he offered.

Alix shook her head. "If you were an ordinary man, with no title and no lands, I would leave all of this behind for you without a second thought. But I cannot live in your world, Nikki." Her voice was firmer than he had ever heard it before. She didn't want an argument, Nikki knew, but he had to try.

"Then why would God put this love in our hearts? Why tell

me you love me, and then refuse me? Alix, we make each other happy." He paused. He could not speak to how she felt. "You make me happy."

"But you will be czar." Alix shook her head. "I cannot marry a czar." Alix touched his cheek, her fingers warm and soft. "I want you. But I do not want Russia."

"Alix, I am ordained by God to be czar. If I want you to be my czarina, then that means it was ordained by God as well. It will be right for Russia, and right for us."

"Says who?"

Nikki gaped. "Wh–what?"

"Who says that you were ordained to be czar?" Alix fixed him with stern, stubborn eyes. In moments like this, he could see the steel in her soul. She hated parties, but she had the heart of a leader. Another reason why Nikki wanted her at his side.

"Everyone. God. The Church."

"You were ordained for this time, this moment. You met me." Alix placed her hand on her chest and drew in a deep breath. "And the thing I want most in the world is to leave this place and never look back. Maybe God is trying to tell you something. Maybe we have a choice."

Nikki shook his head. "You have a choice. I was born to this."

"You can't help loving me. I can't help loving you. Your father has begun to give power to the people. Perhaps ... perhaps this is what you were born for. Perhaps that is why we found each other. We don't want palaces or jewels, just our retreat. So why not retreat?"

He could not find any holes in her logic, even if he knew her words would scandalize everyone in the Russian court. But as Nikki considered the idea, he realized he didn't need their approval. Or his father's. He had always felt most at home with soldiers, humble men from humble families who just wanted to do their job. "What would your grandmother say?"

Alix didn't waver. "I won't know, because we won't be visiting her. It will be just the two of us. A domestic life—all we have ever wanted."

"Where? How?"

"Somewhere else, with new names. America, maybe."

It sounded so simple. "How do we know this is the right thing to do?"

Alix held up a handful of cards. "We let God tell us. Close your eyes and draw. Kings or queens, we rule together. Aces, we take the life we want."

For a moment the night hung still around them, the glowing starlight like something from a storybook.

Nikki closed his eyes and reached for a card.

ABOUT THE AUTHOR

Jennifer M. Roberts earned her BA in history, but she prefers to dream of how things might have been rather than focusing on how things really were. She hails from the Midwest and enjoys sweet corn, contra dancing, and historical re-enactment. This is her first published work. To learn about upcoming and future projects, visit www.jmroberts.com.

13

RUFUS AND THE WIZARD OF WIRELESS

STACE JOHNSON

March 10, 1898
Denver, Colorado
To: Nikola Tesla, 48 East Houston Street, New York

Dear Sir,
I am a civil engineer near Denver, Colorado, and I have heard you are considering moving your lab to Colorado Springs soon. If so, please accept my invitation to meet at the Brown Palace in Denver to discuss a possible application of your telautomaton. I think you will find the idea to be rewarding in many ways.

Sincerely,
Rufus T. Owen
Civil Engineer
Central City, Colorado

Rufus passed the telegram form under the barred window to a man in a bowler hat.

The man picked up the paper, read it, wrote in a ledger, and said, "Forty-five cents, please, Mr. Owen."

Rufus fished the coins out of his vest pocket and laid them on the counter, then pushed them through the opening under the bars. "Will you notify me at the address on the form if I get a response?"

The telegraph clerk nodded and handed him a receipt. "Yes, sir. We make a daily mail run to Central City." He tipped the brim of his bowler back and leaned to look behind Rufus, calling, "Next!"

Rufus turned away from the window, tucking the receipt into the same vest pocket that held his coins, and walked out the west door of Union Station into the cold. Pulling his collar up around his neck, he strode down the platform and checked his pocket watch. On the wind, he recognized the whistle of the mail train to Central City. Good. He could get back to check on the progress of the *Nautilus* soon.

As the train snaked its way up Clear Creek Canyon to Central City, he wondered if he would receive a response to his telegram. He knew reaching out to Tesla was a long shot. After all, Rufus was just an engineer in a small mining town, and Tesla had worked for Edison and Westinghouse. What use could Nikola Tesla have for him?

Still, Tesla had worked in Telluride, so it was worth a try, and maybe Rufus would be surprised. He had mentioned the telautomaton, which most people were not aware of, so perhaps it would pique Tesla's interest. Mentioning the *Nautilus* would have certainly done so, but he didn't want that news getting out just yet. In any event, he would continue with the project. If Tesla didn't respond, Rufus would just have to find another propulsion system.

He disembarked at the new Colorado and Southern depot in Central City, thankful that he no longer had to trek from Blackhawk in the cold, and made the steep climb up

Nevadaville Road to his rented workshop. He opened the three padlocks on the double door with three different keys, then stepped into the frigid darkness of the shop. An oil lamp hung in the gloom to the right of the door; he lifted it off the hook with a well-practiced blind reach, then lit it with a wooden match. In the yellow glow of the lamp, he shook the match out and tossed it into a metal bucket on the floor.

The shop was cut into the mountainside, providing ample workspace and good insulation against the noise of hammers and metalwork. Worktables lined one side of the shop, while the curved side of the *Nautilus* flickered in the lamplight on the other. Propped up on wooden supports, it loomed before him in the dim light, a twenty-foot-long wooden structure clad partly in metal, but with a skeletal frame. Like its namesake from Monsieur Verne's novel, it was shaped like a fish: thick in the middle, narrower than it was tall, and pointed on both ends to cut through the water. Movable horizontal fins extended from both sides, spaced evenly along its length. It had no keel, but rather a small dual rudder, which sprouted from the wooden framework surrounding the propeller shaft. At the highest part of the craft was a small tower with a hatch and an aerial rising into the shadowy rafters.

Rufus looked over the craft, noting the progress his workmen had made soldering the tin plates on the side. He thought back to when he was a young man studying engineering, inspired by the wondrous worlds in Jules Verne's writing, worlds so similar to his in some ways, but so fantastically different in others. To someone with an active imagination living in a landlocked state, a voyage with Captain Nemo was the ultimate escape, and now he hoped to recreate that wonder, at least in some small way.

Turning away from the *Nautilus*, Rufus carried the lamp across the room and set it down on one of the tables, pulling out a stool for himself. From a leather satchel hanging on the wall, he pulled several sheets of paper, a slide rule, a quill, and an inkwell. He lifted two of the pages into the light, one above the other. On the first were three drawings of the *Nautilus* from the side, above, and end on, with draftsman's marks indicating the dimensions. Below that, and flowing onto a second sheet, were mathematical calculations, some intact and some crossed out. Setting the pages down and resting his left hand against his temple, Rufus began the painstaking process of re-checking his figures, occasionally fiddling with the slide rule and writing down new numbers.

∽

It had been more than three months since Rufus's telegram to Tesla. Summer was in full swing, Clear Creek was swollen, the trees were rife with pine cones, and the ice on Missouri Lake was a memory. The mountain runoff was good; there would be plenty of water in the lake for the *Nautilus* test in a few weeks.

Having not heard from Tesla, Rufus had been researching lead-acid batteries, capacitors, and motors for the submarine. He was convinced that electricity was the proper fuel for the propulsion system because it eliminated the problem of exhaust created by internal combustion, and a relatively small battery and motor would suffice for this proof of concept. He had debated purchasing one of England's Hummingbird taxicab drivetrains and adapting it, but transporting it across the Atlantic would cost money he didn't have. His work engineering water systems for the town paid for his home and the materials for the *Nautilus*, but not much else.

Discouraged, he walked down the hill to the post office on his weekly mail run. When he got there, the postmaster handed him an envelope from the Denver Telegraph Office. Rufus tore it open to find a return telegram from Tesla in New York.

> June 13, 1898
> New York
> To: Rufus Owen, Central City, Colorado, via Denver Telegraph Office
>
> Dear Sir,
> I will pass through Denver in two weeks. I am intrigued to hear your proposition and will meet you at the Brown on the 28th. Check train schedules from New York for time.
>
> Believe me to be,
> Yours very truly,
> N. Tesla

Rufus could not contain his enthusiastic shout.

The postmaster raised a bushy eyebrow. "Good news, I presume, Mr. Owen?"

"Indeed, Mr. Randall. Indeed!" Rufus said a little too loudly. "Among the best I've ever received!" He tipped his hat to the postmaster and left the building. He read and reread the telegram as he strode back to his workshop, the wheels in his head already whirring at a frantic pace.

The shop doors were unlocked but barred from the inside, as he had instructed his contractors to do while working on the submarine. He pounded on the wood and yelled, "Mr. Lamont, Mr. Ballard, it's Rufus Owen. Please open the door."

After a moment, he heard the heavy timber being lifted from its iron brackets on the other side, and the right door creaked open. Fred Ballard motioned him in with a furtive look, then closed the door and replaced the bar. Rufus smelled the acrid scent of tin solder in the air. The second workman, Lamont, carefully laid down his soldering iron and walked toward the men, wiping his hands on a rag.

Owen looked over the submarine, gleaming in the lamplight. Only the conning tower and approximately a third of the hull—toward the aft—remained to be covered.

"Gentlemen, I'm pleased with the progress you've made on the *Nautilus* in the last few months. She's looking nearly seaworthy, I must say."

The men laughed at the exaggeration.

He paused and looked them each in the eye, in turn. "There has been a development, and I will need you to complete the work sooner than expected. Will you be able to have it done by the twenty-eighth? I will increase your payment by ten percent if you can."

Ballard looked at Lamont and raised an eyebrow. "What do you think, Billy? We could use the extra money."

Lamont nodded and turned to Rufus. "Yes, I think we can do that for you, Mr. Owen."

Rufus shook hands with the men. "Excellent. It's a pleasure doing business with you both." He turned on his heel and lifted the bar from the door, then nodded "Good day." He heard Ballard reapply the bar as he walked away.

∼

Rufus waited in the tavern of the Brown Palace, sitting upright and trying to keep his left knee from bouncing. He had checked the train schedules, as Tesla had suggested, and expected to see the man with the famous mustache and center-parted dark hair walk through the door at any time. He hoped his enthusiasm wouldn't bleed over too much into his speech; he didn't want Tesla to think him some kind of crackpot or reprobate. With effort, he forced his leg to be still.

A moment later, a mustachioed man in a half stovepipe hat walked through the short hallway from the foyer into the tavern and spoke to the bartender. The bartender gestured to

Rufus, and the man turned to look at him. It was Nikola Tesla!

Rufus stood, startled despite himself, adjusted his lapels, and waved across the small room.

Tesla nodded, removed his hat, and strode purposefully toward Rufus, his heels loud on the tile floor. They shook hands, and Rufus pulled out a chair at the table, gesturing for Tesla to sit. Tesla removed a white towel from his left pocket and wiped his hands, put the towel in his right pocket, and took his seat.

The bartender walked over and said to Tesla, "Welcome, sir. Mr. Owen is covering your tab today. What would you like?"

"Scotch," Tesla said. "Dewars, if you have it." Only a hint of a Serbian accent colored his speech.

"Indeed, sir. And you, Mr. Owen?"

"The same, thank you," Rufus replied.

The bartender bowed slightly, turned, and walked back to the bar.

Rufus leaned forward. "Thank you, sir, for making the time to meet with me. I have to admit, I was not at all sure you would accept my invitation."

"Inventors need engineers, Mr. Owen, otherwise we would get nothing built. But it was your reference to the telautomaton that intrigued me. How—and what—do you know about it?" Tesla's eyes narrowed.

Rufus sat back, one arm outstretched on the table. His fingers tapped idly as he spoke. "As you noted, Mr. Tesla, I am a civil engineer. My specialty is water management, but I am also interested in electricity. I follow your work as best I can from the relative isolation of the Rocky Mountains. I am in regular mail contact with colleagues in New York, and one—who must remain nameless—was a consultant for your upcoming project at the Madison Square Electrical Exhibition this fall. When he saw that you requested a large tank of water for your telautomaton demonstration, he informed me of the details and suggested I visit New York for the event.

"My hypothesis is that you are building a boat of some kind, perhaps controlled by electricity, and you are calling it a telautomaton. The name implies some sort of independent operation, or remote control of some kind."

Tesla arched an eyebrow. "Interesting, Mr. Owen. Your instincts are formidable." The barkeep arrived and gently set two glasses of Scotch on the polished wooden table. Tesla pulled another white cloth out of his left pocket and wiped the rim of the glass as he picked it up. When finished, he put the towel in his right pocket and raised his glass in tribute.

"A toast to you, Mr. Owen," Tesla said. "You are not exactly right, but you are close. The telautomaton is, indeed, a boat, and it is controlled remotely using electricity. It is also powered by electricity, though not through wireless transmission ... yet."

Rufus raised his glass in response and gave a shallow nod. "Batteries, then? Lead-acid?"

"For the time being, yes." Tesla's eyes narrowed again. "You are quite a smart fellow, Mr. Owen. I'm glad to have made your acquaintance. But I must admit, I still don't understand why you wanted to meet. You mentioned an idea for the telautomaton, but I don't understand what application there would be for one up here in the mountains."

"What better place for a proof of concept than the lonely mountains of Colorado, where the air is dry and crisp and sparks jump from your fingers if the carpet is too soft? Where the canyons echo with the concussive thunderclaps of dynamite in the mines? Where no one would be expecting watercraft research to be happening, and therefore, would not be spying on your work?" Rufus sipped his drink, flared his nostrils at the strong caramel taste of the Scotch, and leaned forward. "Tell me, sir. Do you believe that the dry, thin air of

Colorado is more conductive than the muggy, smoky air of the East Coast?"

"I do," said Tesla. "That is why I am building my new laboratory in Colorado Springs, as you mentioned in your telegram."

"A wise move, I suspect," Rufus said. "On a related topic, have you heard about this?"

Rufus pulled a folded piece of newsprint from his breast pocket and pushed it across the table to Tesla, who opened it. Tesla looked over the clipping, a *Rocky Mountain News* story about how the United States government had launched a design contest for a submersible that could be used for military applications.

Tesla nodded. "Yes, the sinking of the *Maine* seems to have motivated the navy to improve their fleet." He paused and looked at Rufus. "You are suggesting the design of the telautomaton could be applied to submersibles and sold to the United States Navy."

"Exactly," said Rufus.

"And you propose to build and test a submersible telautomaton here, in the mountains of Colorado?" Tesla raised an eyebrow.

"I'm already building it. It's under construction in a workshop in Central City. I named it the *Nautilus*, after Monsieur Verne's famous submarine."

"And where would you test it?" Tesla asked, taking another sip of Scotch.

"Missouri Lake," Rufus answered. "A small, isolated lake, a few miles north of Central City. I've begun construction on a dock with a launch gantry there." He paused and sipped his own drink. "Would you like to see the *Nautilus*? The No. 71 leaves for Central City in"—he checked his pocket watch—"forty-five minutes."

Tesla stared into his glass. After a moment, he looked up. "I am intrigued. What, exactly, is it you need from me, Mr. Owen?"

"Propulsion. Nothing more. The craft is nearly built, and I have done all the calculations to determine how much ballast to include, accounting for either lead-acid batteries to drive an electric motor, or, preferably, a motor attached to a resonant transformer of your design."

"You would like to power the craft with an electromagnetic field?" Tesla angled his head and looked Rufus in the eye.

"Yes. I have read your research on high-frequency resonating transformers, and I have already included an air-core transformer with a torus as part of the design. My hope is that you can assist with the design of a primary transformer on the shore to help create the electrical field across the lake. In my estimation, considering the weight of the submarine and the resistance from the water, it would require approximately twenty thousand volts to power the craft, which could be generated from a comparatively small device, as I understand it." Rufus lowered his head and cleared his throat. "But, of course, I defer to your greater expertise."

Tesla leaned back and stroked his mustache. Then he reached for his glass and threw back the remaining contents, curling his lip as he swallowed. "Shall we? We mustn't be late for the train."

∽

Colorado and Southern No. 71 pulled up to the platform at Union Station, venting steam. The silver on her boiler and running boards matched the coupling rods and the rims of the small driving wheels, contrasting with the shiny black on the rest of the locomotive. She was like new, having been renumbered and painted in the silver-accented livery when the C&S rail line was formed, and she was the pride of Central City.

Rufus had the honor of building the sluice that fed her water tower with a diversion from Clear Creek.

Rufus and Tesla showed their tickets and climbed aboard. On the way up the canyon, they sat on opposite sides of the aisle, having agreed on the way to the station to keep quiet about the project. When they arrived, Rufus took Tesla directly to the workshop.

Rufus opened the triple-locked door, stepped in to retrieve the oil lamp from its hook, lit it, and waved Tesla into the workshop. Rufus closed and barred the door behind them. The metal on the side of the *Nautilus* came alive with the lantern flame. The submarine was complete, including a shiny sphere atop the conning tower aerial.

Tesla walked the length of the submarine, examining the control surfaces and touching the smooth tin welds with his fingertips. "Impressive, Mr. Owen." He looked up at the orb on the tower. "You have indeed studied my work. I assume there is a capacitor in the lower part of the craft?"

"Yes! But I will admit, it is not tuned. That is part of the reason I am requesting your expertise."

Tesla walked to the back of the craft, where the propeller extended from the hull. He placed a finger on the blade and turned it. "There is very little resistance," he said. "Is there no motor installed?"

"Not yet," Rufus answered, shaking his head. "I didn't know whether I would be using your method of energy transmission or a more mundane lead-acid battery for power, and that influences the motor choice."

Tesla nodded. "I believe we could easily propel your craft with the twenty thousand volts you suggested. And the scale of your coil is certainly large enough to produce that." He paused in thought. "I also have some ideas for a motor that might work. Eliminating the need for batteries would indeed reduce the weight..." He trailed off, his chin in his hand.

Rufus stood in silence, watching the genius at work. He imagined Tesla's mind as an exquisite machine, like the silver-liveried locomotive, wheels and cogs turning in time with coupling rods and pistons as he churned through his thoughts. Rufus saw the focus return to Tesla's eyes, and then the Wizard of Wireless spoke.

"All right, Mr. Owen. I will help. I will work on a design while on the train to Colorado Springs, and I will mail you instructions on how to tune the transformer and set up a boundary for the electromagnetic field, along with the exact weights of all components for your ballast calculations. I will provide the supply transformer and motor, but I will bring them later—after you have tested the craft's seaworthiness."

Rufus grinned. "Thank you, sir! I will not disappoint you. Do you need my schematics for your calculations? I will happily provide—"

"They are here," Tesla said, tapping his temple three times. "I have everything I need. But I do have one stipulation, Mr. Owen."

"Yes, Mr. Tesla?"

"No one must know of my involvement until we have a working prototype. I told my benefactor that I was building a laboratory in Colorado to research cold light; he would be concerned if it were to come out that I am working on wireless power transmission for a submarine, especially where there is no ocean."

"My lips are sealed, sir," Rufus said, twisting his hand in front of his lips as if he held a key.

With that, Rufus opened the door, and Nikola Tesla walked out into the fading daylight. He looked left and right, and hearing the strains of an upright piano on the breeze, began to follow the sound.

Rufus called out, "Sir! Do you need my address for your post?"

A BIT OF LUCK

Tesla kept walking and, without turning around, tapped his temple three times again.

∼

For the next two weeks, Rufus tuned the resonant transformer and recalculated the ballast required on the *Nautilus*, following the specifications sent by Tesla. When he finished his calculations, he enlisted the aid of Lamont and Ballard over a period of three more weeks to gather the three tons of rocks needed for ballast and place them near the Missouri Lake gantry dock.

When he was sure he was ready to test, he hired a mule team driver to haul the submarine in a covered livery wagon up the four steep, winding miles to Missouri Lake. Rufus chose the first full moon in August for the date of the launch, hoping to maximize nighttime visibility. He invited a few friends to join the project, enlisting them to help him launch the *Nautilus* and swearing them all to secrecy. Lamont and Ballard were included, as was Fred DeMandel, an enthusiastic young man who reminded Rufus of himself in days past.

The night of the launch, the full moon reflected off the water, its image flickering as small waves lapped the shore. The stars stretched unbroken from one horizon to the other in the clear Rocky Mountain sky.

Rufus gathered his friends on the end of the dock. "Gentlemen, thank you for your help on this project. It's a strange thing for a man to ask of another, to help him build a submarine and test it in a shallow lake high in the Rockies. It's even stranger for those people to accept such a challenge. Thank you for your belief in the *Nautilus* project. I'm confident we will be long remembered for our efforts tonight. Mr. Lamont, Mr. Ballard, your workmanship is exquisite, and I thank you for your efforts." He clapped, and the others joined in. Then he rubbed his hands together and said, "Shall we commence?"

Rufus explained his plan for transferring the *Nautilus* from the livery wagon to the gantry using iron levers, where it would be suspended on two wide leather straps before being swung out over the lake. Then they would form a fireman's relay to load the ballast, with young Fred, a man of small stature, as the last link in the chain, carefully placing the rocks inside the submarine.

When all the ballast was loaded and Fred was out of the submarine, they would batten down the hatch, swing the gantry out over the lake, and gently lower the *Nautilus* into the water until the craft reached equilibrium.

"According to my calculations, there should be nothing left above the water but the aerial. Are we ready? Do you have any questions?" When no one answered, Rufus said, "All right, then. Let's make history!"

The men took their assigned positions and put their shoulders into the levers while Rufus slid the leather straps around both ends of the submarine. Then he swung the gantry over until it was above the submarine, and with another heave, the men lifted the craft high enough that Rufus could attach the straps to the gantry hook. The crane shifted with the weight but remained firm. It all went flawlessly.

Then Fred climbed in, and within the hour, the men had transferred three tons of ballast from the shore to the submarine. The thick leather belts stretched about a foot with the extra weight, and the gantry creaked and complained, but held.

Rufus retrieved a bottle of whiskey and some tin cups from the livery wagon and poured each of the men a cup, then one for himself. He raised a toast under the moonlight.

"Well done, gentlemen, well done!"

The men clinked glasses, and Rufus threw back the whiskey in one swallow.

"The hard work is done! All that's left is to move the *Nautilus* over the lake, lower it, and let it float when it reaches equilibrium." Rufus retrieved a pair of heavy leather gloves and a rope from the livery wagon.

After a few minutes of rest and another cup of whiskey, the men gathered at the aft of the submarine. Rufus tied the rope to a loop on the end of the gantry, donned the gloves, and stood on the dock, pulling the rope taut.

"On my mark, push as hard as you can. I will pull on the gantry to swing the *Nautilus* around to the front of the dock. Understood?"

The men nodded, and young Fred said, "Yes sir!"

Rufus wrapped the rope around his gloved hands and blew out a fast breath. "Ready ... and *heave*!" he called. He braced his foot on a dock post and pulled with all his might while the men pushed from behind the craft.

To everyone's surprise, the gantry swung around quickly on its well-greased mount. One of the men stumbled and fell into the water next to the shore as the *Nautilus* rushed away from him.

Rufus himself staggered backward into the railing on the other side of the dock and fell, rope still in his hand, as the looming shape swung around the edge of the dock and out over the lake. When it was perpendicular to the end of the dock, the gantry slammed into a stop block with a loud boom, and the entire dock shook.

The *Nautilus* still had momentum, though, and when the gantry stopped, the submarine became a pendulum, the bow of the craft rising a few feet into the air. The wooden gantry and leather straps groaned in protest, and from deep within the hull of the *Nautilus* came a deep rumble.

"The ballast! It's shifting!" Rufus yelled, scrambling to his feet.

The submarine reached the limit of its pendulum swing, paused for a second, then started swinging back the other way.

Rufus pulled hard on the rope, but he was no match for the heavy craft. The *Nautilus* pulled him forward, and he fell onto the dock again, prone. The rope slid through his gloves, and the craft swung past the center to the opposite extreme. Rufus heard more rumbling from within the *Nautilus*, and before he knew it, the bow slipped out of its leather loop and crashed into the lake below, splashing everyone and pulling the stern under with it.

In an instant, the *Nautilus* was gone.

Rufus stared at the moonlight reflected in ripples and bubbles on the surface of the lake, stunned. After a moment, he rolled over to his back, placed his hands over his eyes, and wept.

∽

Rufus went directly to the telegraph office when he got off the train. He filled out the form, then stood in line while a young man in a crisp US Navy uniform sent a telegram to someone back home before gathering his duffel and heading for the platform.

The man with the bowler hat was there again. As before, he accepted the form, read it, wrote in his ledger, and said, "Fifty-one cents, please, Mr. Owen," without looking up.

Rufus pushed the coins under the teller window.

The man pushed a receipt back, then tipped his bowler back, looked Rufus in the eye, and said, "Have a safe ride back to Central City, Mr. Owen."

A BIT OF LUCK

August 4, 1898
Denver, Colorado
To: Nikola Tesla, 48 East Houston Street, New York

Dear Sir,
I regret to inform you that the project we discussed has come to a halt due to the loss of the prototype during testing. I have neither the funds nor the will to start over.
I remain eternally grateful that you took the time to meet me, and I hope your laboratory in Colorado Springs brings your greatest success yet.

Sincerely,
Rufus T. Owen
Civil Engineer
Central City, Colorado

∼

It had been nearly a year since the *Nautilus* had slipped beneath the surface of Missouri Lake. Rufus had moved to Pueblo. He had escaped Central City in the night, simply because he couldn't bear to continue living with constant reminders of what had become known as "Owen's Folly." He had found work in Pueblo easily enough, maintaining the city's water supply channels, and never spoke of the *Nautilus* again.

One day, he passed a newsstand and, out of habit, purchased a copy of the *Rocky Mountain News*. On page three he saw a picture of Nikola Tesla under the headline "Tesla Wins Navy Submersible Design Contest."

Rufus smiled. Perhaps his *Nautilus* had survived in some small way.

ABOUT THE AUTHOR

By day, Stace Johnson is a mild-mannered IT manager, but at night he transforms into a poet, writer, and musician. He has appeared at numerous science fiction and fantasy conventions as a panelist and parody singer. His written work has appeared recently in the *Animal Magica 2*, *Modern Magic*, and *Drabbledark II* anthologies, and he is currently writing a novel in the Steve Jackson Games *Car Wars* universe for publication with Three Ravens Publishing. Learn more at his Linktree, https://linktr.ee/lytspeed.

14

G-GALS
KENDRAI MEEKS

The black phaeton pierced the veil, allowing the Gals a view of the gleaming mansion through the fog. Rarely had Rosie seen something so simultaneously audacious and elegant. A layered chiffon cake of a house, she thought. If only the reason they were here wasn't so sour, she might allow herself to take in the sweetness of it all.

Cici's hands curled around the corner of the car, her nose crinkling. "What, was Vanderbilt's place unavailable for the season?"

The fervent practitioner of sarcasm expected no answer, but Rosie wouldn't have been inclined to disagree. Whoever had pulled a contract for their services certainly hadn't sneezed at their demanding rates.

Rosie shrugged and pulled a single cigarette from her coat pocket before nesting it between her lips. "New money." She took a few puffs as the tip burned to life. "No one with the loot to afford a place like this should be inviting us out here in the open. If he'd been brought up in wealth, he'd been taught better."

"Unless he's got nothing to hide."

Rosie turned as Cici took a position next to her. "He hired us. No one hires the Gals unless he's got something to hide or wants us to make sure it gets hidden." She looked back over her shoulder. "She still sleeping?"

"Fell asleep the second we got out of the city." Cici pivoted at the hip. "Wake up, Babydoll, or we'll send the car back to the city with you still in it, and I hear there's rats where they park at night."

Blue eyes popped through a cascade of blonde ringlets. "Rats?"

Babydoll was the newest member of their trio, and the most gullible. Rosie thought it all in good humor, but the way the nineteen-year-old bolted up, head whipping from side to side like she expected one of the vile creatures to appear with a pair of house slippers, made her wonder if they'd gone too far.

"No one said anything about New York having rats."

"More them than people." Rosie took a long drag, letting the smoke chew its way through her words. "Relax, though. Out here, even the vermin can't afford the cellars."

The pendulum fell, and fervent eyes focused on fanciful dreams. "Gee, golly!" Her ringlets bobbed as she stumbled toward the front steps. "Who lives here—Rockefeller?"

"No one *lives* here, baby. It's just where the man who's hired us is staying, and I guess, where we'll be staying."

You could count all the stars in the sky in Babydoll's eyes. "Honest to goodness? *We* get to stay in *this* ... *this*... palace?"

"The nice house won't make the work any easier." Cici's voice caught the knife's edge as she straightened, at attention so to speak. "Or cleaner."

"It can be as dirty as Sunday night dishes for all I care." Babydoll held her arms out. "Would you look at this place? It must have cost a gold mine! Who is the John? Must be famous. An actor, or some Wall Street guy, or something. Come on, Rosie, tell me."

Before Rosie could remind Babydoll that all information was given only when needed, she was preempted by the appearance of a very tall, very thin, very sallow man, and Babydoll's words sputtered out like the engine of the car that had delivered them to this Shangri-La beyond the valley of ashes.

He looked them over, judging them as he was judged, before leaning in Rosie's direction. "Mr. W is waiting for you in the library."

∼

Each step across checkerboard floors and through marbled doorways grew heavier, the opulence pressing in. Men with houses like this usually had gardens deep with skeletons. Even Cici, who should have been acclimated to such extravagance, surveyed with a cautious side eye.

Rosie refused to look impressed, even if it took some effort in this case. As the senior member of the Gals, she'd spent ten years being shown in through the servants' entrances of countless 5th Avenue mansions or dressing up as the help to blend into the background of many an ocean liner. Mr. W's portfolio clients included at least two lesser-known Vanderbilts, not that there was any paper trail to prove it. But there was something about those old money shacks that made one bleed into the other. Like all those ancient cathedrals in Europe before the war: each a monument to the Lord built of the same brick, diminished in their grandeur by consequential ubiquity.

Babydoll turned circles. "A king must live here."

Cici cackled. "This is America, child. There are no kings, only titans."

"America is the land of self-made kings." Rosie picked up her pace, challenging the butler who'd fetched them to do the same if he wanted to remain in control. "But this house doesn't belong to anyone that high and mighty."

She'd noticed it the moment they'd pulled up. The house didn't look so much lived-in as it did lived-up-to. Every knickknack at an angle to catch the eye in sequence, like pearls on a cord. Each window framed as if a stage light. Each flower punctuating another bodacious claim. This house was *staged*, and its master a spider trying to draw prey into its web, but a very particular type of prey. It wasn't Rosie, and it certainly wasn't Cici or Babydoll. Which begged the question, whom was it meant to ensnare?

Finally, after several corridors that would shame both saints and sinners, they turned a corner, coming to a set of mahogany double doors. The butler's white-gloved hand wrapped around a handle polished to within an inch of its life.

"Sir, the Gals have arrived."

Rosie rolled her eyes as she pushed past the shadow of a man. "We don't need to be announced, Jeeves."

The library equaled the house that came before it. Only, being filled with books, it held a certain approachability the hallways lacked. Behind the desk was a dark-complexioned man with graying hair and a generous chin, his hands crosshatched.

"My *beautiful ladies*."

Mr. W unwound himself from the desk, hands out wide and welcoming, one stretched toward Rosie. She glared at the fingertips. He knew she hated to touch men. Unless it was to kill them, and then she was negotiable.

Seeming to recall his employee's qualm, Mr. W. pivoted to the darker-skinned beauty dressed in a green walking dress. "Cecilia, my dear." He pulled her deadly hand to his lips and pressed a kiss. "Elegant as always."

Cici closed her eyes and breathed through the discomfort. When Mr. W pulled away, her steely eyes hatched up. "Meyer."

It was a delicate tit for tat. One of things you did not do in this line of work was expose other's identities needlessly. Even here, in the private library of one of East Egg's most luxurious private homes, that protocol still held. Cici liked to remind Mr. W that she knew things about him that could be dangerous if he overstepped boundaries. Namely, who he really was.

Mr. W took the hint. He dropped both her hands and his attempt at flattery, turning at last to Babydoll. "You must be our newest recruit."

The little blonde was all pigtails and bubbles. "Yes, sir. And you must be Mr. W?" She plunged forward, curtseying like she was meeting a head of state. "Name's Hildie Kolder, but you can call me Babydoll. *Everyone* does, and really, I don't take no offense. Honest, I don't. I know I'm young, but I'm just excited to be here, you know? Been waiting my whole life to do something fun and important, and I'm ready. I won't let you down, Mr. W. I'm as reliable as rain in the spring."

With each word, the old man's angular face lost a dab of its brilliance. Babydoll was a strong cup of coffee, but ultimately, well-intentioned. This time, when Mr. W stepped back behind the desk, it was more a shield against her exuberance than to sit. "Ladies, won't you please?"

He motioned vaguely to a nearby sofa, its soft brown leather gentle on their skin as they sat like three little ducks in a row.

Rosie didn't like to beat around the bushes—especially bushes that required one to come this far from the city. "What's the job then?"

Mr. W folded his hands in his lap, out of their view. "Protection."

"Of something or *someone*?"

Cici, for all her fine qualities and physical blessings, often lacked tact. "Let me guess: this is the love nest for some uptown banker with a mistress who can't keep her mouth or her legs shut. We're supposed to school her up."

Their job three clients ago had been just such a situation. Some highfalutin St. Louis alderman whose weekender went about bragging she had him eating out of the palm of her hand, and a few other places too. Mrs. Alderman didn't appreciate that much. Oh, she knew her husband was soaking seed from there to New Orleans, but she didn't care to have it thrown in her face at respectable establishments. The Gals had been asked to deliver a personal message to make sure the bit on the side learned to hold her tongue.

"Nothing like that, Cici." Rosie focused on Mr. W, looking for his face to betray her deduction. "The question we should ask is—are we helping someone seduce, or win back?"

"A little of both." Mr. W rolled his tongue inside his mouth as if sensing something rotten in the air. "It involves someone you've *met* before, Rosie. On a certain boat on a certain lake, traveling with a certain millionaire about twelve years ago. *And it also involves a certain somebody else he almost ran away with.*"

"Daisy." Rosie should have known they were in for a sweet treat wrapped in an old, wet newspaper.

Mr. W looked at the other two ladies in turn, but when he spoke, he pushed his voice high into the air. "Fedor?"

The beanpole of a butler stepped forward. "Sir?"

"Why don't you show Cici and *Babydoll* the pool?"

Fedor leaned in. "The deep end, sir?"

That finally broke Mr. W's expression. He buried a silent laugh in his shoulder. "No, Fedor, just the deck."

Babydoll blushed with a ferocity that radiated heat. Good to see some part of her innocence remained. "The deep end? Like, we can go swimming if we want?"

Cici, however, knew better. She stood, pulling the young

blonde to her feet. "Come on, Baby. We'll twinkle our toes over the edge."

Alone with Rosie, Mr. W pulled a cigar from a box on the side of the desk and took his time to light it. He took a deep pull and savored the smoke before blowing it out in a steady stream.

"You knew the day was coming."

"I knew he always *hoped* the day would come. Between you and me, I wasn't as excited by the prospect." Rosie leaned back in her chair, running her callused hands over the soft brown leather. "Guess I know whose house this is now, and how he affords it. Good job, Meyer. Your great diamond in the rough, your protégé. And to think, after all these years…"

Mr. W narrowed his eyes. "Is this going to be a problem?"

"A problem? Come on, it's me. I'm a professional. I can set my feelings aside and do my job." She swallowed the tiniest crack in her voice. "Just like last time."

"I know you can, Rosie. That's why I kept you on, even after what happened."

"Let me guess, she lives in this neighborhood now." The brunette buried her head in her chest. "She doesn't remember none of it, you know. The heist, the players, the accident." Then, she moved to the edge of her seat. "That probably includes him, or didn't he realize that? That she's going to look at him and not have a single clue who he is."

"Jay's got reason to believe otherwise." Mr. W flicked the cigar, sending a rain of ash falling toward the mahogany desk.

Didn't he know how much that thing cost? Or didn't he care because it was someone else's property?

"He went after her once already," Mr. W added.

"Yeah, and look how that turned out."

"I mean *after* Louisville." The implied *after what you did* remained unspoken.

A chill crept up Rosie's back, setting all the little hairs on her arm on end. "No kidding?"

Mr. W nodded, smug in his knowledge. "And at her wedding, no less. Pretty sure the little stunt he pulled rattled something under those bouncy blonde curls. Reports were she almost left the other guy at the altar."

"Yeah, well, I've done some digging on that guy she married, and I'm telling you, he'd have dragged Daisy up that aisle in tears and a torn dress as soon as let her go. You know how these old-money types are. They consider the goods paid for with promises and cashed in on lies."

"*Daisy's* one of those old-money types, just like you used to be."

A quick gesture, hand turned out and flowing over her head and down into her lap, invited inspection. "And just look at me now."

Mr. W did look. At length. So long, in fact, that Rosie had time to regret her sarcasm. He'd never made a move on her, but a blind man could see he'd thought about it. The thought made her insides curl up. Mr. W was old enough to be her very much older brother.

She pushed away the thought and refocused. "Point being," she said, "wasn't anything going to bring her back into the fold. And you know what? I think it's better that way. Some people are born for this kind of life. Daisy forced herself to fit in to it. It didn't take long after buying in for her to start looking for a way to cash out her chips."

"But she still knows what she knows."

"Does she?" That was enough. This was a job. Nothing more, nothing less. "Look, Meyer, doesn't matter how much luggage I'm lugging behind me. I'm here, I'm ready to work. Just tell me what the hell he's expecting me to do."

～

Babydoll was nineteen, but she looked all of nine with her stockings rolled up next to her on the marble deck, her shapely legs slow pedaling the water.

"What do you think it's like to wake up and look at *this*"—she drew her arms in, like she could gather the wealth around them into her arms and claim it as her own—"each and every morning?"

Cici examined her fingernails and tried to focus on the cracking polish rather than the damning name that Rosie had uttered in the library. Freaking Daisy Fay, after all these years.

"I think it's a lot like waking up in a tenement in the Bronx," she said flatly. "After a while, everywhere becomes background. Even a place like this. I promise you, the guy who owns this place barely notices he has a pool, let alone marble halls and a fancy view."

"Something tells me the view is why he's here." Everything Babydoll said was with the conviction of a child who'd overheard a rumor. Water ran in rivulets over her calf as she held her leg parallel to the surface of the water. "I'd never stop noticing it. And even if I did, I'd hire a man just to remind me once a week. No one should have something this ritzy unless they appreciate it."

"The type of people who have places like this only look one direction: ahead. They never notice where they are, only where they might be next. Once they got something, they forget all about it." That included people. There was a reason you bought a senator, not rented him.

"You're so cynical, Cici."

"This is nothing *but* experience talking, Babydoll." The drag off her cigarette gave such a pleasant burn. "But it don't matter what I say. You won't be able to see truth until you've been lied to one too many times. It ain't no sin and has no shame, but youth is a weakness."

A light breeze picked up the edges of Cici's hair, bringing up her eyes with it. The fog out over the bay had lifted since they'd arrived, opening the view to the horizon. As she'd suspected, their location was on the westernmost of the two juts of land extending out into the Sound. Across the gray-green waters, the marmoreal facades of the society mansions looked like they'd been chiseled out of the surrounding rock, not unlike the temples of Greek gods she'd seen on the eastern edges of Europe. Waves of green skirted their portcullises and promenades.

Same breeze blowing through those trees over there is what's smacking me in the face now.

The sound of approaching footsteps brought up their attention. Rosie's shoes, pale pink patent leather to match her cheeks and white to match her dress, measured her descent from the exterior staircase and down to the rounded pool pavilion where the other two Gals waited. As soon as she was close enough, Cici saw the barely visible grimace Rosie wore whenever she found their assignment less than savory. You'd think that would be every time, but Rosie wasn't the sentimental or emotional type, nor was she the kind of girl who fretted over danger. Cici had seen that gal glare down oafs twice her size and six times her width, barely flinching.

Cici took a draw from her cigarette and blew out the smoke in a stream before turning its butt out in Rosie's direction. "That bad, huh?"

Rosie pinched the cigarette and nodded her thanks. "It isn't great."

"You could just turn it down." Babydoll proved her naivete every time she opened her mouth.

Rosie chuffed a laugh and buried her chin into her chest. "No, I can't. I owe Meyer for this one."

The ash from the end of Cici's replacement cigarette fragmented and drifted down to the deck and mixed with the drops of water Babydoll had splashed on to the deck. She'd only done two jobs so far, neither of them particularly risky nor illegal. Rosie had selected them on purpose until the kid got her legs under her. Truth be told, the boss would have preferred a half dozen small-time arrangements to whatever this was. Maybe the principals in this act came with dollar signs at their door, ones that let them wipe their feet clean before traipsing into their palatial abodes. Babydoll had looks that could make a Baptist preacher take up sin, but she didn't have the brains to know how to use that truth in moderation. The girl didn't realize yet that there were certain jobs you couldn't turn down. Namely, the ones Mr. W brought you.

Still, it couldn't hurt to take a softer approach here if Rosie was wilting this early on. "Mosey on down here, Chief," Cici said, "and unload the facts with your feet in the water. Everything sounds better with your feet in the water."

The white dress twirled as Rosie pivoted, kicking off her shoes at the same time. She settled between them in silence. The breeze brushed the leaves quivering on the trees.

The brunette's eyes closed, and she let out a slow exhale through a grin. "Jesus, but don't that feel nice?"

For once, Babydoll didn't rock the boat. Sedated by the serenity of their surroundings and the view, they enjoyed a moment. That was, until Rose's back straightened, and the words started to flow like the waters of the Sound.

"You know, Babydoll, that we ain't the first Gals."

The young woman kept her eyes on the pool, her legs crisscrossing in lackadaisical fashion. "Yeah, I'm number eight." Said like it was a school test and she'd memorized the bare facts the night before. Then Babydoll lifted her gaze. "But you've never said anything about the ones that came before, or how it all started."

Even Cici, who'd be brought in as Gal Seven, didn't know for sure who had comprised the original three. There were *always* three, except for the odd moments where one of their numbers had either bowed out or been bumped off. There was enough evidence to suggest who their founder had been. Cici had never been able to confirm if Rosie even had the ups on who was sometimes referred to in passing as Prima Donna. Was that meant as a tribute, a clue, or some kind of underhanded insult?

"And I won't, except when it's needed. And right now, it's needed." Rosie seesawed her legs, watching her feet lift in turn and drip water. "Number Five found me in Racine, and Mr. W agreed to pick me up. Not sure what they saw in me back then, honestly. I was just some illegitimate scruff kept comfy and quiet so my daddy's real family wouldn't have their glowing image tarnished."

She lifted her eyes to the blue-gray skies above.

"Despite what they say, it ain't always so bad being a love child, you know? Not when it comes with a steady flow of cash that buys you access into their circles without any of the expectations of staying there. It let me learn things and do things without worrying what anyone thought. Those folks judged me guilty by virtue of being alive, so what did I care if they kept judging me? But Mr. W thought that was an advantage, said I was the perfect chameleon, that I didn't need much training. Maybe that's why I was put on the Great Lakes job before I was ready."

Babydoll's back arched, the equivalent of a dog lifting its ears. She still romanticized big cities. "What Great Lakes job?"

Cici knew this part. It was the reason she was brought into the fold, after all, when Daisy had bowed out. "It was a job about—what, Rosie—a dozen years ago? Long before I was a Gal. Big money, old bachelor, no apparent heir. Mr. W thought it'd be a shame to let that money be buried or, worse, given to a charity."

"I was to play the damsel in distress," Rosie said, stepping back in. "I was the perfect age for it: seventeen. Too old to be a child, too young to be looked at as a woman. Old men love that. They get the fantasy of a dangerously young lover and the emotional fulfillment of being a father figure. Don't look at me that way, Babydoll. Why do you think you're here?"

Not that they'd put the young woman in that position. She wasn't ready to manipulate a lover.

Yet.

Rosie pressed on. "I'd barely moved in when I got chased right back out. Turned out, someone found the mark before we did, some young fella from the Midwest. I knew I should have stood my ground, but I was young and I panicked. I ran out of there, feeling like a failure. Mr. W told me not to worry, that if our bug was already in another spider's web, we'd just go after the other spider. Not right away, though. A little later when he'd had time to grow fat and lazy. Besides, it's easier to con a con. They never think it can happen to them."

Cici noticed how still Babydoll had grown. Listening intently, but in an effort to improve herself or to gain ground on Rosie? It was easier to pull someone off their pedestal if you could build a stool of their failures to stand on.

"Duly noted," the youngster said after a few moments, her eyes simultaneously fixed and distant, building castles out of Rosie's bricks. "So what happened then?"

"Didn't you just hear what she said?" Cici said. "A con never thinks it's going to happen to them."

Rosie nodded. "Years later, Mr. W says he has a job for us in Louisville. We show up, and who do we Gals find but the little spider himself? He should have been rich enough to get a meeting with Rockefeller—only he's heading off to war? Either this guy is the most patriotic bastard this country has ever known, I say to myself, or he's got another con brewing. Either way, I want to know why. But I can't go after him, nor the others. He knows our faces from our last encounter. As luck would have it, one of your predecessors decided it was time to bow out, giving me a chance to add a new pearl to our necklace. And that's when I found *her*."

At this point, Babydoll's eyes had gone wide. She was hooked on the bedtime story. "Who?"

"Her name was Daisy, but of course it was, wasn't it?" Cici pursed the cigarette between her lips and took a deep drag. "Fit her too. All fresh and springy and innocent."

"She was a clean linen sheet, thrilled to be brought into the fold," Rosie took over. "Rich little thing who'd never done a wrong thing in her life. Not according to her mom and pop, anyway. The plan was simple. Daisy was supposed to go after the fella, try to get him to believe she was falling for him. Meanwhile, she'd gently rib him about being able to keep her in the style of luxury she was accustomed to if they were going to have any future together. It gave her an easy out if Mr. America had spent all the loot, or if he'd never gotten his hands on it after all. She'd just say there was no way she could ever be with a poor man."

But that wasn't the part of the story that grabbed Babydoll's attention. "And the old man's money? She find out what happened to that?"

"He'd been swindled out of most of it by a distant family member after Moneybags died," Cici said. "He was broker than a single piece of hardtack split between a platoon. Only by then, it didn't matter. Daisy had convinced him if he *had* money, he could have *her*. Worse, Daisy convinced herself of the same thing."

"She'd gone and fallen in love with the bastard," Rosie broke in. "And she tried to go after him. It was all very romantic, or at least would have been if he'd died in the war. But, no, he's off fighting the Kaiser, and Daisy's back in the States. We tried to get her to move on to a new mark, but she'd lost interest after she lost Jay. Decided she didn't want to be a Gal. That's when Tom swooped in with his ready-made fortune

A BIT OF LUCK

and well-financed charm. Meanwhile, Mr. W sees an opportunity: a hungry man with a proven track record of making over on a rich guy and who'd do anything to get the girl he loved."

Babydoll's face screwed up. "So, this Jay is a Gal?"

Rosie looked off into the distance. "No, Jay's something much worse. He's our new boss." Cigarette between two fingers, Rosie jutted a hand at the Sound, and toward a blinking green light visible in the day under a canopy of black clouds. "And over there sits Daisy, ensconced in her money and memories. Jay wants her back, wants to show her he's become the man he'd promised he would be—fool that he is. See, if Jay lets on to Daisy the way he made his money, he risks exposing Mr. W, and Mr. W isn't too keen on that."

"What are we supposed to do about it?" Babydoll asked.

Both Rosie and Cici gave her a somber look.

"You can't kill rich people," the youngster protested. "Too many ties, too many interested parties. Besides, she knows who you are, Rosie. She'll see you coming."

"But she doesn't know you or Cici." Standing, Rosie flicked the cigarette into the pool. It snuffed out, saturated, and started its descent toward the green tiles at the bottom. "Cici, you still golf?"

The young woman nodded. "Not sure how that matters."

"Apparently Daisy has a thing for women who 'do things.'" The last was said with a snide tone. "Mr. W is going to buy you a way into the local circuit and float a story about how you're an up-and-comer from the Midwest. He thinks Daisy will want to rub up to your fame this spring. Babydoll, you're going to throw yourself at the husband, see if you can't get and keep him distracted."

The blonde pulled her legs from the water and spun Rosie's direction. "And what's your job?"

"Mine? To provide a smoke screen," Rosie answered. "Jay is

going after a married woman and, by all accounts, a mother too. Not an easy thing to do in a place where everyone is looking left and right to see who's running beside them. So this place?" She held her arms up. "I'm going to fill it with people, because when *everyone* is here, it will be like no one is here. Yes, sir, by the height of the summer, everyone—even Daisy—will want to be at Gatsby's."

ABOUT THE AUTHOR

Kendrai Meeks enjoys using history as inspiration but will admit to ignoring (or inventing) it when convenient. She professionally twists truth, myth, and fairy tales across science fiction, urban fantasy, and, as Killian McRae, romance. Her best-known works include the Red Riding Hood-inspired urban fantasy series The Red Chronicles, and the Cinderella-inspired Cyberpunk series, Enter the Kingdom, both complete and available in print and digital formats.

15

COLLATERAL LOSS
FULVIO GATTI

Tomorrow Never Knows.

The words float through my brain as I take control of Lee Harvey Oswald's body.

I know it's a song title, but I can't recall the band's name. Strange.

My host's hands—now mine—are skinnier than expected. I wear a uniform, and the room inside the Texas School Book Depository is nondescript.

I flinch. The rifle with telescopic sight and the .38 revolver are on the nearby table. The familiarity, coming from my host, clashes with my previous knowledge of what the weapons are about to be used for.

I recognize the noise from the crowd in the street below. The pieces of the puzzle come together, tickling my spine. The process is painful only for the first hundred times. Later on, either you die of an aneurysm or you become a Time-Initiative Supervisor.

I take the rifle and weigh it. The time-travel manual says to keep history on track until the very last second. I wrote that manual. Anna hated it, but she knew it was good work. The memory of my lost wife helps me preserve my identity, so I let the melancholy sneak in.

She won't agree, even now. We started speaking at the Academy about saving JFK. Too many, uncountable potential repercussions to change it, she said.

But I had a decade after her death to study Dallas, November 22, 1963.

Millions of possible timeline consequences.

One spark of hope.

I see the car approaching. Through the telescopic sight, I perceive nothing but color contrasts. Jackie's pink dress, the black collar unfolded. JFK's ivory pocket square.

Being here, I make a statement. The days of Time-Initiatives as keepers of a balanced past are over.

It's easy if you try.

More words out of nowhere. I know the melody. I know the voice. I don't know the artist.

I wonder if it's not just a side effect but the Switch, already happening.

JFK's car gets closer, and the scene is almost the one portrayed in the video of the assassination. It's too late to go back. I put my finger on the trigger.

I hold my breath until the car is out of range.

I relax my finger and put the rifle down.

They are safe now.

JFK will live.

Pain invades me. It feels like piranhas eating my flesh from the inside. I collapse on the ground.

I'd scream, if I could, as I realize what I've done.

I can't recall their faces, or their names, or a single song title.

The historian's theory was true. After months of mourning for JFK, the US press needed something happy to write about. They heard about those four musicians from Liverpool who were a rising sensation in the UK and chose to pave the way to their global career.

With Kennedy alive, the band will be nothing but a temporary musical phenomenon.

My name is Ringo Valenti, and I've just made a terrible mistake.

This new timeline will have JFK.

But people will never know about the Beatles.

ABOUT THE AUTHOR

Fulvio Gatti is an Italian speculative fiction writer who has been writing and publishing in his native tongue for twenty-five years. He has been writing in English for the global market since 2018, and his stories can be found in pro magazines, magazines, and anthologies. He's been a SFWA associate member since 2022. He lives with his wife and daughter on the wine hills of Northwestern Italy, where he works as a local reporter and event organizer. Visit him at www.fulviogatti.it.

16

BOULDER CHOKE
CARRIE CALLAHAN

Casey imagined the hardness of the immovable earth closing in as she delved deeper between crevices and boulders. The entrance of the abandoned mine dwindled and disappeared behind her as the narrow passage curved, and it felt safe to be away from the sixth-grade boys who had egged her into the cave—Travis and Mikey and Drake, all pelting her with gravel, jeering at her, daring her to go into the yawning mouth of the mine. It was like this every time her mother moved the two of them to a new town. Bullies were always drawn to the new girl, and it didn't help that the bruise-colored birthmark pressing against her hairline looked like a target.

The rock walls glistened with quartz in the beam of her flashlight, inching closer with each step she took. The outside world had vanished, leaving a heavy silence ringing in her ears, washed by the rush of blood in her eardrums. The air hung fetid and damp, waiting.

Along her route were abandoned lengths of broken chain and miscellaneous tools rusted into smudges on the earth. A murmur of running water rose from inside the earth, and Casey wondered if the shaft connected to the sewer line. The pebbles grew larger under her feet as the end of the cave emerged into her narrow beam. A great big pile of boulders sloped upward, blocking the passage completely.

A small rock clacked to the ground behind her. Casey whirled, shaking the flashlight at every corner and shadow, but no one was there. Sighing, she turned back to the dead end.

Carefully placing each step, Casey climbed the left side of the cave-in. She pointed the flashlight between hulking stones, looking for a passage. Just as she was about to give up, the light disappeared into a particularly wide crack. An opening. A steel support beam had fallen at an angle, stalling the cascade of stone.

She didn't want to keep moving into deeper and darker territory, but the jeers of the boys followed her and she couldn't turn back.

Casey bent to crawl through the wide bottom of the hole, scraping her knees on the rough ground. The flashlight was slick in her hand, earth squeezing her body, pushing, shoving, forcing her into unnatural shapes. The walls narrowed, tugging at her shoulders and arms. She considered turning back, telling the boys that she was too big. Instead, she twisted around a bend, forcing her shoulders into a painful angle, to where she thought the passage ended.

The crevice widened abruptly, the floor giving way to a lower level, and Casey windmilled her arms for balance. She stood, brushing dust from her clothes before shining the flashlight into the cavern. She danced the light back and forth ahead of her, but it barely penetrated the darkness.

"Hello?" she called, her voice echoing on distant cavern walls. Then, louder, "Hello?"

She jumped at a crash of rock followed by a splash. Sunlight crept in through a newly created skylight, revealing a yawning cavern around a massive palace: white marble columns and pediments and statues stacked like a layered cake in the gloom; a curved bridge flanked by dark, rippling pools; roots clutching the structure like dead vines.

∼

The first girl didn't even make it through the cave entrance—the falling boulder spooked her, and she ran. I didn't know who she was yet, and I tried to call out, but I don't think she heard me. The boulder reversed its fall to plug the skylight, and I waited from behind the barrier for it to fall again.

∼

Casey rubbed at her eyes, trying and failing to clear them of the vision in front of her. After watching the building for a few minutes, a flicker of light caught her attention. Perhaps a candle in the window of the palace? But it was already gone. She turned, heart racing, and peered back through the crevice. It looked wider from this side.

If she turned back now, the boys would call her chicken and a snitch and whatever else they could think of while pelting her with stinging rocks. They would probably follow her home.

Casey turned toward the structure looming in the darkness, hurrying to crest the ancient bridge before she could chicken out. She clambered up the stone steps under the watchful eyes of blind statues, all the while looking for something to take back—a piece of carved stone or the glint of treasure.

The climb was steep and riddled with treacherous fractures. Casey slipped more than once on her way to the first level, banging her shin against the harsh angles of crumbling steps. At the summit of stairs, she leaned against the massive columns flanking the entrance to catch her breath and peered down at her progress. The cavern looked almost small from her perch, distant walls disappearing into shadow.

When she could breathe, she stepped between a set of double doors hanging akimbo, crossing the threshold. The doorway was so wide she couldn't reach both sides at once, and the ceiling disappeared into a foggy light that permeated everything. However, once she stepped inside, the palace was less intimidating.

Ahead of her, another set of stairs lead up while marble designs in a rainbow of shades cut into the barrel ceiling overhead. Colonnaded hallways stretched deep into the distance on either side of the stairs. Casey rubbed her foot against the thick layer of dirt and dust on the floor, revealing the gleam of yet more polished marble.

"Welcome."

Casey jumped and whirled at the cracked voice. The flashlight beam shook as she pointed it at the speaker: a gaunt woman wearing a long, baggy dress that swept the floor. Her hair was stringy but neat—streaked with fresh gray and hanging to the woman's shoulders. She was older than Casey's mom but smiled just like her.

"I'm so sorry," the woman said slowly with what seemed like genuine concern. "I didn't mean to frighten you. Are you here for a tour? It's free," she offered helpfully.

Casey stared at the woman. Something about her was so familiar—was it her hair? Her eyes?

∼

By the one hundredth time I saw the flashlight in the cave entrance, desperation clawed at me. It hadn't even been a full day, but I held my breath and hoped so hard that she would see me, hear me, let me out. The drum of falling rock enticed her toward the entrance. As she climbed the palace steps, I saw her face and realized what I had to do.

∼

"Do I know you?" Casey asked, squinting at the woman.

The woman shrugged sadly. "I'm sorry, but I can't be sure. I've met many people as caretaker of this building. What's your name, dear?"

"Casey Winthrop."

Something flashed in the woman's face, but it was gone before Casey could identify it.

"That does not ring a bell. In any event, Casey, would you like a tour?" the woman asked again, smiling.

Casey shook her head. "I don't think so. I have to go—"

"Where to? To meet your friends, perhaps?" The woman's smile thinned.

Casey thought of Travis and the other smirking boys waiting outside with their fistfuls of stones and their taunts. "Not really."

"Then to see your parents? Perhaps they are expecting you."

The house would be empty for hours yet. Her mother worked late, and she only saw her father on weekends. She shook her head slowly. "How do you—"

"Oh, please, let me show you around. You would be doing me a favor." The woman's smile stretched, sweetened until it was cloying. "It's boring being the caretaker of a palace no one wants to see. At the end, I have some free caramels—perhaps you would like one?"

Caramel—her favorite candy. It wouldn't be right to say no. Her mother always taught Casey to be polite with adults.

"Okay."

∼

After so many iterations—so many failures—I started to think some numbers had significance. I was convinced girl 321 would be the one to come in, and I thought 666 would be evil. But 321 only came up to the bridge and threw little rocks in the underground stream before leaving, bored. Girl 666 made it up the stairs, but when I came out from behind the doorjamb, she ran like so many others.

My birthday is April 22, so I thought maybe 422 would be important. She wasn't. Up the boulder went, and I waited for the next significant number.

Eventually I gave up on such a silly superstition. For a while, anyway. After puberty, I started to hope again.

∼

The woman suddenly relaxed. "Good, good! Then follow me this way and let the tour begin. You can call me Alexandra, and I'll be your guide this evening!"

Alexandra—her grandmother's name. It reminded Casey of glass grapes and Tiffany lamps, of days spent on the couch watching soap operas and waiting for her mom to come home from work. It reminded her of home-cooked meals and bowls of her favorite caramels. Casey blanked out memories of the funeral.

She looked back at the exit and the cavern beyond as the woman's footsteps echoed away. She sighed and turned to follow the older woman into the murky palace.

Casey trailed Alexandra as the woman explained the purpose of each room: the parlor for guests, the private sitting room for family, the music room, the chapel, the ballrooms, the mini theater complete with box seats and a frayed curtain over the wooden stage. Alexandra went on about historic preservation and why it was important for the palace to have a caretaker, while Casey kept trying to determine where she'd met the woman before. She was beginning to think Alexandra was a ghost—maybe her grandmother's ghost.

"This is the dining hall," Alexandra continued, waving her hand at another large, gilded ruin of a room. A chandelier, complete with half-used candles dripping wax down the tarnished arms, hung from a spiraling plaster medallion. At the center of the room was a large, oval table. One side of the table glimmered in the light of the lamps that dotted the room, but the rest of the surface was hidden under a thick layer of dust.

"Why is only one side clean?" Casey asked, peering through the doorframe.

"Well, the caretaker has to eat somewhere, right?"

Casey flinched at her tone, but Alexandra smiled benignly. Their footsteps followed them into the hallway.

"And finally," Alexandra continued, stopping in front of a pair of pristine wooden doors. "We find ourselves at the back of the palace and the most important room of all: the library."

∼

Once I was in the tens of thousands, I stopped counting and started making up numbers for each of them. Number 69420 was a good girl, very prim. I didn't remember ever being that neat. She called out politely from the bridge, "Anyone there?" I didn't answer, afraid I would scare her off, but she left anyway, convinced no one was home. Of course, no one was *home, but even I didn't know that yet.*

∼

Carved and inlaid with elaborate patterns, the library doors were the only ones intact that Casey had seen. Alexandra made a flourishing gesture, motioning Casey to open one of them. She leaned her entire body into it, huffing as the door creaked open.

The room beyond was larger than the ballroom, larger than the theater, and stacked from floor to ceiling with books. It was the cleanest room by far, each surface gleaming in the robust lamplight radiating from every corner. She'd always appreciated libraries for their peace and quiet—no bully would risk annoying a librarian. And this was the ultimate library, a collection fit for a fairy-tale princess.

"It's amazing," she said, eyes wide to capture the wooden shelves, the curls of elegant trim, and the ladders that reached to the distant ceiling.

"It truly is. And I have a special book I'd like to show you," Alexandra said. "This way."

Casey followed her guide, eyes glued to the books that were a hundred different shapes, sizes, colors, and materials. Some looked to be a thousand years old, while others were common paperbacks. The shelves were bright wood, echoes of old life in their grain peering out in the lamplight. Vines, columns, and caryatids bedecked the room in every corner. Books lined not only the shelves but also tables and chairs, a fireplace mantel, and even a faded velvet sofa. The smell of dusty paper and aging leather permeated the air, along with the lingering scent of stale wood smoke.

They stopped at a plain wooden podium set against the back wall. It supported a massive tome open to a fading page of ornate lettering. The book itself seemed as large as the sofa, and the paper was a collage of yellow and beige fibers pressed together under thin, black script.

"This is the ultimate book—the book of all secrets. This palace was built, in the end, to house this book above all." Alexandra caressed the page that was open, staring reverently down at its contents. For the first time, Casey noticed the woman's fingernails were ragged and bitten down.

"What does it say?" Casey asked.

"Many things," Alexandra responded, impatience tingeing her voice. "Though no one knows their meaning for sure. You can make out this line right here—" She ran a finger down the page to a specific point. "Go ahead. Read it."

Alexandra's eyes glinted, and the skin around her eyes wrinkled as she smiled wide, encouragingly. The words were unfamiliar, but Casey worked through them, sounding out each syllable when she didn't know a word, just as she'd been taught.

"Coral crepting tempir. Loosentia carbonishing... This doesn't make sense," Casey said. "What language is this?"

Alexandra shrugged. "No one knows. It's been studied, you know—I have been studying it for years down here. Keep reading. It gets more interesting."

∿

You might wonder why I didn't just grab them when they got close enough, but I did. I tried that more than once, but they almost always slipped away. I managed to keep number 32456, but when I brought her to the book, she wouldn't read. She called me a witch! I kept her for a few days before the place started to stink. I decided kidnapping wasn't worth the hassle.

I worried 98457 would be afraid of witches, so I darkened my ragged gray hair with coal ashes from the fireplace. But she was skeptical anyway—didn't even get halfway to the library before fleeing. A piece of wrapped caramel fell out of her flopping backpack as she ran, and I knew it was almost time.

∿

Casey did as instructed, intrigued by the strange words that were almost as familiar as Alexandra. As she read, a breeze drifted down from above. Alexandra breathed deep, and Casey shivered.

"Don't stop," Alexandra said, but Casey didn't hear, pulled into the singsong rhythm of the words.

"...silen distri fugis." The words ended at the bottom of the page, and the breeze faded, lamps swaying on their chains.

"Beautiful," Alexandra said, eyes closed and face content. "Yes—perfect pronunciation. Just as it was, so it must be."

"What was it?" Casey asked, and Alexandra's eyes popped open, suddenly intense.

"It was a spell."

"A spell?" Casey asked, cocking her head. "What does it do?" She stepped back from the book, a strange tension twisting her gut. "What was the spell?" she asked again. *If it was even real*, she thought to herself.

Alexandra ignored her, turning to walk out of the library.

"Wait!" Casey ran to keep up, but the woman strode through the palace toward the broken entrance. She paused at the threshold, peering out at the cavern. Her wrinkles softened in the dim light, eyes wide with anticipation. She pushed back a lock of hair, and Casey saw a darkened patch of scalp.

"You have a birthmark just like mine," she said stupidly.

Alexandra stepped through the doors, and the air around her rippled.

Casey felt as though a stone had dropped onto her chest. The air thickened, closing in on her, choking her, then suddenly loosened. She walked to the door and tried to step through, but her foot slipped at the threshold, as though she were trying to walk through a wall.

Finally, Alexandra turned to face Casey. "I'm so sorry, dear. I had to do it. You'll understand when it comes your time—in an age or two."

"What's happening?" Casey asked, fear setting in as she scrabbled against the invisible wall. She ran her hands down it, cold as marble and just as hard. She slapped her palm against it, and then again, feeling the sting without understanding where it could come from.

"You've refused to follow me into the palace nearly two hundred thousand times," Alexandra responded, ignoring Casey's panicked question. "*Two hundred thousand times!* Can you even conceive of such a number? Or imagine my frustration when you get to the doors and still don't come inside?"

"You—Who are you?" Casey panted, leaning against the invisible barrier.

"Oh, darling—poor thing. I'm you, of course. And now I'm free. I'm sorry to do this to you—to us—but you'll understand when you're older. That I can promise you." Alexandra gave her a bittersweet smile with teeth that crooked with terrifying familiarity.

"The loop will reset, time and again," she continued, hair no longer thin and gray but thick and dark. "Sometimes you walk through the crevice, and sometimes you turn back. Sometimes you get all the way to the bridge before changing your mind. Over and over, you come to this cave. It will frustrate you at first, but eventually you will learn to accept it. Read the books—it helps to pass the time."

"I don't believe you. I would never do this—what you said—to someone. I'm not you!"

Alexandra shrugged, catching her falling dress sleeve as she suddenly seemed too small for her clothes. "Suit yourself. I'm just trying to help," she replied.

"Please, let me go. I promise I won't tell anyone—" Casey started, tears pricking her eyes, but Alexandra was already on the stairs down to the cavern. Something clattered to the floor in front of the doorway: a piece of wrapped caramel, just out of reach. Alexandra might have turned back, but Casey could no longer see the little girl in the gloom. The last of the light faded as a boulder emerged and drifted up from the depths of the water, plugging the skylight.

∼

Did you notice my eyes were the color of your eyes as I offered you the candy? Or as I showed you my precious library? Did you notice me change as you read the words from that one, awful book? Did you feel the blanket of weight fall on you as it fell off me? What despair did you feel as I left without turning back? What did you think when the first girl was spooked from the cave entrance?

Did you know who she was?

∼

Casey slid to the floor, staring into the darkness. A flashlight flickered at the crevice, and someone pushed deeper into the cave.

"Hello?" came the call of her own voice. When the boulder crashed, the girl who'd called out squealed and fled through the narrow passage.

The boulder drifted up.

The cavern darkened.

A light flickered.

"Hello?"

ABOUT THE AUTHOR

Carrie Callahan is a 2019 recipient of the Writers of the Future Award, a 2020 recipient of the Working Class Writers Grant from the Speculative Literature Foundation, and a 2023 finalist for the Baen Adventure Fantasy Award. She is a member of SFWA and has an MFA from the Bluegrass Writers Studio where she was awarded the Emerging Writer's Award in Fiction. You can find her work in *Writers of the Future Volume 35* and *Galaxy's Edge Magazine*.

17

THIS WAS YOUR LIFE (PLAY IT AGAIN, SAM)

MARY PLETSCH

Samantha spent her weekdays alone in an apartment that had become a waiting room, searching for ways to keep herself occupied while the clock ran down. She was grateful for Kevin, but he had a busy job and a wife and three young kids, and he couldn't put his life on pause. So Sam began cleaning out her storage closet as a favor to her son. She could at least accomplish something practical in the time she had left.

She unearthed a huge plastic container that had followed her through most of her life, childhood bedroom to dorm to apartment to house to apartment to condo to apartment again. She couldn't remember the last time she'd looked inside. Years. Decades. It was a time capsule now.

She opened the lid to discover the mementos of a lifetime: battered *Intertemporal Highway* novels, the decorative tin with the fake bottom where she'd stashed weed, a jewelry box containing diamond earrings she thought she'd given away. Way down at the bottom, she found her old boom box with its double cassette decks.

Why not plug it in and let it play while she sorted through the sediment of fifty-eight years? She found cassettes from

This Was Your Life (Play It Again, Sam)

bands who were still touring, cassettes from musicians long dead, a mixtape made by her tenth-grade boyfriend, tape after tape of songs recorded off the radio. And she found a cassette resting in the second deck, a tape she didn't remember. It was tantalizingly blank, emitting nothing but a hiss when she pressed play.

Having discovered a diversion that could draw her attention away from the light at the end of the tunnel—so very close now, and not at all warm—Sam saw nothing wrong with a silly indulgence. She decided to make a soundtrack of her favorite songs throughout her lifetime. When it was done, she picked up a pen and gave her mixtape a name: *This Was Your Life.*

She pressed play, listening as she worked, until she heard the opening notes of the banger she'd danced to at her senior prom, and an old memory came roaring up from the back of her mind. Vicky, age nine, had loved to dress up and dance to this song. Sam couldn't bear to hear it now. She'd be with her daughter soon enough.

She smashed the rewind button. The tape squealed.

It was better for the tape if she stopped it before pressing play, and Sam had always prided herself on taking care of her things, but her son wasn't going to cherish a box of old cassettes so what the hell, Vicky was looming large in her mind, her greatest regret, and she needed a distraction *immediately.* She hit the play button and thought she heard a couple of lines from her high school anthem.

> *Take, take it back, take it all the way back*
> *Too cool for school and we're on the attack*

Sam wakes up in science class on the first day of tenth grade.

Sam has been plagued throughout her life by what she calls *high school dreams*, which always involve some ridiculous pretext for why she, a fully-grown adult, has to repeat high school. In the dreams, it feels humiliating to sit shoulder to shoulder with children and be treated as their peer.

This dream is different. She is a teenager again, and the people around her, also teens, are people she'd really gone to high school with. She wears the red flannel shirt that she'd worn until she'd put holes in both elbows. It's intact now, as fuzzy as ever, and there's something in the front pocket.

Sam takes it out. It's a mixtape with a totally bizarre name: *This Was Your Life*.

Dreams are weird. She puts it back.

Sam's head throbs painfully, which feels a little too real. On the actual first day of tenth grade, she'd dozed off because she'd stayed up late reading *Wrong Way Down the Intertemporal Highway*. Sam's still half-asleep, but she thinks she's seen all this before.

The class will choose lab partners. Sam will make a beeline for Tim Schultz and so will Katherine Davidson. Tim will choose Sam and make her feel like the luckiest girl in the world.

Sam will be sitting in science class again this time next year, her head throbbing from the punch that Tim landed on her temple.

Tim is basically the first big regret of her life.

The back of her neck prickles.

She's already learned her lesson with Tim Schultz. She doesn't need to learn it again.

Sam stays in her seat while Katherine Davidson approaches Tim. Tim glances in her direction—wanting her more than Kathy—and Sam quickly turns away, scanning the room for... who had ended up being Kathy's lab partner?

Sam's gaze lands on a solitary figure wearing an expression

of disappointment and tapping her fingers on her desk. Right. Marta Dyer, the class weirdo. Sam can't remember a single thing she'd ever said to this girl.

Still, Marta's got to be an improvement on Tim.

Sam approaches and Marta quips, "Old Maid, you've got the joker."

From forty-three years in the future, Sam's heart clenches for this girl—child, really—who knows she is everyone's last choice. God, but things hit differently when you were (had been) a mom.

Sam gestures to Tim and says, "I'd rather play Old Maid than President and A-Hole."

Marta snorts laughter. "I thought you liked him."

"Want to hear something weird?"

"Okay," Marta says warily.

Sam can't possibly tell Marta the truth, so she takes a page from *Intertemporal Highway*, remembering too late that in high school she hadn't let anyone know that she liked nerdy stuff. "What if I told you two guys in a time-traveling sports car warned me that in the future, Tim mutates into a huge jerk?"

"DeLorean or Lamborghini?" Marta asks with a hesitant smile.

Could Marta possibly recognize a…

"Lamborghini on the Intertemporal Highway."

Marta's smile broadens. "Roger and Shotgun Roy are *way* cooler than Marty and Doc Brown."

∼

Sam arrives home after school to her childhood bedroom in a house that had been torn down eleven years ago and would be torn down thirty years in the future. She stumbles to her vanity, confirms her suspicions: she is fifteen (again), she still has the mind and memories of a fifty-eight-year-old woman, her pain is gone, and this is not a dream. She takes the cassette out of her pocket and puts it in her stash tin for safekeeping.

Sam (fifteen) just wanted to have a good time, but Sam (fifty-eight) has a lifetime's worth (more like half a lifetime's worth) of regrets and partially realized dreams. Marta and Tim are proof that she can make different choices on this...this replay.

But she has to be careful.

High school didn't change her life in a radical way. University will—that was where she met (will meet) Tony. Her marriage might not have worked out, but she doesn't want to undo her children.

Sam finally understands the gift she's been given.

October 16.

Vicky.

~

Funny thing about Tony.

At first, Sam had been apprehensive about approaching the cute, sandy-haired guy at the football game, knowing full well there could be no happy ending. Thoughts of Vicky and Kevin gave her courage.

God, she'd forgotten how much fun she and Tony had together when they were young. She put thoughts of divorce out of her mind. She and Tony hadn't started fighting until... how old had Vicky been? Twelve? Thirteen? It had always been about money.

Then Tony had lost his job, and that had been the beginning of the end: his withdrawal, his depression, his drinking, his final fatal spiral. Sam had stayed longer than she should have, trying to help him, but he hadn't wanted her help.

She vowed to get out sooner this time, but she could at least enjoy the good times first. She couldn't make too many drastic changes.

Was it a drastic change to decline his offer of diamond earrings—the eventual cause of their first money fight? She'd rather not do *that* again.

Was it a drastic change to take a promotion at work? One she'd used her *insider knowledge* to get? Extra money would do a lot to get her through the rough years after leaving Tony.

Was it a drastic change to tell Tony that he was a good partner and a good father rather than a good breadwinner? To encourage his interests outside of work?

Funny how the little things add up.

~

Valentine's Day. Tony will lose his job in two months. Their marriage will be over nineteen months after that.

Tony comes home with a bouquet of flowers. Over dinner, he tells her that he has been offered a new job by one of his friends in the auto club—just in time, because there's rumors of layoffs at his current company. The new job doesn't pay as well, but Sam's latest raise more than makes up the difference.

Tony looks so worried when he asks what she thinks.

"I think you should take it," she says.

Years scatter like splinters. Sam doesn't get divorced.

~

Just like that Vicky is seventeen, and it's October 16, a date that had lived in infamy. No longer.

"Mom, *why*?" Vicky demands.

Why cannot be spoken. Sam resorts to "Because I said so."

Goes to bed.

Sleeps deeply, awaiting a glorious morning.

Wakes up at the same time as last time, 1:03 a.m. exactly, because the phone is ringing, and before she picks it up, she already knows it's the same police officer and she already knows what he is going to say.

∽

Clearly Vicky had known about Sam's stash tin. It was where Sam had hidden the car keys to make certain Vicky would stay home.

Sam opens the tin up, still half disbelieving. Sure enough, the keys are gone. There's nothing in there but an old cassette tape: *This Was Your Life*. The ribbon is wound around the right spindle, as though it's been played through to the end.

The sight of it drops Sam down a hole to another world where she was—will be—still is a fifty-eight-year-old woman looking down the barrel of a terminal diagnosis who does not want to—*cannot*—bury her daughter again when she is so close to burying herself. She goes to the basement, to that time capsule of a plastic tub. Plugs in the boom box. Slides the cassette into the deck and nudges it shut.

Presses rewind.

Prays lightning strikes twice.

Presses play.

On the stormy days
In the sultry nights
When I find myself
Zeroed in your sights

If at first you don't succeed
But you know the things you need
Throw back to remember when
And try, try again...

This Was Your Life (Play It Again, Sam)

~

Sam wakes up from a late afternoon nap on October 16, a day that is not going to live in infamy if she has anything to say about it.

She goes out to the garage. Slashes all four tires.

~

October 17. Vicky is surly at breakfast. Sam is riding high on happily-ever-after. Even the prospect of telling Tony about the car can't bring her down.

The phone rings.

Sam, of course, thinks of the police. But the police have nothing to say to her when her husband and two children are wolfing down scrambled eggs. Sam summons her courage to answer.

The voice on the other end is a teenager, asking for Vicky and sniffling loudly. Sam's heart sinks as she passes the phone to Vicky and waits with a growing sense of apprehension.

She braces herself for the worst. Her imagination fails her.

It's so much worse than she guessed.

~

Roger told Shotgun Roy, "It's the things you don't know that'll get you in the end."

Michael Donohue had still had too much to drink at the field party. His older brother Shaun had still been determined to take him home before he got too rowdy. Shaun had still begged a ride home, and in the absence of Vicky, he'd asked Cindi McMaster. Sam had not known that Cindi had been at the party.

Michael had still found it funny to kick the driver's seat,

even after Cindi, like Vicky, had asked him to stop. And Cindi, like Vicky, had finally turned around to yell at him. And Cindi, like Vicky, had not seen Frank Bertrand pop up from behind the hill ahead, driving up the middle of the road in his rusty blue pickup, drunk as a skunk and high as a kite.

Shaun survived, as he survived before, in a wheelchair for the rest of his life.

Michael survived, though he hadn't before.

Cindi McMaster died in Vicky's place.

Meaning she'd never grow up to marry Kevin Tanahill.

Meaning Sam has saved her daughter and erased her grandkids.

∼

Sam has no reason to feel sad. It doesn't count when you can take it back.

Press rewind.

Aim for the third song on the cassette.

Press play.

> 'Cause we're getting the knack, and we're on the right track,
> Take, take it back, take it all the way back.

Sam rolls out of bed, opens her plastic storage tub, and puts *Breaking Speed Limits on the Intertemporal Highway* into her backpack. It is October 16, and she is in the tenth grade.

∼

Marta Dyer is Sam's best friend, despite the weird hobbies she developed on account of growing up on a farm in the middle of nowhere. One of those hobbies is target shooting with her dad's .308 Winchester. She goes hiking in the bush pretending to be Shotgun Roy. She invites Sam to come along and play Roger.

On the first replay, Sam had reluctantly agreed to give it a try. If she made Marta hang out at the mall with her, it was only fair. Turned out she liked it about as much as Marta liked hanging out at the mall, namely, a lot more than she thought she would.

On the second replay, Sam still plays Roger, but this time she puts a lot more effort into refining her aim.

∽

Sam wishes she'd taken the time to learn more about Frank Bertrand in the past twenty-seven years, but she'd been more focused on having a(nother) good life and hoping Frank was (would eventually be) burning in hell, so here she is in the stupid forest with a .308 Winchester slung over her shoulder, binoculars around her neck and her boom box in her hand, finally doing something she's been putting off for far too long. Had she really believed that Frank would add something of value to the world before his time was done, or was that just an excuse to delay a task that made her feel sick whenever she thought about it?

She had told herself she didn't want to carry guilt around any longer than she had to. Instead she'd carried a sense of doom hanging over her head and an obligation to maintain her marksmanship skills. She is no longer certain she chose wisely.

Her back aches and her knees throb, and this would have been easier a decade or two ago. It's already October 14. Frank is supposed to be an avid hunter, and she hasn't seen him once since deer season opened. If he doesn't show up in the forest today, she might shoot the bastard in his own bed tonight and worry about the cops later.

She shouldn't be worried. Fresh batteries in the boom box

and a certain cassette in the deck means there is nothing to worry about.

She will save her family no matter how many tries it takes.

Something rustles in the bush. Sam sets the boom box down in the fallen leaves. She lifts the binoculars and holds her breath. A figure swims into view: dirty blue baseball hat, gray plaid coat, beer bottle in hand.

This one's for Victoria Rebecca Tanahill.

Sam lowers the binoculars. Lifts her rifle. Takes aim.

Pulls the trigger.

∼

Ten minutes feels like forever. Frank just won't die.

Sam throws up.

It's too much—she can't—

Rewind.

Play.

> *Honey, it's no lie*
> *And it's no mistake,*
> *'Cause you miss the shots*
> *That you fail to take.*
>
> *If at first you don't succeed...*

Sam wakes up on October 12 and doesn't bother to go hunting. She has two more days to wait.

∼

Two days later, Sam centers the crosshairs on Frank's head and freezes.

She can't shake the way Frank had lain there, writhing,

smearing brownish-red into the sticks and leaves. She couldn't take the way he'd rolled onto his side and sobbed and called out for his mother. She'd put the barrel to his head but couldn't pull the trigger. She'd thrown the rifle away and vomited instead.

She'd broken then, and she broke now. No force in this life or the last could lift the rifle off her shoulder. She watches Frank's gray plaid coat disappear into the bush.

She can't.

What kind of mother am I?

Rewind.

Play.

And you had me, babe,
With a single kiss.
'Cause when you take aim,
Ain't no way you miss.

Sam wakes up from a nightmare on the morning of October 14. She can still smell the flowers at Vicky's funeral.

∼

Third time lucky. The shot is clean.

∼

There was an investigation, of course, and Sam had no alibi, of course, but the police had nothing to say to her. Everyone knew Frank and his pals drank a lot when they went hunting. It was really no surprise that there had been an accident and no surprise none of them would admit to it.

With no conclusive evidence and no confession, the Frank Bertrand case went cold and the boom box remained unplayed in a plastic container in Sam's basement for eleven years.

∼

Until Kevin and Cindi break up. Sam has always secretly suspected there would be some price to be paid for killing a man, even a man like Frank Bertrand. A hollow feeling fills the pit of Sam's stomach when Kevin tells her that Cindi has been cheating on him. Their marriage—their as-yet-childless marriage—is over.

"How did you find out?" Sam whispers, already trying to sort it out in her head, shuffling through faded memories, looking for the turning point.

Kevin's answer should not surprise her as much as it does. "Vicky. She's friends with one of Cindi's friends and word got around."

Sam sleepwalks through the rest of the conversation. When it's over, she stumbles to the basement, to the time capsule. This is her punishment for playing God: a choice between Vicky and her grandchildren.

Except nothing's ever that simple.

Cindi might have cheated the first time too. Kevin didn't find out. They stayed together. They had kids.

How was Sam going to stop Cindi from hooking up with whoever it was?

Or stop Kevin from ever finding out?

And then make sure it didn't happen again with someone else?

Sam had always had a friendly relationship with Cindi, but nowhere near close enough to guess what Cindi had been thinking.

Sam is going to need some time to figure out how to fix this mess. Maybe a lifetime's worth.

This Was Your Life (Play It Again, Sam)

Press rewind.

Press play—except her finger slips and the tape is still rewinding and what happens if it reaches the beginning and Sam tries again and presses play just in time to hear the first verse of

The itsy-bitsy spider...

∼

Sam's first wedding was very nice.

Her second wedding was perfect.

Her third wedding was totally outrageous.

Funny how the little things add up.

Her fourth wedding is...kind of boring, actually. Soon her marriage feels much the same.

Been there. Done that.

∼

Tony comes home for just one night between business trips. It's how Sam knows that this is the night when Kevin will be conceived.

Tony isn't in the mood.

She plies him with wine, which backfires spectacularly when he falls asleep on the couch.

There's no point in a world without her son. She's not trading Kevin for Vicky.

Rewind.

Play.

∼

They were supposed to get engaged today. They broke up instead.

"I'm sorry," Tony says. He searches for words. "It's like you've become a different person."

But it doesn't count if you can take, take it back, take it all the way back.

Rewind.

Play.

~

"So what if Tony says you have no chemistry?" Marta asks over the phone. "I don't even know why you're chasing that guy. You've got nothing in common."

Sam curls up in her dorm room, a thousand miles away from her best friend, and grieves her husband and children and grandchildren and then realizes at least she doesn't have to sit here alone.

Rewind.

Play.

~

This has happened every time:

- Marta is offered a full scholarship to a prestigious university.
- She takes it.

This has never happened before:

- Sam applies to the same university as Marta.
- Gets accepted.
- Chooses a different major, on a whim.

This Was Your Life (Play It Again, Sam)

~

Jason.
 Walter (Kevin's middle name).
 Jessica (couldn't face Rebecca or Victoria).
 Miscarriage.

~

Jason.
 Alexander (let him be his own person).
 Your secretary? Really?

~

Jason? David.
 Sally (stepdaughter).
 Jessica (doesn't look at all like the first Jessica).

~

No kids this replay. Marta and the folks at the animal rescue feel more like family than any of her partners ever did.

~

The day after Sam receives her diagnosis, Marta turns up on her doorstep. Sam's surprised. This hasn't happened before. Sam dredges her memory and stirs up Jessica (which one?) and Alexander/Walter and Kevin. It was always one of her children, before.

These days it's harder to remember her children. Especially Kevin.

Sam asks herself why she hasn't pressed rewind yet and

comes up with stupid excuses—the dogs, another year before the pain gets really bad—but the truth is she's just not looking forward to another run through high school, nor is she eager to have new children who will be (become) strangers to her.

But she's also not ready to die. God help her, even after this many replays, she's still afraid to die.

Marta sits down on the sofa, and Sam has the wildest idea. A prickling sensation sweeps over her as she wonders if she's really going to do what she's about to do. If she *can*.

She starts by assembling a digital version of her playlist. The first few notes of an alternative song crawl out of her speakers—the beginning of the B-side of *This Was Your Life*.

Marta makes a face. "You like this song?"

"Actually...no." Sam presses stop. "This is something my friends listened to in a world where you and I didn't talk to each other."

"What?" Marta laughs, and Sam tells her everything. Vicky, Cindi, Frank Bertrand, the works.

~

"You don't believe any of this," Sam says.

"No, but if you prove me wrong it'd *absolutely rule*."

"But it's not just about choosing a...a different door. It's all the doors closed by the aftershocks." Sam takes a deep breath, thinking of Tony and Vicky, roads not taken and roads washed out. "There isn't always a way back."

"Sam. I don't have kids, I'm single, my tarantula died last month, and I haven't talked to my family in years. I have nothing to lose. If I wake up in high school, why the hell not?" Marta flashes her an impulsive grin. "But I think we need to do something a little differently right from the start."

Sam isn't so sure. She's scared in a way she hasn't been in decades. She might be making a huge mistake, and she doubts

This Was Your Life (Play It Again, Sam)

there's going to be any taking it back when Marta puts *This Was Your Life* in the second deck, a heavy metal cassette in the first deck.

Play on deck one. Record plus play on deck two.

Sam knows the song, all right. On the first replay, she'd told Marta she didn't like metal. Hilarious, all these concerts later.

If they were doing this, why not go for broke? "Hey, tape over the next song too."

"Why? What's the next song?"

"It played at my wedding when I married..." Sam breaks off. It takes a moment for her to remember his name.

∼

Marta scribbles out a letter with a ballpoint pen and slides *This Was our Life* into the boom box.

"Don't play the A-side," Sam warns. "If I have to 'Itsy-Bitsy Spider' again I'm going to kick your ass."

Marta cracks up. "We've practiced. We'll get it right."

They place their fingers on the buttons, exactly as they've rehearsed.

Together, they press rewind. Count out loud.

Together, they press play.

∼

Sam wakes up in a sleeping bag in an old green tent that smells like heavy metal and eternity. She rolls onto her side and sees Marta sitting upright, clutching a cassette.

Marta turns to her with a huge, stupid smile. "It worked. We're on the camping trip, and we start university in three weeks."

Sam grins back. "Hi there, Shotgun Roy. My name's Roger. Want to ride with me?"

A BIT OF LUCK

~

Marta bets on sports, which has *got* to be cheating. Or maybe Sam simply envies the ease with which Marta embraces her rebirth.

Marta's not really the sort to do the same thing twice, which is just the boost Sam needs to find some fresh excitement in her life (lives). They take different jobs, try different hobbies, go on different vacations together.

There's one exception.

On each replay, Marta places the same bets and wins the same money and buys the same vintage Lamborghini, and the license plate always reads

Ontario
R3WiND
Yours to Discover

~

Back road. Late night.

"Sam, the what-if game will drive you crazy if you let it. Stop trying to manipulate the future and live in the present for a change." Marta is laughing behind the wheel of the Lamborghini. "'Cause our present is gonna be really, *really* long."

Been there. Done that. At least Sam can replay the good parts. "Hey. Let's go back to Hawaii." She takes *This Was our Life* from her purse and slides it into the boom box in her lap.

A corona of light illuminates the hill in front of them as another vehicle approaches.

Marta reaches for the rewind button. "Play it again, Sam!"

They hit rewind together. Press play together.

For just an instant after she wakes up on Waikiki Beach,

This Was Your Life (Play It Again, Sam)

Sam wonders what the other driver saw.

∼

"It's not what you've forgotten," Roger said to Shotgun Roy. "You can always re-learn what you've forgotten. It's what you don't *remember* you've forgotten."

"Yeah, yeah, I know. It's the things we don't know that'll get us in the end."

∼

The Lamborghini races down a back road on an unseasonably warm night. Again. How many times?

Marta's just been dumped, and she's sitting shotgun, wiping away tears and hugging the boom box. Again. How many times?

"You want to rewind so you can patch it up with Katherine?" Sam's lost count of how many replays it's been: ten years here, ten weeks there, memories blurred by the cumulative sediment of time. It has to have been decades since she was last in high school and centuries since she last heard the diagnosis. Sam prefers the part in the middle, even if she's seen it so often already.

"Nah. Kathy's actually kind of a bitch. Can't believe I was into her so many lifetimes in a row."

"In my first life, you two were lab partners." And, honestly, Sam can't remember how that worked out. "You need to get over that girl."

Marta manages a wicked smile through her tears. "Then let's rewind so I can dump her first for a change."

"Why not?"

They press the button together.

Rewind—

And the horrible sound of the cassette player eating the tape.

Sam swears as Marta frantically hits eject. Marta grabs the cassette and carefully pulls the tangled strands of tape out of the player. The hill ahead begins to glow with the lights of an oncoming vehicle.

"Oh my God," Sam says, the weight of a thousand lifetimes finally catching up to her, pressing down on her, because she's just remembered what she'd forgotten, and this time is for keepsies.

"I can fix it." Marta Dyer: always stubborn, always a fighter. "I've got a pencil in my purse."

Marta bends over to get it, and maybe that will save her. Sam chooses to believe it will.

Sam urges the Lamborghini toward the shoulder, but it won't be enough because it's just about midnight on October 16 and coming over the hill is a rusty blue pickup truck driving right down the middle of the road. Frank Bertrand is behind the wheel, drunk as a skunk and high as a kite.

Sam's tired.

She can't really complain. It's been one hell of a ride.

∼

Marta Dyer has spent months learning how to move her fingers again. Now she slides the battered cassette into her old Walkman and prays for a miracle.

Marta is not about to let Frank Bertrand hurt Sam, or anyone else, ever again. She knows where he lived-lives-will live, and she's a good shot with a .308 Winchester.

And this time she's definitely dumping Katherine Davidson first.

She just needs a bit of luck. Enough to make lightning strike twice.

Enough to take her back, take her all the way back.

ABOUT THE AUTHOR

Mary Pletsch attended the first Superstars Writing Seminars in 2010 and learned from the best. In the years since, she has published short stories and novellas in a variety of genres, including science fiction, fantasy, and horror. Superstars holds a special place in her heart; it made the difference between writing as a hobby and writing to be published.

18

THE UNNAMED

GAMA RAY MARTINEZ

Thomas tapped his Bluetooth earpiece to mute the call just as the ball of lighting zipped over his shoulder and crackled into the steel girder behind him. The gremlin who'd thrown it growled a series of incomprehensible sounds. Its two companions leaped from the window to the unfinished wall and back again while some middle manager blathered on about quarterly earnings not being as high as they should.

One of the creatures launched itself at him, but Thomas twisted out of the way and slashed with his sword. The lightweight blade barely slowed as it sheered through the creature's wrist. A leathery hand fell to the ground and evaporated in a puff of green smoke. The creatures shouted at him in unison. Thomas resisted the urge to laugh. They weren't much bigger than rats, and their ears, each as big as his palm, flapped as they jumped up and down. Gremlins had a penchant for messing with technology, and they had driven the workers to abandon this site. Fortunately, no one had been killed. Yet.

Thomas stepped forward and swung his sword at a gremlin standing on a pile of bricks. It danced out of the way, avoiding his strike easily. It didn't, however, see the heavy dagger in Thomas's left hand. The weapon slammed into the creature's face, and Thomas pulled it out as the gremlin disappeared into mist.

A question buzzed in his ear. Thomas ducked under a gremlin's leaping attack and unmuted his headset.

"I didn't get the reports until late last night. I'll get—Ow!"

The one-handed gremlin slashed his nails across his arm, tearing his sleeve and leaving three lines of blood. Thomas's dagger clattered to the floor.

"What was that, Thomas?" his boss asked.

"Sorry, Mike, paper cut. I'll get to them this afternoon."

He hurriedly muted his phone before slamming his fist into the creature who had wounded him. It flew back and crashed into its companion. Pain shot up his arm, but he took a step forward and thrust with his sword before they could untangle from each other. His blade pierced them both. One growled something before they both vanished.

"Thanks, everybody," Mike said. "Thomas, are you going to make it for the eleven o'clock status meeting?"

Thomas rolled his eyes and pulled his phone out of his pocket to check the time—9:30. He sighed and tapped his headset again. "Yeah, I'm done at the dentist. I should be back to the office in about an hour."

"All right. See you then."

There was a round of goodbyes as the conference call ended. Thomas pulled off his earpiece and stuffed it into his pocket. He looked at his wound. The cuts weren't deep and had already started to heal, as spirit wounds tended to do. Still, it could've been a lot worse. He must be getting old. It had been years since anything as minor as a gremlin had scored a hit on him, even while he was on the phone. He shrugged.

"It happens to the best of us," he said under his breath.

He reached into his pocket and pulled out a crystal hanging

from a silver chain. He stared into it, but it remained clear and motionless, an indication that there were no other supernaturals nearby. It was only then that he allowed himself to relax.

He walked to the nearby alley and got into the sedan parked toward the back. He pulled a first aid kit out of the glove box and sterilized the wound before wrapping it. That done, he got his phone and spent the next few minutes disabling his GPS, his data, and every other app that could be used to track him. Then, he pulled out the false patch in his jacket and retrieved his other SIM card. He switched it out with the one in his phone and dialed. It rang twice before someone picked up, though no one spoke.

"Conundrum," Thomas said. "Omega three-two-seven."

"Who is this?" a distorted voice said.

"I have no name."

"Confirmed Unnamed. Status?"

"Just a couple of gremlins. They've been dispatched."

"That's the eighth incursion this week."

"Eighth?"

There was a pause. "We had one in London a few hours ago and another in Sydney just before that."

The line remained silent, but Thomas could guess at what they were thinking. Ever since the Unnamed had prevented the Mayan apocalypse of 2012, supernaturals had been coming into the world at an alarming rate, and not all of them could be vanquished as easily as gremlins. They wouldn't be able to keep them secret much longer.

"I'll log it with the others," the voice said. "Keep in touch."

He hung up and switched out his SIM card again. His phone chirped when he turned it back on. He groaned. Mike had scheduled another meeting for noon, right after the status report meeting. It was going to be one of those days.

Thomas just barely had time to shower, clean his wound again—you could never be too careful with gremlins—and put on a fresh set of clothes. He sped to work and arrived just as everyone was taking a seat around a large conference table. He sank into a chair and made a show of paying attention.

The status meeting, like many others of its kind, was filled with people who didn't really need to be there. Of the fifteen people, maybe five had something relevant to say. The rest, including Thomas himself, would've better spent their time actually doing their jobs. To make matters worse, the air conditioning had gone out again, and the windowless room was quickly becoming unbearable. Mike seemed oblivious to their discomfort and continued with the pointless meeting. Thomas let out a long breath. In his experience, giving up your common sense seemed to be a prerequisite for going into middle management.

That and gaining a few pounds, he thought as Mike waved his pudgy hands at a chart projected on the wall.

The meeting droned on. A few people started paying more attention to their phones than to the pointless reports. Thomas found himself nodding off and decided playing a game was better than the attention he would draw if he started snoring. As he reached for his phone, he felt a vibration. He assumed it was another meeting request, but he didn't have any new notifications. He shrugged and opened a puzzle game he'd been working on.

His pocket vibrated again. A sharp point poked at his leg, and his blood went cold. It was the crystal. He glanced down and saw a flash of bright green light. He closed his fingers around the stone before he could make out a pattern. It felt warm, and he cursed under his breath. Vibration, light, and heat. Three signs. This was no gremlin. He had to get out of here. He pushed back from the table, and every eye turned to him.

"Sorry," he stammered. "I have to go."

"Thomas?" Mike asked.

Thomas got up and rushed to the door. The crystal was hot in his pocket.

Mike got up, too, but Thomas didn't wait for him. He left the conference room and half jogged past the receptionist. He had just pushed the button on the elevator when Mike poked his head out of the conference room.

"What's going on?"

"Sorry, it's a message from my dentist." Thomas spouted the first thing that came to mind. "I have to go."

For a moment, Thomas thought Mike would insist he come back. Thomas wouldn't, of course. It wouldn't be the first time he'd lost a job for his duties as an Unnamed, but Mike gave him a slow nod. "I hope everything is all right."

"Thanks," he said. "I'll try to get back this afternoon."

The elevator dinged, and Thomas stepped through the door, wondering if he had misjudged Mike. As soon as the door closed, he pulled out the crystal. He had to hold it by the chain to avoid being burned. It still glowed bright green, but every few seconds, it flickered red, and once there was a flash of white. He searched his memory for what kind of creature that could be, but he came up empty.

The elevator reached the ground floor, and Thomas shoved the crystal into his pocket, gritting his teeth against its heat. He nodded at the security guard in the lobby and rushed out to his car. Once inside, he replaced his SIM card and called in. They went through the same security measure, and the voice on the other side asked for a report.

"I've detected a major supernatural," Thomas said.

"Signs?"

"Light, vibration, and heat. A lot of heat. I can't hold the crystal without being burned." Suddenly the crystal began to hum. "Do you hear that?"

The voice sputtered for a second. When it spoke again, there was fear in its tone. "Sound?"

"Yes."

"Elements?"

Thomas waited until the pattern of lights repeated themselves. "Earth mostly, but there's a little fire and a touch of air."

Muffled voices came from the speaker as Thomas hung the crystal over his rearview mirror. It drifted to one side, and he pulled out of the parking lot, following its direction. It only pointed to the source; it didn't tell him how to get there. He wound through streets that were relatively empty, it being before the lunch rush. He was so focused on the crystal that he missed the red light. A car missed him by inches, the driver honking and flipping Thomas the bird.

Finally, the voice came back over the phone. "We think it's an earth dragon."

"What?" Thomas swerved in his lane, but managed to control his vehicle. "There hasn't been a dragon in fifteen hundred years."

"That's what the signs point to."

"Are you sure? What does the child say?"

The silence lasted almost a full minute. "The child is gone."

Thomas suppressed a shiver. It had happened before. It was almost impossible to hold someone who had as detailed knowledge of the future as the child did, but for it to happen now, with so much supernatural activity happening worldwide, couldn't be a good sign. Time to worry about that later, though. Command was usually right about the signs. Usually.

He took several deep breaths to calm himself. It didn't work. "If I'm going to be fighting a flying, fire-breathing lizard, I'm going to need backup."

"Earth dragons don't fly, Unnamed."

"Does it still breathe fire?"

"Yes."

"Then I'm going to need some backup."

There was the sound of rustling pages. "Nine-five-seven is in town."

Thomas cursed. "Anyone else?"

"How long?"

Thomas stared at the crystal a few seconds, timing its pulses. "Under an hour."

"No one else can get there in time."

"Fine. Give me a minute, and I'll get you a location."

The crystal led him across a series of turns before he finally ended up at an old warehouse. Graffiti decorated one wall, but no one seemed to be around. He gave the voice on the phone the address and waited, taking the crystal down and putting it in his pocket, lest it be seen.

Unnamed 957 took less than ten minutes to arrive. He parked a beat-up old pickup next to Thomas and glared. Both men got out of their cars, and Thomas stood face to face with a man tall enough to fit in with a professional basketball team.

"Dmitri," Thomas said, inclining his head.

"Thomas. What's this about?" He spoke with a heavy Greek accent and wore a long trench coat, the kind that would immediately attract the attention of any police officer who saw it and make them worry that it hid all sorts of deadly surprises. Of course, in this case, it did.

"Didn't Command tell you?"

Dmitri shrugged. "Something about a prime supernatural."

"Haven't you checked your crystal?"

"I lost it in Moscow fighting against those vampires. Haven't had time to get a new one made."

Thomas pulled out his crystal and showed it to the other man. Dmitri blanched and took a step back, bumping into a beggar neither had seen. Dmitri retained his balance, but the other man fell to the ground. Dmitri reached into his coat, but Thomas grabbed his wrist.

"Leave him alone. We have other things to worry about."

The beggar looked from Thomas to Dmitri, apparently unaware of the danger he had been in.

Dmitri gave Thomas a level look. "You should have checked for that."

Thomas's eyes seemed to slide off the beggar, which meant he probably had some sort of supernatural ancestry, making him hard to notice. Of course, about a quarter of humanity came from one mystic bloodline or another. Thomas glanced at the crystal, but this man was nothing special.

The beggar picked himself off the ground and brushed away some of the gravel that had gotten onto his oversized coat.

"Mer's not here," he said in a raspy voice. "He's not here yet. He was supposed to be here. He told me, but he's not here." He shambled away, and his voice faded to mumbles.

Dmitri sniffled, but Thomas quirked an eyebrow. "You really shouldn't act that way toward the people we're defending."

"We're not defending him. His kind are a drain on society." Dmitri reached into his coat and pulled out a shotgun. "Did they say what kind of creature it is?"

"Where's your sword?"

Dmitri groaned. "You guys really need to come into the twenty-first century." He opened his coat and revealed a long thin blade. Like Thomas's weapon, it gleamed light blue from the fairy magic used to enchant it.

"Actually, I was thinking it would be a bad idea to fire that in the middle of the day inside the city limits. The police get annoyed at that."

Dmitri smirked. "Whatever is necessary."

"Command thinks it's an earth dragon."

Dmitri laughed, putting away the shotgun and drawing his sword. "That'll be a story to tell. The legends are awakening, it seems."

"Do they always have to wake up grumpy?"

The crystal pulled Thomas to an aluminum door. It wasn't locked. A pentagram had been spray-painted on. Thomas leaned close and sniffed, but it was only paint, not blood. It had probably come from some fool who didn't realize how much power that symbol could have if done correctly. Of course, no one who knew how to do it right would waste their time painting it so far from ley lines or other sources of power. He opened the door and stepped into the warehouse.

It was little more than a large room with a bare concrete floor. A couple of worn boxes sat in the corner with assorted odds and ends scattered around, the sorts of things a homeless man not entirely right in the head might collect. They probably belonged to that poor fool outside.

The crystal took on a vague gold outline. The creature wasn't here yet, but it would be soon.

Thomas wiggled his fingers in a simple ritual, and the crystal dimmed and cooled. He stuck it in his pocket and drew his own sword. All they could do was wait.

As the seconds stretched to minutes and then to half an hour, Thomas found it difficult to remain alert. Dmitri's stance never wavered, though, and his eyes continually scanned the warehouse. Though he never would've admitted it, Thomas admired the other man. Of all the Unnamed, he was probably the rudest and least likeable, but few would deny he was one of their best.

The ground trembled, sending adrenaline through Thomas. He tried to force down the fear rising in his throat. Cracks spiderwebbed through the concrete, and the middle of the warehouse floor bulged upward.

Dmitri motioned to him, and they moved to opposite sides,

prepared to come at the dragon from two directions as soon as it appeared.

The floor exploded upward in a shower of dust and rocks. A growl that sounded more like a dog than a dragon came from the rubble. When the dust cleared, a reptilian head was rising out of the hole, swiveling back and forth to take in the room.

Thomas and Dmitri charged, each swinging in a wide arc.

The creature's slitted eyes looked at Thomas as he drove his blade at its head. The monster didn't even blink as Thomas hit it. The force of the impact sent pain shooting through his arms. He drew back and gaped. The creature didn't have a mark on it.

Dmitri delivered two other slashes in quick succession, but each strike was as ineffective as the first.

The dragon lashed out at Thomas, but he was already out of the way. The creature climbed the rest of the way out of the hole. Its serpentine head was about five feet long. Then, its scales gave way to orange fur dotted with black spots and a lean, feline body. Its legs ended in cloven hooves.

Thomas cursed.

Dmitri kept his sword between him and the creature while he slowly circled it. "That's no dragon."

It was a hundred times worse than a dragon. A thousand times worse. Dragons had been fought and killed by heroes throughout the ages. It was never easy, but it could be done. This thing, on the other hand...

"That's a questing beast," Thomas said.

"I thought they killed that thing at Camelot a thousand years ago."

"They tried."

Its head darted toward Thomas, but he caught its long teeth on his blade. A clear liquid dripped off its fangs and splashed on the ground. Its rotting breath almost made him gag. Thomas forced his sword up, hoping to cut the soft flesh inside its mouth, but even that was too strong.

Dmitri dashed in and thrust at its body but succeeded only in cutting away a thick tuft of fur. Both men backed away, and the creature hissed.

"How do we kill this thing?"

"The eyes?" Thomas ducked under another attack.

"Are you sure?"

"Not even a little bit."

"Right. I'll be the bait."

Before Thomas could respond, Dmitri charged with a battle cry on his lips. The beast's head turned to him. Thomas drew his dagger and stabbed in the same motion, plunging the blade into the creature's left eye.

The creature roared so loud Thomas thought his head would explode. He pulled back, leaving the dagger embedded in the creature's eye.

Blood spattered on his hand, sizzling on his skin. He tried to shake the blood free of his hand, but it ate a small pit into his flesh, cauterizing the wound as it sank in. A second later, the dagger's hilt fell free. The blade had melted.

The beast turned its lone eye to Thomas. He could practically hear its teeth grinding. It started to move, but Dmitri ran up behind it. He held his sword in both hands and thrust downward as hard as he could. The blade didn't go in, but a patch of blood no bigger than a fingernail spread from the point of impact.

"So you're not invincible," Thomas said under his breath.

The creature turned around and reared. It slammed its hooves into Dmitri, sending him to the ground. His sword slid across the floor and clattered against the wall.

Thomas moved to help, but the beast anticipated his maneuver and rounded on him in time to catch his sword in its teeth. It twisted its head, tearing the blade from Thomas's grasp. Its jaw shifted, and the sword broke in half, releasing a dim flash as its magic dissipated.

"No!"

A loud boom drowned out Thomas' shout. He looked up and saw the shotgun in Dmitri's hands. The other man pumped it and fired again.

The creature twitched, then roared and charged, barreling into Dmitri. It brought its hooves down on him, and Thomas heard a sickening crack.

"So that's a questing beast," a soft voice said. "I always wanted to see one."

Thomas turned to the door and gasped. A child, no more than six years old, stood there with wide eyes. His pale skin seemed to shimmer in a way that wasn't quite human, and his blond hair could have been made from woven gold.

This wasn't just a child. This was *the* child, the one who could see the future, though how he had gotten here, Thomas had no idea.

The beast looked up and roared even louder than when Thomas had stabbed it. It thundered toward the child.

Thomas cursed and threw himself at the creature as it passed, but he bounced off it with no effect. He picked himself up and ran toward Dmitri's sword, but it was too far. In horror he watched as the questing beast neared its new prey.

Then the beggar, who had apparently entered without being seen, stepped in front of the child. He reached into his beer-stained jacket and pulled out a shining sword with a jeweled hilt. He spread his legs wide, holding the sword like a man trained to use it.

Thomas froze and stared as the man sidestepped the creature's charge, slashing as it passed. His blade cut a long line down the monster's flank. It reared, but with another quick slash from the shining sword, its front legs came off. The beast tried to stand, but the stumps couldn't bear its weight, and it crashed to the ground. It lashed out, but the beggar moved like

A BIT OF LUCK

a cat and had no trouble avoiding its attacks. He let out a long breath and shook his head.

"You never fought with me," he said. "Just with Pellinore, Palamedes, and Percival. I always wondered what would happen if we battled."

The monster growled and tried to bite him, but the beggar flicked his blade in an almost casual fashion. The beast's head fell free of its body, a pool of blood spreading on the ground.

The man sheathed his sword and looked at Thomas. For a second his gray eyes and sharp features made him look like a soldier in his prime, but then the image was gone, and only the beggar remained. His gaze moved to Dmitri. The other Unnamed was a bloody mess, and Thomas was sure he was dead.

Then Dmitri groaned, and Thomas rushed to his side. He knelt down and looked at the beggar, who was talking to the child.

"Mer. I knew you would be here. You told me. Now, I need to tell you something."

Dmitri coughed. "What did I tell you? Legends are awakening."

He continued to mumble, but Thomas couldn't make anything of his words.

"I didn't know Morgause was my sister," the beggar continued. "You have to tell me that."

The child nodded. "I will."

"No!" Thomas cried out as it all came together in his head. The questing beast. That sword. Pellinore, Palamedes, and Percival: the names of knights who had been dead for more than a thousand years.

"Mer," Thomas said, not daring to believe what he was about to say. He spoke louder. "You know him. You know Merlin?" He looked at the beggar. "Are you Arthur?"

Arthur looked up. He wore a strangely peaceful smile. "I

told Mer what I was supposed to. Now, everything will be better."

He stepped through the warehouse door. Thomas was about to go after him when Dmitri groaned, drawing his attention. Thomas tore his shirt to make makeshift bandages and called Command.

"It wasn't a dragon," he said after he'd gotten through security and requested aid for Dmitri. "It was a questing beast. The child is here, and he confirmed it."

"The child?" There was stunned silence on the line. "Wait, did you say a questing beast? You killed a questing beast?"

"Negative, it was some guy off the street. I think—" His words caught in his throat. "I think it was Arthur. King Arthur."

The voice on the end of the line sputtered. "Say again."

"We were saved by Arthur Pendragon."

"We thought he might have awakened. Please tell me he didn't speak to the child."

Thomas hesitated, as if by not saying it out loud, he could make it so it had never happened. But it *had* happened. Arthur had spoken to Merlin. Merlin, who aged backward. He could foresee the future because he had lived it, though he had no knowledge of the past.

"Yes. He told the child about Morgause."

The voice on the other side of the phone whimpered. "He... what?"

Morgause had been Arthur's half-sister, but neither had known that at first, and the pair had had a child, Mordred, who had been largely responsible for the fall of Camelot.

Thomas looked at the child, who smiled. The Unnamed had worked for centuries to prevent Merlin from learning any part of Arthur's story before it was time, lest that knowledge change history in unpredictable ways.

"Maybe it won't be so bad," Thomas whispered into the

phone, desperately hoping it was true. But you never could tell when it came to manipulating time.

The crystal in Thomas's pocket went ice-cold. He didn't have to ask Command what that meant. The past had been changed, and that change was rippling through time.

Thomas held his breath as the change overtook him, rewriting the history of the world into one where Camelot had never fallen.

ABOUT THE AUTHOR

Gama Ray Martinez lives near Salt Lake City, Utah, with his wife and kids. He moved there solely because he likes mountains. He collects weapons in case he ever needs to supply a medieval battalion, and he greatly resents when work or other real-life things get in the way of writing. He secretly hopes to one day slay a dragon in single combat and doesn't believe in letting pesky little things like reality stand in the way of dreams.

19

THREE TIMES THE POWER, FOUR TIMES THE PAIN

AKIS LINARDOS

The engine of my chronobike revs up with a machine-gun groan as I twist the rough metal handle and suck a lungful of gasoline air, readying myself to leap through time.

Ba-ba-bup. Ba-ba-bup. Ba-ba-bup.

London's bridge is empty of life, save for the abandoned cars pressed against the sides, hulls cracked and stained with demon blood that reeks like moldy tomatoes. The way the metal shells form a straight path for me to bike across makes me feel like Moses.

"Third time's the charm, eh, Lucy?" I whisper to my chronobike.

She replies with a warm, motherly voice, emitted from the perforated surface on the purple frame . "I'm sure we'll save Sylvia this time, Magnus."

I tap the hull. Her AI is kind enough to melt butter. Ten years ago I'd never imagined myself playing best-buddies with a chronobike. But, well... life happens.

I put on my goggles, and the street ahead turns purple through the lenses, while the crumbled buildings beyond the bridge lay like sandhills of amethyst. "We got the time in our hand. All we need is a bit of luck. Now, eyes on the horizon."

Another twist and the engine revs louder.

Ba-ba-bup. Ba-ba-bup. Ba-ba-bup.

"Off we go," I whisper and charge across the long bridge, the purple lenses showing my blurry visions of flashing lights like trains passing by as cold air whips my face. By the time I reach the end of the bridge, the familiar twist of time-warp nausea knots my stomach.

The crumbled buildings are now erect as if they were just built. Citizens pass along the zebra crossings and Big Bus Tours continue unfettered by time or demons.

Past is present, present is past, and everything is future.

Ready to be remolded for the third time.

∼

Ten minutes later, Lucy and I are in front of Kingston University, where Sylvia works. I dismount and push through a throng of chattering students crowding the entry. I catch a whiff of a pumpkin latte one of the students seems to be holding, and my mind is flooded with warm memories of my first date with Sylvia. Our first date, our first kiss, our first—

The glass of the entry door forms a crack, and moisture suffuses the surface as the air suddenly grows colder.

Shit.

Have we arrived late this time?

I shove the students aside and yank the door open with such force the cracked glass shatters completely and showers me and the nearby students in smithereens. I'm vaguely aware of voices calling me names, and I respond by turning over my shoulder and yelling at them, "Run if you know what's good for you."

My boots smack the wooden floor, echoing through the

large hall. More cracks form with razor-sharp sounds on the glass panels covering the walls. I run across the white-plastered corridors of the uni until I finally reach the biology department. I stop in front of Sylvia's lab. The one where she does her PhD in behavioral neuroscience.

I open without knocking, greeted by the thick smell of iodine and the surprised gasps of students in lab frocks working over a humming centrifuge machine.

Sylvia is among them, and her features contort as if trying to decide between frowning and opening her eyes wide. Knowing her, she's seething at me invading her work space. I wonder if that overwhelms her surprise of seeing gray hair on my temples and the hints of wrinkles around my mouth. Or maybe it's my long blue leather coat that strikes her. Twenty-five-year-old me would never have worn leather.

"Magnus? What?" Her mouth works, but she doesn't produce any more words as I rush to grab her by the wrist and pull her away.

"No time," I say, realizing she'll be further surprised at the aged roughness of my voice, untethered from that of my younger self by a distance of a thousand-or-more cigarettes.

"What happened to you?" she says, but it's a statement, not a question.

"Life," I say, almost surprised at how willing she is to follow me this time.

The first time, I was young and busy with my own studies on quantum physics, too far away to reach her before the invasion began.

The second, I leaped back in time, rushed into Kingston with the chronobike, forming a time-warp right inside the lab. The distortion incited such panic as to disorganize the whole uni, and she was convinced I was some alien that had invaded her boyfriend's body, aging it in the process.

Three Times the Power, Four Times the Pain

She yanks her hand away. "Magnus, what the *hell* is going on? What happened to your voice? Your hair? Your...ear?"

Ah, I forget about the ear. A demon bit it off the second time I was here.

"Trust that I'm the same man you remember. A lot has happened. But I'm here." I cup her hands into my palms. "I will save you this time."

"Save me? From what?"

Another loud glass *crack*.

The floors shudder.

"An earthquake?" she says.

I grasp her wrist again and pull her with me as I fumble for my chronobike keys. "No."

"You're hurting me."

We stumble as the building shudders again, fissures snaking across the wooden floor and up the walls. I produce the chronobike key from my pocket and click the button, summoning Lucy. On the key-screen, the number twenty-six appears, counting down to twenty-five, twenty-four.

The left wall bursts open like an eggshell, and out comes the sledgehammer, hoisted by a muscled black giant three times my size. The giant's jaw is square and black beneath the skull of a goat, teeth clacking and showing pale gums between them.

Sensing Sylvia's knee-jerk reaction, I coil my arm around her and shut her mouth with my palm. "Don't scream. It will only summon more of them."

The giant takes a few slow steps toward us, cocks his head, doglike. *"Distorter. Of. Time?"*

Its voice is like metal grating against metal, and shivers crawl down my spine. "What are you on about, man?" I try to act cool, but my voice is tremulous.

I eye the key. *Five. Four.*

"Time meddlers." The giant hoists his sledgehammer high,

A BIT OF LUCK

ready to crash us. *"Timecrushers."* His breath smells like rat urine.

Three. Two.

"I've no idea what you're saying. Can't we discuss this?"

The sledgehammer forms a downward arc.

One.

Lucy's saw-toothed front wheel crashes through the wall and, with a continuous *crunch*, grinds the goat-head of the demon, scattering bone fragments across the floor.

The giant drops, feet twitching like a squashed cockroach.

The teeth recede from the front wheel, and Lucy lands in front of me.

"Took you a while," I say.

"I came as fast as I could," she replies. Her motherly voice is oddly fitting to the deed, like a bear mangling a predator to protect her cubs.

"Jesus Christ, Magnus. What the f—"

"Yes. It's a lot to take in. I understand. Now climb aboard."

I take the handle, nest on the seat, and pull Sylvia behind me. As I rev up the engine, the sound of crushing walls surrounds us, and skittering creatures swarm the corridor, rushing toward us on long, muscled spider-legs.

∼

Gunning the speed to the maximum, we crush spider-shaped demons beneath the wheels as we rush out of Kingston. The streets are already a parade of calamity harbingers: giants bearing twisted sledgehammers, demon hounds leaping at screaming pedestrians, and vampire-faced bats warping down from wormholes in the sky.

And that goddamn reek of rotten tomatoes.

"Lucy," I say. "We need a long empty street to rush forward

Three Times the Power, Four Times the Pain

in time again. Think the bridge might already have space for it?"

"Unlikely. It will be chaos now. You need to leave the city."

"All right," I say and twist the handles. As I wheel down the streets, I pull out my pistol to shoot at the flailing bat creatures rushing at us. "You all right back there?"

Sylvia is quiet. Then her hand snatches my second pistol from the holster and fires at a bat rushing from my blind side.

"Good shot," I say.

"I c–c–can't believe I did this."

"Not surprised. You always had fire in you."

She puts the pistol back on my holster, and I feel her arms shaking against my ribs.

We're at the edge of London. North Circular Road. Men and women scream desperately as they are torn apart at the hands of demons, the armored police barely managing to protect the children, hailing bullets against the monsters.

Wish I could save them all.

"Are you from the future?" Sylvia says.

"How'd you figure?"

"You said, *rush forward in time*. You look old. You smell different—tobacco, whiskey. Did someone discover time travel?"

"Yes. And that someone put a crack in the world so sharp it made a portal to an adjacent universe. Just so happened the adjacent universe is the embodiment of hell. Figures, right? Just the bit of luck to make all the difference. All the litanies in the world could not armor us from this."

"What happens to you? I mean to the you we leave behind now. I just talked to you this morning. You were so excited about the new developments in your quantum leap experiment. You were—"

She stops talking, and the weighty silence between us becomes so heavy it seems to overwhelm the sounds of calamity. An absence of words so dense it absorbs everything around it.

"Magnus," she says slowly. "What happened today?"

I exhale the weight of the world. "I was on the final round of experiments. A single broken glass marble the size of a thimble in the testing tube. Who'd have thought such a flimsy, tiny thing could do so much damage?"

I gun the engine, crushing through an incoming demon hound. "My machine reoriented all its particles. Perfect alignment to its prior condition. The marble was whole again. For the first time in the known universe, I *reversed* entropy."

Her warm arms coil around my belly. Embrace me tightly. "It's not your fault. You couldn't have known."

"Great-ass excuse. I broke time. And with it, I broke space too."

As we reach the end of the road, a sledgehammer smashes against a car, sharp metal fragments raining over us like hail. It snaps on the chronobike's hull, wrenches between the front wheel and its cover. The bike topples over, leaping in the air, and like a stone skipping over water, it bounces twice along the road, then hurls us off.

Pavement scrapes my knee and elbow, but I grit my teeth against the pain and limp up to one foot, scanning for *her*. By the time I find her, it's all I can do to unsheathe my pistol and fire at the twin bats that are tearing at her belly as I rush to her side.

One bullet. Two. The bats are down, and I'm over her, hoisting her up in my arms as she bleeds all over my chest.

A cold hand seizes my heart. "No. We were so close. So *damn close*. Sylvia, please don't die. *Not again!*"

She reaches out her hand and caresses my cheek. Her mouth works, and I lean closer to hear her whisper, "It's not your fault."

Three Times the Power, Four Times the Pain

∼

I bury her at Epping Forest, by the redolent oakwood trees she loved. The trees beside which we first lay to make love, when we still lived with our parents and had no place to call our own.

"What now?" Lucy says softly as I leave the dirt mound covering the Sylvia of this timeline behind. Another Sylvia I failed to save.

I place my hand on Lucy's hull, feeling the warm hum of the quantum engine within.

"We try again," I say, putting on my goggles and climbing on board. "As many times as it takes."

Ahead of me, the trees are purple pillars with iridescent leaves. And the chronobike's engine revs up with a machine-gun groan as I twist the rough metal handle.

Ba-ba-bup. Ba-ba-bup. Ba-ba-bup.

ABOUT THE AUTHOR

Akis is a writer of bizarre things, a biomedical AI scientist, and maybe a human. He's also a Greek who hops across countries as his career and exploration urges demand. Find his fiction at Apex, Dread Machine, the Martian, and visit his website https://linktr.ee/akislinardos for other dark surprises.

20

ENTROPY RANCH
KEVIN J. ANDERSON

Dallas Morning News, May 20

"A single-engine plane collided with a DC-10 jet during takeoff from DFW airport Tuesday, killing 93 people. The pilot of the Cessna 172, Lawrence Stilwell, 42, of Dallas, apparently received conflicting instructions from the control tower and was unable to avoid the collision. The crash killed Stilwell and 92 passengers on the DC-10."

< pause > < rewind > < play timeloop B >

Dallas Morning News, May 20

"A single-engine plane narrowly missed collision with a DC-10 jet during takeoff at DFW airport Tuesday. Looking shaken, the pilot of the Cessna 172, Larry Stilwell, told reporters after the incident, 'It was real close. I got clearance from the tower the same time the jet did.' This is the third such near miss in four months at DFW, and the National Transportation Safety Board plans to investigate. 'I paused for just a second,' Stilwell said. 'Somebody had put one of those religious pamphlets on my pilot seat, and I took the troubleKevin J. Anderson to throw it away. Maybe it was a miracle, or maybe just a coincidence. You tell me.'"

Green-uniformed bellmen hovered around the hotel entrance, ready to pounce on anyone carrying luggage. Jersey glanced again through the angled glass of the revolving doors. If the shuttle-bus didn't come soon, he'd be late getting to the Dallas Convention Center.

He dutifully snapped open his briefcase to check the sheafs of Grovemont Industrial Gloves leaflets, computer printouts of permeability characteristics, and a stack of business cards held together by a red rubber band. Killing time.

Jersey withdrew the Hi! My Name Is: badge from the conference and pinned it on. They had gotten the first name wrong, again. Edmond Jersey, not Edward Jersey! Why did people always assume that someone named "Ed" was a -ward and not a -mond?

It would have felt so good to shout at the convention registration clerk, but Jersey calmed any such response before it could jump out of his mouth. Another dagger-headache threatened to take center stage in his brain pan. It was their mistake, not his, right? Jersey had taken the badge in silence as he wandered off into the vast convention center crowded with other industrial hygienists, posters, and exhibits.

Now, the following morning, he sat waiting in the hotel lobby. The A shuttle bus supposedly showed up every fourteen minutes; he had been sitting there for eleven.

With a snap of his wrist, he dusted a comb through his thinning brown hair and adjusted his tie. Jersey still didn't feel comfortable in a suit, but he did his best to keep up the corporate image. The conference schedule had some interesting papers being presented in the third session, but

A BIT OF LUCK

Jersey would have to man the display table in the Exhibit Room. Time to pay his dues, to banter statistics, to coax new customers, and to give the good old Grovemont Gloves cheer.

He pressed his briefcase shut and stood up, brushing the seat of his pants. *Better wait outside,* he thought. He eased his way through the revolving door under the Hilton's wide awning. One of the green-uniformed bellmen moved toward him, but Jersey ignored him.

When the shuttle-bus had missed its scheduled rounds by a full minute, Jersey scowled, but he quelled the annoyance. *It doesn't matter. Damned if I'm going to be an ulcer candidate before I turn thirty-three.*

But the conference did start promptly at eight. He looked at his watch again.

One of the fat yellow buses pulled up to the curb with a groan of brakes. Jersey hustled toward it until he saw the bright "D" in its window. Wrong shuttle. With an effort, he made his face become calm again. He wouldn't risk bringing on another dizzy spell. They had been getting worse and worse over the past month, and Jersey didn't want to look like a fool by fainting to the sidewalk in front of everyone.

The traffic light changed at the corner, and other cars came flooding past the hotel. He could hear the D bus revving up. Its doors hissed shut, like a monster gobbling prey. The muggy air smelled of oily exhaust.

Bright blue-mirrored skyscrapers clustered around the downtown, peeking over the older buildings that still remained like fossils in limestone. Across the street from the Hilton stood a three-story-high Cokesbury Bible bookstore, flanked on either side by a pawn shop and "ABC Bail Bonds—Guaranteed!" Jersey smirked. Here, in the very midriff of the Bible Belt filled with this "holier than you-all" attitude, what God-fearing Texan could ever possibly need "Bail Bonds Guaranteed"?

Entropy Ranch

Out of the corner of his eye, he saw a plump fiftyish woman. She wore a baggy print dress that obliterated all sexual details, and under one arm she carried a stack of printed leaflets. Her face bore a beatific yet militant smile that said "The Lord is my Shepherd, and don't you forget it, buster!"

Jersey looked away quickly, trying to avoid her gaze, but she came toward him anyway. At another time he might have bantered with her, but not this morning—he had to save his rhetoric for potential customers, not waste it on a salvation zombie. He made up his mind to cross the street and look in the window of the pawn shop until the bus came.

He didn't look, didn't pay attention to where he was going as he flashed a glance behind him at the woman. The street seemed clear, and he clutched his briefcase as he scuttled around and in front of the waiting D bus, directly into the path of the second bus swerving around.

Jersey turned, had time to gawk at the giant yellow-and-black wall of metal slamming into him. He felt his nerves suddenly disconnect, as if short-circuited. No pain came into his head, but he sensed dozens of bones breaking at once—his arms, his rib cage, his skull. Then his vision turned all red, as if his eyes were filling with blood from the inside.

< pause > < rewind > < play timeloop B >

Out of the corner of his eye, Jersey saw a plump, fiftyish woman dressed in a baggy print dress. Under one arm she carried a stack of printed leaflets.

He quickly tried to avoid her gaze, but she came stumping toward him anyway. *Oh, not this morning!* he thought, wondering if he could dodge back into the hotel. He flicked his eyes back and forth. It might be easier to go across the street, stand by the pawn shop—a good Christian lady would never be seen by a sinful establishment, would she? Jersey made up his mind instantly.

"Wait!" she called. "The world is coming to an end!"

A BIT OF LUCK

He turned his head and quipped back, "Yes, and I have soooooo much to do before it does! Can't stand around talking!"

Hah! Got off a zinger! He snickered and skipped out into the street, directly in front of the accelerating D bus. He missed the curb, stumbled, and pinwheeled his arms, trying to back up. Jersey saw the bus driver's head turned away, chatting with one of the passengers. Jersey dropped his briefcase. The giant vehicle looked like a prehistoric monster rearing up as it struck and rolled over him.

< pause > < rewind > < play timeloop C >

"Wait!" she called, "The world is coming to an end!"

Jersey groaned to himself. Couldn't she see that he didn't want to Know the Lord at eight o'clock in the morning? He scuttled toward the street. Maybe if he cut across against the traffic, she'd give up and seek easier prey.

The street seemed clear. The D bus began to move, lurching forward as it gained momentum. The woman hurried desperately, reaching out to clutch his arm and scattering a few of her leaflets on the sidewalk.

Startled, Jersey looked at her hand on his arm and glared at her. "Do you mind?"

The woman seemed surprised at her own action and quickly released him, abashed. "I . . . I'm sorry, sir. Sometimes I get a little carried away in the service of the Lord. I just wanted to have a word with you."

"Kindly keep your words to yourself." He didn't like someone intruding upon his morning. Now he'd probably be annoyed for hours.

He stepped off the curb, almost walking into the D bus as it passed. The bus driver honked at him in annoyance, then pulled out into the traffic.

With relief, Jersey saw the A shuttle-bus arrive in a hissing of air-brakes and a belch of oily smoke. The missionary woman dropped back, and he was surprised she gave up so easily.

But as he grabbed the rail of the bus, Jersey felt a painful blackness swimming up between his ears, like a crowbar on his temples. A deep-seated sickness clawed its way from his heart and his solar plexus. He thought he was going to vomit. Disorienting pain burst from all the nerve endings in his brain.

Oh, not here, not here!

He slumped and sat down heavily on the steps of the bus. His face turned a discolored white, like a melted vanilla milkshake.

"Hey man!" the bus driver said.

The missionary woman stood over him, looking astounded and concerned. She moved quickly, holding his chin, peeling his eyelids back and staring at his eyes, his pupils. She held his wrist as an expert would, taking his pulse. With the back of her hand, she felt his forehead.

Then all the pain and dizziness passed, as it usually did. The woman's appearance changed, a mask dropping back into place. She returned to her role as a formless old Bible-thumper. "There, there," she said. "Maybe you'd best just go lie down?"

Jersey thrust her away and stood up again, blinking and embarrassed. "Just moved too fast, that's all. Now please leave me alone."

She frowned, but dropped back. Jersey made his way to an empty seat. He closed his eyes and breathed deeply, in and out, as the bus pulled away from the hotel.

~

Jersey tugged his tie loose as he fumbled for the hotel room key in the pocket of his slacks. *Thus ends another typical day at the convention.* The suit jacket hanging over his arm steamed with perspiration in the afternoon heat. The Hilton had no swimming pool, only a couple of hot tubs on the roof—ninety-five frigging degrees outside, and they had a hot tub.

Inside, the maid had shut off the air conditioner. He tossed his jacket on the bed. Jersey rubbed his temples, feeling the aftermath of hour upon hour at the Grovemont Gloves booth. He arranged and rearranged the colorful brochures. He plied the customers like an old carny huckster, holding forth his computer printouts of comparative permeability characteristics as if they were sacred scrolls. During a self-imposed break, Jersey wandered around the other exhibits, picking up a plethora of free pens, kitchen magnets, key chains. The spoils of war.

Jersey unbuttoned his shirt. Tonight, the conference would be having their banquet—Texas-style barbecue, of course. He could find dozens of better barbecue places up and down the street, within walking distance from the hotel. But he had come to the conference to enjoy himself—and everybody else would be going to the banquet.

Then he noticed the neat white envelope on the bed, propped against the pillow.

For a moment, he felt a touch of amused annoyance. Probably one of those "thank you for staying at the Hilton" cards. He snatched up the note, then sat on the bed, puzzled.

The letterhead said simply, Entropy Ranch. His mind pondered the ludicrous notion, as if redneck Texas ranchers concerned themselves with "entropy." The note was handwritten, careful and neat, and made out to him personally. The paper itself smelled of faint perfume.

Dear Mr. Jersey,

We would like very much for you to visit us this afternoon. We are concerned about the dizzy spell you had this morning on the bus. This is not a sales pitch—it's a personal invitation extended to you alone. Please take the time to come.

No signature. The only other thing he found in the envelope was a map.

~

The teeming madness of the Dallas freeway system finally fell behind, and all of Texas seemed to spread out in front of him. Ranch houses, fields, the roadside dotted with mesquite, corn flowers, and occasional stands of live oak and cottonwood. He drove with one hand on the steering wheel of the rental car, one hand holding the sketched directions.

How the hell had they known? Jersey didn't know whether he felt more amazed or frightened. It took him nearly an hour and a half to get to the last turnoff, a thin unpaved road branching off from a county highway—unmarked, and not much different from similar roads he had been passing for a dozen miles.

The rental car trundled along the gravel, raising dust. Jersey glanced at the odometer, ticking off seven-tenths of a mile as mentioned on the map. An alfalfa field spread out on either side, heavily overgrown with weeds. The unpaved drive hooked around a slight view-blocking hill, and then Jersey saw a barbed-wire fence and an ornate wrought-iron gate. Red-brick posts flanked the gate on either side.

Down the driveway, a large, well-kept farmhouse towered like something out of a Faulkner novel. Three cottonwood trees spread voluminous boughs in a protective shell around the house.

Jersey pulled the car to a stop outside the gate. He took his keys and stepped out of the car. How did they know? Why did they pick him? What did they have in mind?

Barbed wire stretched out for half a mile in either direction, enclosing nothing of significance, as far as Jersey could see. Several signs hung from the fence, alternating between KEEP

OUT and NO TRESPASSING, in a typical Texan welcome. On the iron gate a small metal plate bore only the plain engraved words, Entropy Ranch.

Jersey stood on the metal slats of the cattle guard under the gate and punched the intercom button mounted in one of the posts. "Excuse me? My name is Edmond Jersey. I . . . received a note."

A filtered drawling voice drifted up from the speaker. "Yes, Mr. Jersey. Please come on up to the house." The lock on the gate clicked open electronically. "You can leave your car where it's at. We're not expecting nobody else."

Uneasy, Jersey pushed open the gate and entered. His dress slacks were starting to get dusty. He strode up toward the house and paused, but forced himself not to turn back, as the gate swung shut behind him. He wiped sweat from his forehead.

When he reached the farmhouse, Jersey noticed a thin Black woman reclining on a porch swing in the shade of the cottonwood trees. She stood up, smiling, as he approached. She wore a crisp white lab coat over worn blue jeans. She had soft, wide eyes, high cheekbones, and a hard smile. Her hair was cropped close to her head.

"Welcome, Mr. Jersey. I'm pleased to meet you after all this time. I am Lilith Semper." As she extended her hand, he noticed that she wore no rings, that her nails were clipped close to the fingertip and scrubbed clean. Her voice was cool, educated.

"You sent me an invitation and I came," he said, sounding more impatient than he wanted to. He calmed himself; he'd already had the mother of all dizzy spells today, and did not wish to experience another. "Now what's this all about?"

Lilith Semper smiled invitingly. "Step inside. We've already saved your life twice today, but we'd like to check out a few things, if you don't mind."

Before he could mutter a baffled question, she opened the front door of the farmhouse.

Inside the house's facade stood glass double-doors, behind which sprawled great banks of computers, clean white walls, and giant viewscreens the size of picture windows. Cold, dry air came out at him, heavily air-conditioned to shield computer units from the humid heat. Jersey counted five other technicians within sight, moving, checking instruments.

Lilith Semper startled him by placing a hand on his elbow. "Come on inside—have a look around. This is Entropy Ranch."

He followed her across the threshold between the two doors. He stepped on a square of sticky gray material that grabbed the soles of his shoes.

"For the dust," she explained. Then, from a bin in the foyer, Lilith pulled out plastic booties—instinctively, he scanned for the Grovemont label—and slid one set over her own shoes. She reached into a locker and handed him a stiff lab coat that smelled of bleach. Jersey shrugged into the lab coat and worked the plastic coverings over his shoes. He forced himself not to say anything. She waited for him, then opened the second set of doors.

On one wall, the large viewscreen simulated a detailed sequence of an airplane collision. Most of the technicians stood by a monitor that showed three children trapped in the blazing interior of a burning house. A screen on the far wall, partially hidden behind a bank of control panels, displayed the scenario of some kind of bus accident. Near the door, a police scanner crackled and occasionally spat out a string of words. A notepad and a dot-matrix printer sat beside the scanner on the same table.

Jersey swallowed, feeling a thickness in his throat. A dull ache began to pry at his temples again. Movie special effects? No, that wasn't it. Actual film? Or detailed accident simulations ... What kind of morbid interests did these people have?

Lilith Semper gripped his upper arm. "I know what you're going to ask, Mr. Jersey. But wait a second—let it all sink in."

He continued to stare. One of the technicians, a freckle-faced and sunburnt young man, smiled at Jersey knowingly, then turned back to the freeze-frame image of the burning house. Jersey could see the gruesome detail, the graphic portrayal of the children dying in the fire. The sunburnt technician spoke to his companions, who seemed to be pondering deeply.

"It's time travel, Mr. Jersey," Lilith leaned over and said into his ear.

Startled by her voice, it took him a moment to realize what she had said. "What?"

"We can go back to change the past, or the future, depending on how you want to look at it. As I said, we've already saved your life twice today."

She took his arm and steered him toward the back of the room. The buzzing sounds of the air-exchangers began to make Jersey dizzy. "I'm sorry we have to show you like this—it'll be unpleasant, sure enough. But if I can convince you at the outset, we'll save us a lot of doubts later on."

She took him to the large screen showing the bus accident. As he looked at the image of the yellow shuttle bus, Jersey felt a chill creep inside him. It looked too familiar. He could recognize the front of the Hilton; he thought he even recognized the shadowy bus driver behind the windshield. But the mangled pedestrian under the bus tires—

"Rerun timeloop 0804 A," Lilith said to the attending technician, then turned to Jersey. "We can stop this at any time, if it disturbs you too much."

A new scene appeared, then began to move: the bus arrived, people stood in front of the Hilton. Jersey watched in horror as he came into view, looking around, distracted. Then the missionary woman walked up to him. He tried to escape across the street, and stepped in front of the bus.

Jersey did not even think to cover his eyes.

"That's our original attempt. We tried to stop it from happening, but we weren't aggressive enough at first. We have to change as little as possible each time, you see."

A new tape played. Jersey appeared on the screen again, the missionary woman came, they bantered, he snickered and tried to dash across the street—and, again, the bus struck him. But Lilith froze the image on the screen before the picture could actually show his death.

"Have faith, Mr. Jersey," she said with a beatific smile. "We'll tell you everything, of course."

Jersey felt beads of sweat standing on his forehead, dampening his hair. The inside of his skull began to throb. He took several deep breaths, forcing the nausea away. Not another dizzy spell.

She patted him on the shoulder, failing to comfort him. "It'll be fine now. We just go back in time and do a little tweaking, here and there, to prevent such tragedies from happening."

"But...why?" Stupid question! Nothing else came to mind.

Lilith Semper looked at him with a confident smile. "Why, it's our Christian duty."

She seemed ready to defend her assertion, but Jersey refused to take his eyes from the image on the screen—the expression on his reflected face, the oncoming bus, the deadly impact hanging only a second away.

"But how can you change what's already happened? Isn't it set in stone? If time is . . ." He faltered, not sure what he wanted to say.

Lilith stiffened, and her voice carried a sudden sharp edge. "We are Baptists here, Mr. Jersey, not Calvinists. If you want to talk about predestination, you'll have to find a Presbyterian."

She scowled, but before Jersey could understand how he had insulted her, Lilith's expression softened again. "If you feel up to it, let me show you something, like a demonstration."

Jersey fought down his unsteadiness as she led him to the screen displaying the burning house. He could see toys littered about, a pair of bunk beds and an extra twin bed on the opposite side. One set of sheets had begun to smolder. The boy's form underneath sprawled half out on the floor, but he lay motionless. One girl retched on her knees, choking and screaming; her hair caught fire. The girl in the upper bunk lay mercifully still, apparently strangled by the thick smoke. The paint on a small blue rocking chair in the corner bubbled away from the wood.

Jersey glanced at Lilith. Her eyes glistened with tears, but her voice came out strong and angry. "Meet Tammy, Cindy, and their brother, Brett. The door is locked. You see, Tammy, Cindy, and Brett forgot to come home before six this evening. They were playing down by the creek, catching crawdads and waterbugs. They lost track of time, that's all. But they . . . they came home late, and all muddy, and their daddy got angry. Ten swats for each one of them, and then to their room with no supper." She drew a deep breath, then blew it out slowly. "He locked them in while he went off to play softball.

"We don't know how the fire started yet. The children are going to be killed—they already have been killed—but how can we just leave them? What kind of world can let that happen?" Lilith stared at him as if demanding an answer.

"Now, by changing a few parameters, we might be able to save them. We can influence precursor events so that this tragedy does not happen.

"Ethically, we have to interfere as little as possible to achieve our results. We don't want to damage the future. We have developed our own rules, set ourselves a time limit of ten 'subjective' hours to fix a disaster. You see, if we go back only an

Entropy Ranch

hour or two, it shouldn't set up significant ripples in future events. But the longer we wait, the greater a chance for a backlash. You must have heard plenty of stories about time-travel paradoxes."

She fell silent for a moment, almost brooding. "That means if we can't find a way to save these children soon, they're gonna die like this, in flames."

Jersey stared at the screen, mulling over Lilith's words. "What do you mean, subjective hours? And how can you sit here and manipulate events—once you change something, then it never really did occur, so how can you know about it. I mean . . . this is confusing."

"Believe me, Mr. Jersey, all of us here have studied paradoxes until our heads spin. We're safe because we're in this place, Entropy Ranch. Within the boundaries of our fence is a sheltered area, like an island in the timestream. All timelines come here, ripple around, and move on. We can reach in, stir the waters where we like, and watch what happens."

She shrugged. "We've got operatives on the outside, like the lady who distracted you this morning. These operatives change little things, interact in tiny ways, and we observe from here. Sometimes we have to do it over and over again until we achieve what we want.

"For instance, maybe we'll have someone give the daddy a rose on his way home from work, get him in a better mood when he sees his kids getting home late and muddy. Maybe then he won't lock the door, and they'll be able to get out of there. That's the type of thing I'm talking about."

"But why did you pick me? What have I ever done for you?"

Lilith shrugged, and somehow that infuriated him. "Entropy Ranch is just starting out—we need test cases, success stories. Right now we can only respond to local accidents, whatever we pick up on the Dallas-Fort Worth police radio.

"We heard on the scanner that you were killed in an

accident this morning. We thought we could fix it. We sent one of our operatives to the scene and, after three attempts, finally managed to distract you long enough so you didn't step in front of that bus. You were very persistent about being killed, Mr. Jersey."

Her eyes took on a passion. Jersey could feel her perspiration as she gripped his hand. "Think of it—we can eliminate awful fires like this, prevent plane crashes, terrorist attacks, stop all those stupid accidents that"—she faltered, then pushed on—"that needlessly claim so many lives. We can do something about it, even after it's happened.

"But we need to know the effects of what we do. We need to study you, Mr. Jersey, because after we had changed time to save your life, you suddenly collapsed on the bus. What did we do to you—have you uncovered some very peculiar side effect? We have to know before we go on. That's why we broke our secrecy and called you here."

Lilith led him away from the image of the burning house. "The techs need to get on back to work. Come over here—I want you to meet someone." She motioned to one of the other workers.

The man was thin enough that the lab coat sagged around him like a discarded skin, but he moved with an effeminate grace. His silvery gray hair had been swirled and molded with generous amounts of hair oil. A braided bolo tie hung around his neck, secured by a garish lump of turquoise.

She introduced them. "This here is Dr. Barens. And Mr. Edmond Jersey."

Automatically, Jersey extended his hand. Barens shook it and then took his cue, moving over to the third screen, which still showed the image of Jersey on the verge of death. "We want to check you out, Jersey. Maybe we set up some backlash when we sidestepped you from your appointed meeting with death."

Barens called up a file from the terminal. The image on the

screen dissolved and returned to show Jersey climbing the steps of the shuttle-bus. The missionary woman chased after him. Suddenly, the other Jersey's expression turned gray and waxen. He stumbled against the railing, sinking to the bus steps. The missionary woman hurried up, looking professional now, feeling his pulse, checking under his eyelids.

"We've never seen anything like your attack before," Barens continued. "It looks serious, and we want to check it out, to see if our tweaking caused some unexpected physical response."

Jersey chuckled a little to himself. "You're both jumping to conclusions. That was just one of my dizzy spells—I've been having them for a month. I doubt they have anything to do with your, er, activities. Not unless you've been 'rescuing' me since April."

Lilith Semper's face wore an almost comically shocked expression. Barens himself cringed, as if stunned. The noise of the air exchangers grew to a loud buzzing as Jersey felt the other techs in the room fall quiet. Some of them watched him openly; others glanced out of the corners of their eyes.

"We never did consider that, Lilith," Barens mumbled. She pursed her lips and finally turned to Jersey but continued to speak to the doctor. "Then we got to find out what's wrong with him anyway. It's our Christian duty to help, remember?

"Mr. Jersey, won't you please go with Dr. Barens and give him complete details of your symptoms? He may want to do some tests after all."

Barens reacted uncertainly, but Lilith glared at him. The doctor motioned Jersey out another set of double doors into a small sitting room. Barens began to interrogate him in detail about the history and background of his dizzy spells. About halfway through the discussion, the doctor grew concerned enough to start taking notes.

Jersey fidgeted on the sofa as Barens sat in silence. The doctor got to his feet, concentrating on his notes and his thoughts. "Wait here," he said and began to walk back toward the main control room.

"Bullshit!" Jersey said. "I want to know what's going on."

"All right, come on then."

Lilith Semper watched them, hopeful. She raised her eyes, waiting for the doctor to speak. At the other viewscreen, the technicians working on the burning house scenario chattered to themselves about a possible solution. "Well?" she asked.

"His symptoms are pretty clear, but I can't tell how serious it is without different equipment." He continued, as if intentionally ignoring Jersey. "You know, I'm supposed to put in a thousand qualifiers that say 'maybe' and 'possibly' and 'some symptoms suggest'—it's standard bedside manner. But the patient never listens to them anyway, so why bother? I think it's either an aneurysm or a brain tumor. But I'd need a CAT scan to verify it. We're not set up for that kind of sophisticated stuff here—this isn't a medical research lab, you know."

Lilith looked stricken and turned an ashamed expression at Jersey, but he felt too sickened himself to answer. Finally he muttered, "I've got to get out of here."

"He's right," Barens agreed. "If this has been going on for a month, then he should get himself into a hospital soon."

Lilith looked around in anguish for support from the other technicians, but they rapidly turned their heads away. "But we can't let him go. Not now!"

∽

Jersey, Dr. Barens, and Lilith Semper joined the technicians in the large dining room. Stripped of their lab coats, the people took on a more relaxed air. Lilith helped some of the techs bring in empty bowls, baskets of bread, and two large pots containing green or red chili. Dr. Barens brought him a can of cold beer, and Jersey savored it.

"This is a dry county we're in, but somebody runs in to Dallas once a month to pick up a couple cases of Pearl." Barens sighed. "We can't be expected to sacrifice ol' demon alcohol for science or for God, you know."

Three of the places remained empty as they all sat down. "Somebody had another idea to save the children," Lilith said. "Not much time left, so they couldn't take a meal break."

She opened up the windows, and the sound of grasshoppers came from outside. Everyone sat quiet for a moment. Jersey reached for the basket of bread. Then Lilith started intoning a prayer, which grew to several minutes in length.

Jersey had little appetite. Aneurysm. Brain tumor. Possibly malignant—fatal. Now he felt angry and helpless, upset at the people of Entropy Ranch. He should be back in a Dallas hospital, undergoing real tests, seeing what the best medical techniques could do to save him. Instead, they wanted to keep him here for a couple of days—"We don't have the facilities for more than a blood test and some other high-school chemistry experiments"—where he would only grow worse, hour after hour.

When Lilith Semper finished her rambling prayer, and the others had echoed "Amen," the technicians began to serve themselves, ladling out chili and breaking off chunks of bread.

"The green is hot, the red is milder," Dr. Barens said in his thin voice.

Jersey took a small bowl of the red chili, sniffing it suspiciously. "Since I already know too much for you to ever let me get out alive," he said, "why don't you tell me how you managed to put this little research facility out here without anybody knowing about it."

"Oh, Mr. Jersey," Lilith said, "don't you be so melodramatic."

"Am I?"

She took a spoonful of chili and followed it with a bite of

corn bread. "Entropy Ranch, this entire giant project, is funded by one of the better-known TV evangelists. Don't look so surprised. We're taking that money and turning it to the benefit of all of us, as God wants us to do. Our scientists were able to do work with a more open mind than all them party-line physicists, and they found a different way to look at relativity. You see, our people start out with the assumption that miracles can happen, and they look for an explanation. Most other researchers break their backs proving that things are impossible, not possible. Our engineers came up with a way to map the timestreams, and once you get to seeing something, it's a relatively simple step to manipulate it.

"So, rather than just learning from our mistakes, we can now go back and fix them in the first place. Just like we saved you this morning. Love one another, strive for peace, do unto others, and turn the other cheek. Those are all admirable goals, aren't they?"

"No other reason, huh? No profit? No glory?"

"No publicity whatsoever. Now that we have the technology, how can we not use it to help other people?"

Jersey ate his chili, keeping a sour expression on his face. "Well, I thank you for saving me—but if you don't mind, I'd best be saving myself. Get to a hospital, you know?"

"We're trying, Jersey," Dr. Barens interrupted. "But we need a little time to work out some technical difficulties."

"What's to stop me from just leaving? Are you going to force me to stay? Whatever happened to Christian charity and doing all that stuff unto others?"

Lilith sighed and met his eyes with a sympathetic expression. Barens pushed himself away from the table and went into the kitchen to get Jersey another beer.

"It's easy to get into the Ranch," she explained, "because all timestreams converge here. But we're reaching out, manipulating dozens of different futures that all intersect right here and then branch off in their own directions, swirling around the fenceline. At the moment, our most crucial problem is to save the children in the burning house, and we may have to try something desperate, something unorthodox." Her dark eyes went distant for a moment, then she stared back at him.

"But bear in mind that we are working for your best interests. Give us time to put everything straight. We can set you back down at a point in time that everybody'll see as 'this afternoon.' Nobody will even notice you've been gone."

Jersey still felt indignant. "You're going to erase my memory or something?"

Lilith lowered her eyes. "We would like to hypnotize you for our own protection, but that needs your complete cooperation. If you choose not to cooperate, well—we are Christians, you know, and we do prefer to think the best of people."

He ate the last of his chili and concentrated wholeheartedly on finishing the beer.

"We'd like you to stay in our guest house tonight."

∼

Jersey lay back on the unfamiliar bed, listening to it creak as he moved. He could see the oak bedposts in the moonlight that came through the window. A sluggish breeze stirred the curtain, but Jersey felt sweaty and uncomfortable. Though they had provided him with a pair of light cotton pajamas, he preferred to sleep in his own underwear.

How long did they really want to keep him there? He closed his eyes, turned his thoughts inward—he could sense the alien presence of something growing inside his head, like a parasite. Even if they put him back a day into the past, the tumor would still have grown a day's worth in his "subjective" time or the aneurysm would have worsened. If he could only get to a hospital.

Outside, crickets thrummed, but otherwise the ranch seemed quiet, asleep. He got up and crept to the door, certain he would find it locked—but the door swung open, revealing the small sitting room in the guest house. No guards either. These people were absurd in their trust. Feeling exposed, he slipped back into the bedroom and pulled on his slacks, holding the car keys and coin purse in his pocket to keep them from jingling.

How could he possibly benefit by waiting? His life lay on the line, after all, not theirs. It seemed an ironic denial of their own Christian charity. They couldn't do anything for him here —they said as much. Holding him for an extra day or two was just a stalling routine. Pointless. Maybe an extra day would make the difference for him in a real hospital, if things were as serious as Dr. Barens suggested.

He buttoned his shirt and took a deep breath. What would they do if they caught him trying to escape? Not that it mattered—he had to try. He pushed open the screen door, careful not to let it slam, and stood on the porch. Just to his right, the tall white farmhouse blotted out the stars, surrounded by the black masses of giant cottonwood trees. He saw lights on inside, a thin figure silhouetted in the window; it looked like Lilith Semper, watching. But, standing in the bright room, she would not be able to see him.

He paused, listening and waiting. He expected some kind of security, but he'd seen no evidence of dogs, not even the typical ranch-hand German shepherd wandering the grounds. None of the doors were locked. *We are Christians, you know, and we prefer to think the best of people.* He wondered if they'd be interested in buying some nice swampland in Florida.

Jersey began to walk down the drive, walking on the grass to avoid crunching the gravel. His heart beat heavily, and he drew air in short, quick breaths. He moved faster, but forced control on himself, making sure he didn't run in panic.

Down at the bottom of the hill, he neared the wrought-iron gate, but he stopped, suspicious. If anything, the gate might trigger an alarm or tied to a motion sensor. If he was going to have to climb over the wrought-iron, he might just as well scramble through the barbed wire instead.

Jersey saw the outline of his rental car on the opposite side of the gate, and that reassured him. If they had truly meant to keep him trapped, they would have moved the car first thing. This was laughably easy—did they want him to leave?

He waded through the weedy alfalfa until he came to the barbed-wire fence. Jersey had made up his mind that he wouldn't tell anyone—explaining Entropy Ranch would be too awkward, and he did owe Lilith Semper that much, for saving his life the first time. Turn the other cheek, and all that.

With a last glance at the spectral silhouette of the ranch house, he pried the strands of barbed wire apart and, careful not to snag his slacks, he climbed through—

—and landed in the middle of the burning bedroom. Flames licked at the side of a child's rocking chair. Clotted smoke in the air blurred the outlines of a pair of bunk beds and an extra twin bed. Stunned disorientation made him lose his balance as intense heat blasted him, singeing the hair on his arms and head and scouring the insides of his nostrils. He whirled, staggered back, but the barbed wire fence, the ranch house, all had vanished, leaving only an impenetrable bedroom wall.

How could he have fallen into a different timeline? His eyes filled with water and then, it seemed, with steam. He dropped to his knees. When he drew in a deep breath to scream, the hot air scorched his lungs

If he died, would the people at Entropy Ranch know where to look? Would they come back to rescue him again? Then sick despair slammed into him with double force. Their ten-hour time limit to save the children had expired—Lilith Semper wouldn't look at all.

Or had they somehow set this up for him? Was this the "something desperate, something unorthodox" plan Lilith Semper had concocted? Because they had saved him once today, did that give them the right to throw him into this?

Jersey lurched to his feet, pawing his hands in front of him. The fire roared, blistering in the air. He could smell the awful reek of incinerating wood, plastic, paint. The door would be locked; he knew it was locked.

And then, in deeper horror, he saw the three children. The boy Brett sprawled half out of his bed, stricken down while trying to escape. One girl lay motionless in the upper bunk; the other girl was coughing on the floor.

He would not refuse to help them, just to spite Lilith Semper if she was watching. Edmond Jersey could Do Unto Others as well as anyone else. His anger made him want to curse Lilith, but it wasn't worth wasting precious seconds. Recklessly, he yanked at the girl on the upper bunk as he dragged the other girl to her feet. He jerked the comforters off the beds, then slapped the boy several times, rousing him from his unconsciousness.

"Come on! Come on!" He tossed the thick comforter around himself and the motionless girl. He blanketed the other two children and hustled them along with him.

Jersey's brown hair seemed to be flaking off in silky ash, and his face burned, raw. He did not hesitate as he savagely kicked at the door with his heel.

The door shuddered in its frame, and he stepped back to kick again. He felt something crack in his leg, but wood splintered around the doorknob. He struck out one last time, and the wood around the lock bolt shattered to pieces. The door swung open to another sequence of the inferno.

The hallway looked alien, filled with a jungle of flames.

Never having been in the house before, Jersey hadn't the slightest idea where he was—he couldn't even tell if they were upstairs or downstairs. They could never get out that way.

He didn't blink, but lowered his head and pulled the comforter around him as a shield. "Out! We have to get out!" Jersey held tightly to Brett and the girl Tammy as Cindy choked and cried. She sobbed and almost fell to her knees again, but he jabbed her in the ribs and shouted harshly. "Dammit! Cry later!"

He pulled them back into the room. Opening the door had been a mistake. Stupid, Jersey! On the opposite wall of the bedroom, a small window stood partially covered by the frame of the bunk bed. That would have to do. He hoped they weren't on the second floor.

He had to let go of the children. Cindy managed to stay on her feet, but the other two children slid to their knees, choking. Jersey burned his hands as he picked up the small rocking chair, but he smashed it through the window. A crossdraft roared through the room, sucking heat along with it.

Jersey heard noises outside—axes splintering wood, shattering glass. He pushed Brett toward the window blindly. The boy crawled over the frame, cutting himself on the glass but seeming not to notice. Jersey turned to drag Tammy to the window without watching Brett disappear.

He had to wrestle the girl up to the sill. She squirmed, just moving and not cooperating. On the floor behind him, Cindy continued to cry. He could hear her even over the roar of the fire.

Tammy fell to the ground. Jersey saw a glimpse of Brett managing to crawl away across the lawn.

Then he saw moving figures, like monsters from outer space. Echoes of stray thoughts ricocheted through his head. *Is my life flashing before me?* After he had broken open the door, the heat in the room had grown ten times worse. The comforter on his back burst into flames. He could not breathe at all anymore. He needed oxygen, but he felt his lungs burn. He couldn't see anything right.

But he still needed to get Cindy out the window. Jersey could barely move—every step pushed the hot wind against his face. His feet seemed like someone else's appendages. The girl was hot to the touch, but his fingers were beyond feeling. She seemed incredibly light, like a rag doll he tossed out the window.

He leaned through the window himself. He tried to shout for help, but his vocal cords seemed to have been turned to ash. The cold air outside felt like heaven, allowing him to breathe. But the window was too narrow. His shoulders wedged against the bunk bed frame and the side of the window. Glass cut into his arm as he pushed, but he could not fit through the window.

All right, he would just die here then. Keep Lilith Semper happy. Breathing the air and looking outside. That was a better way to go than a brain tumor anyway. He didn't want to die, but he couldn't make any more effort. He surrendered entirely to the fire and slumped forward.

Someone grabbed his arms, his shoulders, pulled him through. He screamed as the glass cut into his biceps, then in a last anguished moment, he fell outside into the early-evening air.

For a moment, Jersey blinked stinging tears out of his eyes, then barely discerned the shapes of fire trucks, people moving about, water being sprayed onto the flame-filled shell of the house. The three children lay collapsed on the ground, but they were being taken care of. They would be all right. Jersey knew he had saved them, and that filled him with an overwhelming sense of wonder.

He preferred his way to the subtle manipulation of Entropy Ranch. Jersey's breath hitched in his burning throat as he whispered, "While you were biting your nails, I was saving them!"

He collapsed and began to sob, but he could feel only the monotonous symphony of pain all over his body. But that was good. The pain meant he would survive, the pain meant that he was not burned as badly as he imagined

"... delirious," a voice said.

Jersey's ears still rumbled from the roaring sound of fire.

"He's in shock, I think. But he'll be okay—those burns will heal."

"Better get him off to a hospital."

Jersey tried to sit up, but other hands grabbed his arms, lifting him. It hurt him deeply, but that didn't seem to matter anymore. He heard one of the girls, Tammy, begin to cry.

"Yes," he sighed, looking up and trying to see faces. Everything remained a blur, but they were going where he wanted to be. He had done his good deed. He had earned it. Everything would be all right now.

"Take me to a hospital ... a hospital."

ABOUT THE AUTHOR

Kevin J. Anderson has published more than 175 books, 58 of which have been national or international bestsellers. He has written numerous novels in the Star Wars, X-Files, and Dune universes, as well as a unique steampunk fantasy trilogy beginning with *Clockwork Angels,* written with legendary rock drummer Neil Peart. His original works include the Saga of Seven Suns series, the Wake the Dragon and Terra Incognita fantasy trilogies, the Saga of Shadows trilogy, and his humorous horror series featuring Dan Shamble, Zombie P.I. He has edited numerous anthologies, written comics and games, and the lyrics to two rock CDs. Anderson is the director of the graduate program in Publishing at Western Colorado University. Anderson and his wife, Rebecca Moesta, are the publishers of WordFire Press.

"For Want of a Hat" © 2024 Kate Dane

"Not on Our Watch" © 2024 Kevin Ikenberry

"Syracuse, the Eternal City" © 2024 Stephen and Carolyn Stein

"The Doom of Egypt" © 2024 Julia V. Ashley

"Divine Calm" © 2016 Charles E. Gannon (Originally published in *101 Stumbles in the March of History*. Edited by Bill Fawcett. [New York: New American Library, 2016].)

"A Ruinous Rent" © 2024 L. A. Selby

"A Brother's Oath" © 2024 Laughing Briar Books, LLC

"Xiào Shùn" © 2024 Lehua Parker, LLC

"Kutuzov at Gettysburg" © 2024 B. Daniel Blatt

"The Notorious Lawman Billy the Kid" © 2024 Edward J. Knight

"Out of Habit" © 2024 Julie Jones

"Aces High" © 2024 Jennifer M. Roberts

"Rufus and the Wizard of Wireless" © 2024 Stace Johnson

"G-Gals" © 2024 Kendrai Meeks

"Collateral Loss" © 2024 Fulvio Gatti (Originally published in *Tick Tock. Five Hundred Fiction #1*. Edited by Ben Thomas and D. Kershaw [Black Hare Press, 2020].)

"Boulder Choke" © 2024 Carrie Callahan

"This Was Your Life (Play It Again, Sam)" © 2024 Mary Pletsch

"The Unnamed" © 2024 Gamaliel Martinez (Originally published in *Parallel Worlds: The Heroes Within*. Edited by L. J. Hachmeister and R.R. Virdi [Lakewood, CO: Source 7 Productions, 2019].)

"Three Times the Power, Four Times the Pain" © 2024 Akis Lindardos

"Entropy Ranch" © 1990 WordFire, Inc. (Originally published in *Starshore*, Winter 1990.)

All Rights Reserved

ABOUT THE EDITOR

Lisa Mangum has worked in publishing since 1997. She has been the Managing Editor for Shadow Mountain since 2014 and has worked with several *NewYork Times* best-selling authors. While fiction is her first love, she also has experience working with nonfiction projects.

Lisa is also the author of four national best-selling YA novels (The Hourglass Door trilogy and *After Hello*), several short stories and novellas, and a nonfiction book about the craft of writing based on the TV show *Supernatural*. She has edited several anthologies about various magical creatures, pirates, and food for WordFire Press. She regularly teaches at writing conferences, including hosting a writing weekend in Capitol Reef National Park through UVU. She lives in Taylorsville, Utah, with her husband, Tracy.

IF YOU LIKED ...

If you liked *Of Wizards and Wolves*, you might also enjoy:

Monsters, Movies & Mayhem
Edited by Kevin J. Anderson

Unmasked: Tales of Risk and Revelation
Edited by Kevin J. Anderson

War of the Worlds: Global Dispatch
Edited by Kevin J. Anderson

OTHER WORDFIRE PRESS TITLES
EDITED BY LISA MANGUM

One Horn to Rule Them All

A Game of Horns

Dragon Writers

Undercurrents

X Marks the Spot

Hold Your Fire

Eat, Drink, and Be Wary

Our list of other WordFire Press authors and titles is always growing. To find out more and to shop our selection of titles, visit us at:
wordfirepress.com

facebook.com/WordfireIncWordfirePress
x.com/WordFirePress
instagram.com/WordFirePress
bookbub.com/profile/4109784512